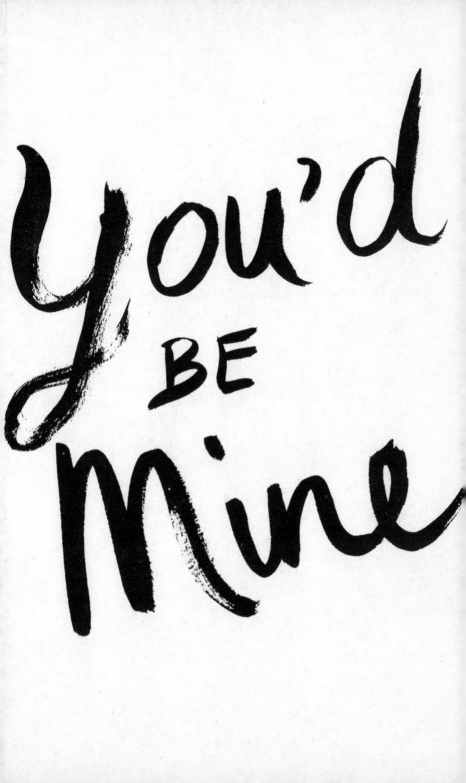

erin hahn

You'd

BE

Mine

WEDNESDAY BOOKS
NEW YORK

YOU'D BE MINE. Copyright © 2019 by Erin Hahn. All rights
reserved. Printed in the United States of America. For information,
address St. Martin's Press, 175 Fifth Avenue, New York, N.Y. 10010.

www.wednesdaybooks.com
www.stmartins.com

Designed by Anna Gorovoy

Library of Congress Cataloging-in-Publication Data

Names: Hahn, Erin, author.
Title: You'd be mine : a novel / Erin Hahn.
Other titles: You would be mine
Description: First edition. | New York : Wednesday Books, 2019.
Identifiers: LCCN 2018029191| ISBN 9781250192882 (hardcover) |
    ISBN 9781250192905 (ebook)
Subjects: | GSAFD: Love stories.
Classification: LCC PS3608.A444 Y68 2019 | DDC 813/.6—dc23
LC record available at https://lccn.loc.gov/2018029191

Our books may be purchased in bulk for promotional, educational,
or business use. Please contact your local bookseller or the Macmillan
Corporate and Premium Sales Department at 1-800-221-7945, extension 5442, or by email at MacmillanSpecialMarkets@macmillan.com.

First Edition: April 2019

10 9 8 7 6 5 4 3 2 1

For Cassie Vrtis.
Behind every author is a younger sister who read
all their terrible early work and still told them to not give up.
My younger sister puts the rest to shame.

Also, this is for my late grandmother, Patty.
Thanks for giving me your way with words.
I hope I've made you proud.

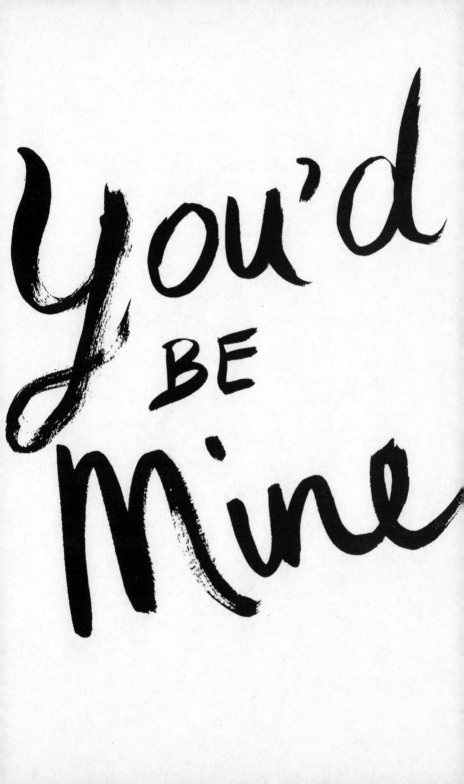

1
Clay

If I die, it's Trina Hamilton's fault. She's hard to miss; statuesque blonde with angry eyes and tiny nostrils wearing top-of-the-line Tony Lamas so she can kick my ass at a moment's notice. When the early-morning sun finally burns through my irises and kills me dead, she's the one you want.

"Christ, Trina, it's barely seven."

My road manager flashes cool gray eyes at me while pressing her matte red lips into a thin line. Her expression hasn't changed in the minutes since she came pounding on my hotel room door. She's a study in stone, but not for long. Better to get this over with.

I mumble another curse, yanking the frayed brim of my baseball hat lower. "At least slow down. I have a migraine."

Trina whirls around and shoves a manicured nail in my face. "Don't," she spits, "pull that migraine bullshit, Clay. You look like death, smell like sewage, and if you think those glasses are doing anything to hide that black eye, you're sorely mistaken."

I scratch at the back of my neck, playing for time. "Are those new Lamas? Because *dang, girl,* they make your legs look incredi—"

She grabs my chin in a painful squeeze, her sharp claws digging into my bruised cheekbone. "Don't even try it. What happened to you last night?"

I wrench my face away. "Nothing serious. A little scuffle with some fans after the show."

Trina stares at me a long minute, and I start to fidget. It's her signature move. I might be a country music star, but Trina makes me feel like a middle schooler who just hit a baseball through her window.

"A little scuffle," she repeats slowly.

"Yeah. A scuffle."

"Really. Just a few good old boys shooting the breeze, probably," she offers with a too-bright smile.

"Right."

She nods and starts walking, her heels clacking on the asphalt and ringing in my ears. A couple of middle-aged tourists halt, curious, midway through loading their golf bags into a rental car to watch us. I tug the brim of my hat even lower and hustle to match her strides through the hotel parking lot.

"So, that's it?" That can't be it.

"No, Clay. That's not it. Your face is all over TMZ this morning. We, as in you and me, because *I'm irrevocably tied to your fuckery,* are due at the label at 8:00 A.M. sharp."

I release a slow breath. "Trina, I have a contract. They already started presale on the summer tour. It can't be that bad."

Trina's cackle is edged with hysteria. "That guy you punched after throwing a beer in his face and waving a knife—"

"Knife? Really? It's a Swiss Army pocket tool. Every self-respecting Boy Scout owns one."

She plows on. "*He* was the SunCoast Records CEO's youngest son. His legally old-enough-to-drink son, as a matter of fact. Which you are not. How you manage to get served time and time again—"

I roll my eyes. "I've been playing bars since I was fifteen, Trina."

"—when you are so publicly underage—"

I lift a shoulder and wince as pain shoots down to my elbow. Must have tweaked it last night. "I'm a celebrity."

Trina grunts, her derision clear, just as my phone chimes in my pocket. I pull it out, ignoring her.

SAW TMZ. ON MY WAY.

"Is that Fitz?"

I nod, texting back.

TOO LATE. TRINA'S HERE.

"You can tell that good-for-nothing fiddler he's on my shit list, too. He promised he'd watch out for you after the last time."

SORRY, BRO.

"I don't need a babysitter, Trina."

MAYDAY, MAYDAY.

"Obviously. Just get in the car, Clay."

We pull into the lot of SunCoast Records fifteen minutes early. Trina slams the door with her bony hip and pulls out a cigarette, lights it, taking a long drag, and leans back against her outrageous banana-yellow convertible.

"I thought you quit." Fitz Jacoby lumbers over from where he's parked his crotch rocket and tugs the stick from between her lips. He stomps it out with his boot, and she glares but doesn't protest. Trina might have said Fitz was on her shit list, but she'd never hold to it. No one could.

"I did, but then Clay happened. He's fixing to kill me and my career. I wish I'd never agreed to manage you guys."

"Aw, now, Trina, that ain't true. You love us." Fitz pulls some kind of fudgy granola bar from his pocket and hands it to her. "Have some breakfast. Have you even taken a second for yourself today? I bet not," he croons. "Probably been up since dawn fielding phone calls and emails. You take five right here. Have a bite, find your chi or whatever. I'll make sure Boy Wonder here makes it up to the office, and we'll see you there."

Before she can protest, he silences her with a look and a waggle of his rusty brows and grabs my arm, tugging me along. "One, two, three, four . . . ," he mutters.

"Clay needs a clean shirt!" Trina yells, and Fitz holds up a plastic shopping bag without even turning.

"How the hell did you have time to stop for a shirt?"

"I have spares," he says, his jaw ticking.

I blow out a breath, trying to shrug out of his grip. He doesn't let go, just keeps dragging me to the glass doors of the lobby. "It wasn't as bad as they made it sound."

Fitz doesn't say anything. Instead, he leads me straight past the security desk to a men's room. He checks the stalls before locking the door and shoves the plastic bag at my chest. "There's deodorant and a toothbrush in there. I suggest you use them."

I remove my hat and glasses and pull my bloodstained T-shirt over my head before leaning over the sink. I turn on the *cold* full blast, splashing my face and rubbing the sticky grime and sweat from my neck. Fitz hands me a small hand towel, and I pat my skin dry. I use the deodorant—my usual brand—and brush my teeth. Twice.

"I like the shirt," I say.

"You should. You own three of them already."

"I have a contract."

Fitz laughs, but it's without humor. "Man, I don't care about your contract. You could've been seriously hurt. You could've been shot. You could've got in a car accident. You *did* get in a fistfight like some kid."

"He started it," I say, but Fitz is already holding up a calloused hand in front of his face, cutting me off.

"We don't have time for this. We're going up there, and you aren't gonna say shit in your defense. You're gonna say 'Yes, sir' and 'Yes, ma'am,' and you're gonna eat whatever crow they throw in your face and pray to God Almighty they don't sue you for breach of contract. Do you hear me?"

I sprint to the toilet. The coffee burns as it comes up.

"Christ," Fitz is saying when I come back to the sink, but he doesn't seem as mad. I splash more water and brush my teeth again, and then he holds the door open for me. As I pass, he grips my shoulder and gives it a squeeze.

Time to face the music.

I "yes, sir" my way through twenty solid minutes of lecturing done by three men in meticulous black suits. I manage not to throw up again. I manage to keep my contract. For now.

"Under one condition," the CEO, Chuck Porter, a balding man with wire frames says. "We have a little side job for you."

"Okay?"

"We've had our eye on your opening act for several months now. She's been giving us the cold shoulder, but we thought if we sent you in . . ."

I slump back in my seat, relieved. "You want me to convince some singer to come on my tour?" Piece of cake. Last year, my tour grossed higher than any other country act across the nation. Who wouldn't want in on that? It's the chance of a lifetime. "Who?"

"Annie Mathers."

A phone vibrates somewhere. Trina inhales softly. Fitz uncrosses his legs, sitting up.

I laugh. "You're serious?"

Chuck Porter's smile is all lips. "Perfectly. She's been hiding out in Michigan since her parents' untimely death. She's been touring the local circuit—"

"I know," I say. "I caught a show of hers last summer outside Grand Rapids."

This seems to surprise Chuck. "Well, then, you know she's special."

"She's talented as all get-out," I concede. "So why is she giving you the runaround?"

Chuck looks at his partners uneasily. "We're not sure. She's recently uploaded some clips onto YouTube and garnered quite a bit of attention, including from our competitors. Her mother, Cora, had originally signed with us. We'd love to have the pair."

I raise a brow at his wording. A *pair*, like they're collecting a matching set. Except Cora's been dead five years, so not much chance of that. I take my time, considering my odds. Annie Mathers is huge. Or, at least, she will be. It took approximately ten seconds of her performance for her smoky vocals to sear themselves into my memory. And with her famous name, she might just make everyone forget my recent indiscretions. Next to me, Fitz pulls up her YouTube videos on his phone, and even through the poor phone speakers, her voice draws goose bumps on my forearms.

We all sit, listening, before Fitz lifts his head and looks at me. "They're pretty amazing." He passes the phone to me, and I watch her figure on the small screen pluck out the melody on an old guitar. She is framed by a tiny brunette playing a fiddle and a Puerto Rican guy with black curls and bongo drums.

"Jason Diaz and her cousin, Kacey Rosewood, round out her band. They've been playing together for years."

I can't drag my eyes from Annie's long fingers skillfully manipulating the strings as though they were an elegant extension of her limbs. Her wild brown curls spring in front of her closed eyes. Suddenly, she opens her eyes and stares right at me through the screen, and my stomach squeezes uncomfortably.

"So, what's her hesitation?" I ask again.

"The past few years, school. She wanted to finish high school in one place."

I nod. I was the same way, but the label wore me down my senior year. It helped that my brother died. I had no reason to stay home.

"More recently, it seems psychological. She's wary of the industry after her parents."

I shrug back into my seat, passing the phone to Fitz. "Not much I can do about that. I don't blame her."

Fitz presses the screen of his phone, turning off the voices and putting it in his shirt pocket. "Which is why you might be the best person to talk to her. You're currently in the industry."

"Yeah, but it's different. Singing was an escape for me, my ticket out."

Fitz shakes his shaggy head. "Maybe so, but you can see it, can't you? You recognize her passion? Because I sure as hell can, and I have maybe half as much as you and that girl. She's a performer. It's written all over her face." He sits back and re-crosses his knee over his leg. "Go up there and get her."

Chuck clears his throat. "You forget. We're not asking.

We're telling you. Either you tour with Annie Mathers or you don't tour at all. I'm willing to take the loss on your contract. We have plenty of eager young talent ready to fill your spot."

I narrow my eyes as Fitz tenses next to me. I still him with a hand. The thing is, I don't think that's the complete truth, but I'm not willing to risk it. If that means I have to go to Michigan to convince a girl to tour with me, so be it.

"When do I leave?"

2
Annie

may
michigan

The first time I saw Clay Coolidge, I was fifteen. It was at a summertime music festival in Chicago. There was a Young Stars competition that was little more than a gathering of braces-faced kids from farm towns who came up together in their church choirs. He hadn't become *Clay* yet. He was singing under the name Jefferson Clay Coolidge. A girl doesn't forget a name like that. It sounds like something out of a vampire book or some Civil War–era hero. On a beautiful sixteen-year-old boy from Indiana, it translated into a honey accent and swooping hair, imprinting on every teenage girl in the audience.

I haven't seen him since, until today.

Now he's sitting at my kitchen table. His eyes are as dark and lovely as ever. His sandy hair is wavy across his forehead, and his long legs are stretched out and crossed at the ankles. My cousin, Kacey, is sitting across from him, sighing. My seventy-year-old gran is bustling around in her frilliest apron making hand-squeezed lemonade of all things.

Let the record show, the Rosewood ladies have no chill.

"Gran," I start, trying to keep the exasperation out of my voice, "I think Clay would be just fine with concentrate."

To his credit, Clay straightens. "Oh yeah. For sure. In fact, Mrs. Rosewood, I'm great with water. No need to fuss."

My gran waves a dripping hand near her ear, ignoring us. Kacey shifts in her seat, flicks her dark hair over one shoulder, but it falls flat since she cut it to a bob over the weekend. She sighs again, her eyes not moving from Clay's handsome features.

He squirms, and part of me glories in his discomfort. Kacey is a lot when you first meet her. My gran starts muttering about someone not refilling the trays in the freezer, and I decide to throw the guy a bone. "Hey, um, Clay? Let's take a walk and discuss whatever it is you came all the way out here to discuss."

Clay scoots back his chair with a loud scrape and is up before the words have half a chance to settle. I shoot Kacey a look and speak slowly. "Why don't you go fetch Jason? I sent him a text, but you know his phone is on silent. Probably up all night on his PS4 again."

She makes a petulant grab for her keys. "I'm not his momma," she says.

I push through the screen door without responding. "We'll be back, Gran." I lead Clay down a mown path that winds to the back acres that will be hayfields come harvesttime. My grandpa hasn't farmed in years, but he rents out the land to a few different neighbors. Right now, it looks like the Logan boys are planting.

Once we're out of earshot, I turn to Clay, still a little in awe that he's here. "So, they're really pulling out the big guns if they've flown you out to the middle of nowhere."

He doesn't deny it. "Does that surprise you? Even if you sucked, your name alone would guarantee butts in the seats."

I snort, despite myself. "Classy."

He shrugs, and somehow, it's charming rather than indifferent. "I only mean you had to know it was coming. You released the clips, after all. Label's probably had someone on the lookout for you since birth."

"Yeah, well. I don't much care for the inside track. I can make my own way, thanks."

Clay nods, reaching down to pick up a large stone and tossing it under the tree a few yards away. It's a telling move. One showing a familiarity with farm life. Stones can wreak havoc on expensive equipment.

"You're a conundrum, Annie Mathers. A natural artist, clearly talented, with a name that would open any door and an offer that's likely the best you could hope for. Why're you playing coy?"

"You just said it. My name," I say. I reach down and pluck at one of the billions of yellow dandelions dotting the grass. "They want Cora Rosewood 2.0." I roll the stem between my fingers before meeting Clay's penetrating gaze. "Did you know the *Late Night* duet with my mom was the most-viewed episode of all time? I was six. I thought Willie Nelson was my actual grandpa until I was ten. I knew the words to 'Coal Miner's Daughter' before I learned my alphabet. My freaking birth announcement was on the cover of *People* magazine's country music issue."

Clay motions his head to keep walking. We step high on the already soft grass. Michigan is a special kind of green in the spring. Green on top of green, edged with more green. I wonder idly how my home looks in his eyes. He's probably used to fancy hotel rooms and has a loft in New York or Nashville. Maybe both.

After a minute, he says, "Look, the way I see it, you can be a martyr and let all of that keep you from your destiny, or you can embrace it and come on my tour."

"And the Mathers/Rosewood name holds no appeal for you?" I say, dubious.

His lips quirk. "No offense, but Clay Coolidge ain't a bad name in its own right."

He has a point. It's not as if he's some unrecognizable upstart. He's young, maybe a year older than I am, but he's been around long enough.

"So, what do you need me for?"

He tips his head back, squinting in the morning sun. "I don't. To be honest, I had nothing to do with the decision. For some nefarious reason, yet to be determined, my tour manager insists we need to sign you for this summer. And apparently, Grammys and gold records don't carry the weight they used to. So here I am, in the middle of nowhere, as you said, hours before I care to be awake, asking you to sign the fucking papers so I can be on my way."

I swallow back the sting of his retort. I asked for it, after all. Still, he doesn't have to be an a-hole.

"Well, by all means, don't let little old me keep you from your hangover," I snipe.

He groans. "Don't be so sensitive."

The weed crushes in my fist, painting my palm gold. "I'm sorry, are you supposed to be convincing me to sign?"

He's silent for a beat, and I wonder if I've blown it. He reaches for my arm, and I ignore the electric jolt in my nerve endings at his touch. "Look," he says, exasperated, though his grip is gentle. "It shouldn't matter what I want. This is about you and your future. Do you want this? Forget your name, forget your history, forget me and the label. Do *you* want this to happen? Because once you sign your name, it's *going* to, and you can't go back."

I press my lips together, considering carefully. It shouldn't matter what he wants, but it sort of does. It irks me that he's playing it off like he doesn't care whether I sign, when he so clearly needs me to. I've been fielding phone calls from Sun-Coast for the last six months. Still, I almost want to turn him down out of spite.

Except I want it too much. At the end of the day, there is little I love more in life than to perform a song of my heart—to pour myself into a melody—to share that piece of myself with a stranger. Everything in me speaks music with a fluent tongue. Surely it's genetic, but my parents certainly haven't done me any favors. If anything, their deaths nearly killed the music in my soul.

But the music won't be stifled. *I* won't be held back any longer. I knew when I let Jason post those videos. I knew I was going to cave and accept an offer because I couldn't *not*. I'm a little surprised SunCoast went this particular route, sending one of their top-grossing artists to my doorstep, contract in hand, but hell, it's *Clay Coolidge*. I mean, it worked.

"Do you ever feel like you're hurtling across the continent on one of those high-speed trains and you find out the brakes are broken?"

"Every day," Clay admits.

I nod slowly. "I'll do it."

"That's what I thought." And I can tell he means it. Understanding passes between us as the breeze shifts. I break first, turning back the way we came.

I don't know what I expect to find when we get back. It's not like I figured my gran would throw a party in our honor, but I guess I hoped for something more than the sad smile I got when Clay unfurled the contract and laid it on the kitchen table. Scribbling out my signature, on the line above where Kacey and Jason have already signed theirs, feels like the inevitable conclusion to a childhood of pretending I had a choice in the matter.

"We need a band name," I say, plucking at my dad's old shaded Martin. A fishing pond rounds out the far corner of my grandparents' property, and Jason, Kacey, and I are sitting in our favorite spot on the shore. Some bands practice in garages; we practice on tree stumps under the covering of weeping willows, their branches sweeping low along the surface of the water.

"Jason and His Argonauts," my best friend offers as he idly taps the heels of his calloused hands on a set of small bongos.

Kacey snickers. "That sounds like a porno."

"But, like, the worst porno ever," I say.

"Orphan Annie?" Jason tries again. Kacey and I both groan. He thumps out a beat. "Let's see what you come up with."

"How about no real names?" I say.

Jason rolls his eyes. "No offense, but I don't think you can keep it a secret."

"That's fine, but I don't need to shove it in everyone's face either."

"You mean like *Clay Coolidge*?" Kacey offers, waving her bow in the air and tracing the letters in the sky.

"Exactly like that," I say, and I swipe my hand as though his name is a gnat I can flick off my conscience.

Jason leans back in the grass, placing his hands behind his head, his shirt rising slightly to reveal abs he didn't have last summer. He's grown up nicely. I'm weirdly proud that he's so good-looking and talented. Like, it's nothing to do with me. Unless you count the times I've kidnapped him to the salon for a haircut when he's hopelessly shaggy.

"So that's a no for Annie and the Mathers, then?"

I try to throw a clump of grass at his face, but it lands embarrassingly short. "What does that even mean?"

"It's existential," he insists, his fingers tapping a hollow rhythm on his chest.

"You're existential," I mutter.

"Children, enough." Kacey drags her bow across the freshly tuned strings of her fiddle, Loretta. The shadows speckle her bare shoulders and play across her toned biceps as her nimble fingers dance out a melody. Kacey is a year older than Jason and me. She fully embraced an artful bohemian style in high school I've always envied. When I initially came from Nashville to live with my grandparents, Kacey was my first friend. She's technically my cousin, but that only made it so the whole celebrity thing never got between us. She couldn't care less who my parents were. She only cared that they were dead and I was alone. The first time I saw her play was at my mom's memorial service, and I've never forgotten the way she was able to put every gloriously mournful feeling I'd had into a song without words.

"The first time I kissed a boy was under these willows," she says after a minute.

I raise a brow. "Just kissed?"

She winks. "A gentlewoman never tells."

"Ah, but you do. More than anyone needs to know," I say.

"Our first kiss was under here, wasn't it, Annie?"

I strum once, sharp. "Nope. That would have maybe been romantic." Jason scrunches one eye, trying to remember. "Jaysus," I say with a snicker. "We only had two kisses. In your basement while watching *Superbad* and then in your car when you dropped me off two hours later. You're lucky I even bother talking to you anymore, let alone invite you on a national tour."

Jason doesn't bother to apologize, just grins lazily. "I remember now. That was a good movie!" Kacey jabs him in the chest with her bow, and he rubs at it absently. "Ow, you wretch."

"It was a terrible movie and a terrible first kiss. Thankfully, Craig Logan was happy enough to help me practice the rest of that summer."

Jason snickers. "I'll just bet he was."

"What about Under the Willows?" Kacey says.

"Sorry?"

"For a band name. It's where we practice—where we spent our summers."

I repeat the name, testing it on my tongue. "It's not terrible. I've always liked the symbolism of willows—they have super-strong root systems allowing them to hang so close to the water."

Jason tilts his head. "I don't know. Now that I know Kacey lost her virginity here, it sort of loses its charm."

Kacey swats him again, and he laughs.

"I would think that would be the selling point for you," I say.

"Good point. Let's call it. All in favor of Under the Willows, say, 'Aye.'"

We all "aye" in unison, and I pull out my phone, tapping a quick email to the label. "That's that, friends. We're officially a band."

It's not like we haven't been playing together for years already, under any number of names that never stuck. And it's not like we didn't already sign our summer away to the record label two weeks ago. But, suddenly, the world feels thicker around us. The air we're breathing laden with expectation.

Jason breaks the silence. "I feel like we need to go get matching tats or something."

"Tramp stamps," I agree dryly. "You first, Jason."

———

Two weeks later, I'm packing up my things when my gran finds me. She places a small stack of folded clothes on my bed. "These are off the line," she says.

I start to sort through them, pulling out a hoodie and a pair of cutoffs to throw in my already overly full luggage. "Thanks, Gran." She sits down, looking around my room. She grabs a frame from my nightstand. It's a candid photo of my parents on their wedding day. Neither of them are looking at the camera, instead staring into each other's eyes as they dance.

"You know when that boy turned up at our door, I couldn't help but think of Robbie knocking on the same door twenty years ago to pick up my baby."

I huff out a breath. "Hardly, Gran. Clay Coolidge wasn't here for a date. He was here because his label paid him to be."

Gran traces a weathered fingertip across my mother's beautiful features. "Had the same kind of feeling, though, in my gut. Cocky cowboy strutting in and taking my little girl away."

I take the frame from her hands and put it facedown on the bed. Kneeling in front of her, I place my hands in her lap and look up into her crinkled eyes. Some of those lines are recent, but most were there long before I came to live in my mother's old room. "I'm not her. I'm not running after any cocky cowboys. I'm going into this with my head on straight. I know what fame can do to a girl, and I know what love can take away. This isn't the same situation at all. Besides, I'll have Kacey and Jason with me."

My gran chuckles once, humorlessly. "Hardly a comfort. My Kacey is a free spirit if ever there was one, and Jason is halfway to cocky cowboy himself. That reminds me." My gran reaches into her back pocket and pulls out a folded sheet of paper, passing it to me. I stand up to read.

"It's a list of churches," she says.

"I see that."

"I had your grandfather find a congregation at each stop of your tour. He used the internet," she explains unnecessarily. I'm taken with the image of my crotchety grandfather googling "where to find Jesus in Pittsburgh." "Never let yourself get too far from the Lord, Annie."

I refold the paper, tucking it into my pocket. "I won't." I don't bother explaining I'll be playing late and traveling through the night most weekends.

I try again. "Gran, I mean it. I'm not like her." I hate the pleading in my voice, but it's so important to me that of all people, my gran sees there is a difference this time around—that this isn't history repeating itself. After all, if I can't convince her, how can I expect to convince the rest of the world?

She smiles sadly, patting my hand. "I know it. You aren't like Cora. You're better than she was. It's why I worry so. You've got even more to lose."

Swallowing hard, I turn away, making a point of returning to my packing. After a minute, she leaves, closing my door softly behind her. At the click, I crumple to my bed, curling in on myself, hot tears streaming down my face. I'm not even sure why. Is it because I'm leaving the only real home I've ever known? I know I can come back, but it won't be the same.

Is it because no matter how much I argue, my gran will only ever see Cora when she looks in my face?

I've spent the last five years trying not to be me. Five years spent planning for a life that didn't include music, all the while performing in small venues like some kind of adulterer. I planned for college. I planned for normal. I really, truly tried. But the pull was too strong.

I know the consequences of signing that contract.

You've got even more to lose.

My mom lost her life to country music. How could I lose more than that?

3
Clay

may
outside indianapolis, indiana

I don't like being home. In the last two years, I could probably count on two hands the number of nights I've spent in
this old house. It's too empty. Years of folks running in and
out and now it sits, dusty and dried up. I make a mental note
to drop a key off at Taps for Maggie. Maybe she or Lindy
can air the place every now and again so I don't come home
to a mausoleum. Except I know I won't. It's not that Maggie wouldn't be willing. She's known my family for years
and would love nothing more than to help. But asking for
help feels dangerously close to initiating contact, and initiating contact is a rocky slope to *family* in a small town like
mine.

   The thought of my brother's fiancée, Lindy, and her mother
always makes my skin prickle with unease. I haven't seen
Lindy or my niece in probably six months. I stopped back
for Thanksgiving but barely made it through the afternoon
and left straight after dinner. At Christmas, I saved us all

the trouble and just sent them a text from a resort in Cabo San Lucas.

Danny would punch me in the gut if he knew how shitty I was being to his girls. Lindy didn't know she was pregnant with Layla until after Danny was already in Iraq. He hoped to be home for the birth but instead died before he had the chance. Lindy sends me a card with pictures every few months. One arrived this morning, and I spent hours staring at images of a chubby toddler with Danny's blue eyes until my own eyes threatened to dry up and shrivel into raisins.

I wish she'd quit. I don't know what she's playing at. I'm not uncle material, and I'm nothing like my stalwart big brother. We'd all be better off if they would let me be an occasional check in the mail.

I toss an empty bottle, and it shatters on the cement floor of my grandfather's old woodshop. My legs dangle over the edge of the loft, and the late-afternoon sun slants through the patchy roof. I watch, transfixed, as the dust particles catch the rays and spin. It's been at least three years since the last time my grandfather filled this space, larger than life. He would stand at his lathe, somehow shaping a spindle for a rocking chair out of a piece of rough-hewn wood.

He taught me how to see the potential in the scrap pieces—how to find the beauty in the ordinary. My grandfather would play his old Carter albums in this shop. He'd close his rheumy eyes and say, "They don't make music like this anymore, my boy. You've been given a gift, Jefferson. Don't waste it."

He was the only one to call me Jefferson. He and Danny. It's my real name. One I left behind once no one was left to call me by it.

I reach behind me and pull out my guitar. I strum the opening chords of "Can the Circle Be Unbroken" and shut my eyes, conjuring up the smell of sawdust and varnish in my mind. I don't hate what I do. I sing songs about cold beer and cutoffs. Pretty girls and Dixie cups of homemade wine. It's my thing. I sing songs people hook up to, and I get paid well for it. I travel the country making people feel good.

Sometimes, though, I like to imagine I could sing something different—something real. Something true, straight from the hills. Or the harvested patchwork of green in Indiana. Or this woodshop, even. A melody, sweet and simple, stirs in my throat. Lyrics swirl in and out of my brain, fuzzy as yet but becoming clearer each day. A song is coming. I only need to open myself up to it.

I still the strings under my hand, shutting down the muse. I'm already on thin ice with the label.

I leave for Nashville in the morning and from there, the tour. For a second, I consider going to the cemetery. No doubt that's where Fitz is. He and Danny were best friends growing up. Closer than, even. If I know him, he'll visit Danny first, then Maggie's place next. He's probably got a gift for Layla.

I can see them all sitting together, shooting the bull. Fitz will give my excuses—say I'm busy songwriting or practicing or doing radio interviews. Or hungover, which is more likely these days. They'll tsk about how I'm never home—completely undependable.

I just can't be home. I can't face it all. So I don't. I pull myself up, proud that I'm not yet too unsteady, and make my way over to the ladder and climb down before I regret it. I almost froze to death up here over Thanksgiving. Accidentally knocked over the ladder trying to get down. Waited too long.

Fitz found me. As usual.

Fitz has a home, with his momma, but he moved in when

Danny left for the Marine Corps, since I was barely sixteen at the time. He has a room and just hasn't ever really moved out.

I get back on solid ground, and my phone *dings*. I curse. It's Trina.

She starts talking as soon as I answer. "Where are you?"

I look around, like she's in front of me. "The shed."

She curses. "I had to move up your flight. A car should be there already."

"Hold on." I stumble out into the light, and sure enough, a sleek black town car is sitting in my drive.

"I see him. Did you call Fitz?"

"He's here with me, Clay. At the airport. Didn't you read your email or get my texts or anything?" Her voice is getting shriller, and I wince, holding my phone a few inches from my ear.

"Isss fine, Trina."

She curses again. "Are you kidding me? Are you drinking? It's the afternoon, Clay!"

I don't bother answering. I'm perpetually packed. Just have to grab my duffel and go. She's still screeching on the phone.

"Put on Fitz."

"Hey, man," Fitz says easily.

"I'm on my way. Hold the plane," I say.

He chuckles. "Sure thing."

I sleep the entire ride to the airport and then the flight from Indy to Nashville. Trina puts me in a cab to the hotel and tells me she'll arrange my wake-up call in the morning so I'd better stay out of trouble until then. After all, we're meeting up with Annie tomorrow.

She shouldn't worry; Babysitter Fitz won't leave my side.

We're in the hotel bar, eating bacon cheeseburgers with french fries and drinking Diet Cokes. A few girls sit at the bar and have tried more than once to catch my eye, but my chaperone ain't having it.

"Not tonight, Clay. We have some place to be."

I snort into my drink, the ice clinking as I forgo the straw and tip it back. "Where?" I mutter. "Room 502 with a couple of dirty movies?"

He rolls his eyes. "Grow the hell up, man. No. Lula May's. I wanna show you something. In fact"—he glances at the time on his phone—"we should get the check."

I finish the last of my fries, intrigued. Lula May's is one of those legendary bars in Nashville. Old as the country music scene. All the greats got their start there. It's a dive nowadays, but just as sacred to the locals. Which I'm not.

We pay our tab and decide to walk to the bar. It's a warm night, though the breeze is cool and feels good on my face. I tilt the rim of my ball cap up and then spin it around backward, allowing the fresh air to wash over me. I love this town. The bright lights and city streets so full of history and straight-up soul. The air smells like barbecue. We pass a dozen different patios playing a dozen different versions of Southern into the night. Laughter rings out, couples kiss in dark corners, and girls clatter around in heels and boots. No one recognizes me. At night, on the street, I'm one more barhopping kid. Everyone's in the business. Either in front of the mic or behind it, but they are involved somehow, someway. No one pays attention to Fitz and me, and I relish the feeling. We cross, turning down a side street that's less crowded. A small neon sign reads LULA MAY'S in old-fashioned script.

Fitz pulls open the door, and *her* voice pours out. The bar is a seedy kind of dark, and once the door closes behind us, it takes more than a moment for my eyes to adjust. At first, I think she's alone onstage, because there is a dim blue spotlight focused solely on her and casting the bar in an ethereal glow. But her hands are clasped on either end of the stool she's perched on, and I reluctantly look past her to the guitarist strumming off to the side.

Patrick Royston, former country mega-superstar, is playing backup, unobtrusive and 100 percent acoustic. This guy was making millions while I was still in braces. Annie winds down a song, and it's completely silent. My face tingles hot in sympathy for her before Patrick transitions into the next song. But she doesn't seem uncomfortable at the lack of ovation. She doesn't even open her eyes.

Fitz nudges my shoulder and points to two chairs in the back of the room. I head for the table, and he goes to grab us a few drinks at the ancient bar. Every inch of the walls is covered in bric-a-brac and framed photos of Nashville's earliest celebrities. I slump into my seat and pull my cap around and tug it farther down over my eyes. The history is palpable in this place, and I'm an imposter in overpriced clothes. The song I'm working on comes back to me, and I have a sudden urge to pull out my guitar and play it right here right now—to prove myself to this silent and assessing crowd. After all, if she can do it . . .

She's singing again, and I recognize the lyrics to "I'll Fly Away" and swallow hard. It was my granddad's favorite hymn. I shut my eyes, focusing on Annie's smoky voice. She doesn't sound seventeen. She sounds timeless. No showy vibrato, no *American Idol*–worthy runs. Her voice is pure. Unadulterated. Untainted.

It's the sound of sweet salvation.

I don't realize until she gasps for breath, I'd been holding mine along with her. I'd been mouthing the lyrics without even realizing I remembered them. When she finishes, she's met with silence again, but as I open my eyes, I find it's not because they don't care for her. They're overcome. There isn't a dry eye in the place.

I startle as Fitz slides a soda in front of me. I nod to him, and he opens his mouth to say something, but the music starts up again.

"I'm gonna play just a few more tonight. If you'll indulge me," Patrick says with a humble grin. "Today's this talented young lady's eighteenth birthday." Small cries of enthusiasm ring out, along with a loud hoot in the front row. From the mess of dark hair, I'd guess it's Jason, the drummer, though I've only seen him on video.

Patrick blows into the mic, rubbing at the back of his neck. "There's lots of things I wish for you, Annie, not in the least that Robbie and Cora could see you up here. They'd be so proud. We're all so proud of how you've grown. But—" He drops his hand and looks at Annie. The light reflects a blue sheen in her eyes. "But your momma used to tell me the strongest roots grow through adversity. You're a hell of a young woman, Annie Mathers."

Everyone breaks into cheering and applause, and Annie throws her arms around Patrick's neck, placing a chaste kiss on his cheek before returning to her stool.

"Thank you," she says in her simple way. "Now, enough of that. I've got one more song for y'all before I pass this mic back to Patrick. I want to thank you for coming tonight. I see a lot of familiar faces, and I'm tickled y'all turned out. It's no secret I've been in hiding these past five years or so. Truthfully, I never really was sure I'd make it back to Nashville, but . . . well . . ." Annie scrunches up her face and releases a slow breath into the mic. "Performing's in my bones . . . so . . . here I am. I don't usually like to sing my momma's songs. In fact, I *never* sing my momma's songs—but since I wouldn't be here today if she hadn't given birth to me, I suppose I could just this once." At that she looks back to Pat and counts down from three.

I recognize this one, too. Of course I do. Cora Rosewood probably had a collection of Grammys to rival Prince's. I prefer Annie's version, though. It's softer. More hopeful. She stands and cradles the mic stand between both of her hands. It almost looks as though she's going to kiss it.

I shake my head and swallow the last of my soda. "I should get out of here before it's over," I say.

Fitz's eyes widen, but I get the impression he approves. He leaves his drink, barely touched, on the table and leads the way out. When we get to the door, I look one last time right as Annie's eyes open, and then I duck out.

I don't know how to feel about what I've witnessed tonight. It was the most beautiful thing I've ever seen, and yet, I'm feeling sick over it. Annie is meant to do this. If ever there was a person on this planet meant to perform, it's her. But at what cost? What are we asking of her? This city swallows so many. It's already stolen her family.

I recognize that haunted look in her eyes. It's the same one I wear every single day—the look of someone outrunning their demons.

When the label sent me to Michigan, I told myself I was doing us both a favor.

Now I'm not so sure.

4

Annie

I've barely landed in Nashville, and I'm kicking myself already for the half decade I've spent tucked away in the north woods of Michigan. I've flat-out lost my immunity to Southern boys, and Clay Coolidge is fixing to kill me with his dangerous charisma. In my kitchen, Clay was arrogant and hungover, but now, just yards away onstage, he's an enigma. He wears dark shades, broods always, and makes love to his mic. He's cornered the market on females age thirteen to ninety.

Of course, he is *so* aware of it, which puts a slight damper on his appeal. For me anyway. I mean, objectively, my dad was plenty swoon-worthy in his time, if his hordes of admirers were any indication. He was also a raging pill junkie with control issues and a mean jealous streak.

We arrive early for sound check because I was too antsy to sit in my hotel room all day. I toyed with the idea of hanging out in a coffee shop until noon, but Jason has the manners of a toddler in public, and I'd rather not risk the extra attention. I have plenty of contacts in Nashville. My parents' old friends—the few I've kept in contact with over the years—have offered everything from a place to crash to any greasing of palms I might need. I don't know why I don't take them up on it.

Well, maybe I do. I just feel plain stupid about it. The truth is, my parents ran in a pretty tight circle in their heyday. And by tight, I mean practically incestuous. After my parents' deaths, I had multiple offers from "aunts and uncles" to take me in. To raise me up in Nashville. To carry on my parents' legacy. But I can't think of a single one who didn't see me as anything other than their bankroll. Imagine the boon to their careers, taking me in as their own? I'd be dressed up in Cora's clothes and taught Robbie's swagger, and then, when I'd reached the ripe age of sixteen, I'd be pushed the label's drugs and they'd own me. The tragic heiress in their silk-lined pockets.

So, no, thank you very much. My way might be clumsier and less lucrative, but I may make it out with my old age intact. There's just one tiny hitch I hadn't counted on, and he's laughing into his mic, making my palms sweat. Truthfully, high school boys held little interest for me. Aside from Jason, I barely dated, and I only kissed him because it seemed the natural thing to do at the time. But I didn't get so much as a spark out of it. The next morning, I found him hanging around Meredith Norgaard and it barely stung. I wasn't in love with him, and besides, I got a great song out of it.

But high school boys had nothing on Clay Coolidge and his jeans.

"Annie Mathers?" An elegant blonde with six-inch stilettos strides toward me, her bloodred manicure outstretched. I take her hand, and she does that thing where she brings her other hand around so I'm wrapped in her embrace. She beams a matte shade of hot pink, and I can't help but gape at her. I don't know whether to feel underdressed or plain intimidated.

"Holy hell. Are you for real?" Jason blurts next to me, and the magic is broken.

"*I am*, thanks," the blonde answers with a wink. "I'm Trina Hamilton, your tour manager. I can see you three have been up north for too long. Don't worry, you'll get used to the hair spray and Botox."

I think I like her. She has a refreshing bluntness I dig. "It's nice to meet you in person, Ms. Hamilton. Please just call me Annie." I can feel my accent already drawling out even after being gone so long. It makes me a little self-conscious. "This blithering sack of hormones here is my old friend and drummer, Jason Diaz, and this little talented beauty is my cousin, Kacey Rosewood."

I turn and keep turning. Kacey's gone. Out of the corner of my eye, I see she is already shaking hands with a stocky, bronze-haired man in a faded green T-shirt and well-fitting jeans. Wherever these boys are finding their denim, I want a lifetime membership to their mailing catalog.

"Ah, yes. That's Fitz Jacoby. He's fiddle and banjo and basically all strings for Clay. He's been on the lookout for your cousin. Fell in love with her YouTube videos." Trina gives the couple a cursory glance like a major musician hitting on my cousin was a totally normal occurrence.

Which maybe it should be. Kacey is a catch, after all. But that was quick even by her standards.

Jason is still gaping after Trina, and Clay is onstage doing a sound check. He huffs, bleeps, and checks into the mic before belting out a line a cappella. I recognize the lyric, but hearing it live and up close sends chills along my spine. His vocals are razor sharp and burn going down. I feel them deep in my bones and reverberating in my skull in only the best possible way.

Sweet mercy. I don't even realize I'm fanning myself until Jason snickers next to me and my hand stops midair.

"And that, boys and girls, is the story of how stone-cold Annie Mathers found her lady parts."

I smack Jason in the arm with a loud *thwack* and shake off my reverie. A quick look over my shoulder confirms no one else was close enough to hear. I shoot him a glare. "Hush, you."

He stifles his smirk just as Clay jumps off the stage and heads in our direction. His long legs eat up the distance in three strides, and I'm not really ready. He tugs a ball cap out of his back pocket and stuffs it on his head before holding out a hand. "Glad you didn't chicken out."

Something about his tone jabs. Not quite condescending but not quite friendly either. More like how your big brother's best friend would talk to you. Not a business partner. This time I let loose on my accent—making sure it's sweet as spun sugar.

"As if you could scare me away."

He raises a dark brow under the shadow of his cap, and I catch a glint of something in his gray-blue eyes. "Good, then."

Jason clears his throat and reaches out a hand. "Jason Diaz."

Clay shifts his focus and shakes Jason's hand. "Right, the drummer. Nice to meet you. Where's your third?"

Jason grins in his affable way and jabs a thumb to where Kacey is still chatting it up with Fitz in the Jeans.

Clay's lips quirk to one side in an almost grin. "Right, Kacey Rosewood, the fiddle prodigy who stares a lot. Looks like she's gotten past that."

My stomach slips a little at his seeming admiration of my cousin. How come she's the prodigy?

How come I even care? Ugh. I will not be one of those

chicks on this tour. Clay is just another guy with a guitar who thinks he walks on water. I knew something was up when the label sent him directly. Kacey confirmed it, telling me he got into trouble when a fight broke out after his show a few weeks back. Apparently, it was all over the news. Turns out Mr. "Clay Coolidge ain't a bad name" almost lost his tour if it hadn't been for me and my sparkling-clean image.

He needs me. *He* needs me. Of the two of us, *he's* the one taking advantage of *my* name. I'd be smart to remember that and quit losing my head over the way his voice raises the little hairs on my arms.

"You're welcome to the stage for sound check after lunch. We've called in catering," Fitz offers with a wide grin, finally making his way past my cousin, though I notice she's close behind.

"Not so fast. I'm gonna need Annie for a photo shoot this afternoon. Someone from the label will be taking publicity shots of Annie and Clay, and then they'll follow back to get some shots of the sound check afterward. So meet back here at three?"

"Photo shoot?" I ask, my voice squeaking a little.

"I thought that was for headliners only," Clay murmurs to Trina.

Her answering grin is slightly manic. "That was before, Clay. Now, they want Annie's pretty face right there next to yours."

He yanks off his hat and bends the rim between his long fingers. "How long are they going to hold that against me, Trina? It was one night."

She flicks a glance at the rest of us, but he's not budging, so I don't either. Might as well know what I'm in for. "It was more than one night, Clay. It was the culmination of many nights, which makes you a calculated risk for the label. So either you cooperate and hold on to your career or you don't. Make your mind up now so I can write my resignation of your Dumpster fire of a career before you take me down with you." Trina's smile is fixed as ever, but her voice carries a lash, and Clay cringes a little under her scrutiny.

He sighs. "Christ Almighty, Trina. That's not what I meant."

She glares.

"Let me grab a water, okay?"

"Fabulous." She turns to me. "You're coming with me, honey. Flawless takes time, and we've only got a few hours."

Trina leads me through a back door—a solid, no-window affair—and down a dreary hallway. If it wasn't for the fact I'm worth more alive than dead after her lecture to Clay, I'd be concerned. This place is shady as all get-out.

Like a low-brow movie set. Or a local access television studio.

Eventually the soft murmur of voices breaks in, and as we approach a well-lit hallway, I release a slow breath. A young black woman in smart eyewear grabs my arm from Trina and pulls me into a dressing room. She's wearing sensible flats and cropped skinny slacks, and next to Trina, she looks like the student class president with her smooth hair and muted style.

"You're late," she says. She readjusts a clipboard under one arm and pushes me gently toward a stark vanity and one of those rickety-looking folding chairs. It seems I've stumbled upon the not-so-glamorous underbelly of show business. That took approximately two hours.

Trina examines her nails next to me, unfazed. "Good to see you, Beth, as always. I'm doing marvelous, thanks for asking. Just got engaged last month." Trina flashes a giant, sparkling diamond. "Melody Parker? She's an entertainment lawyer." My eyes flicker over to the smaller woman, whose expression sours comically, and I make a mental note to never, ever get on Trina's bad side. "Anyway," Trina plows on. "Blame Clay. Pretty boy needed a little come-to-Jesus." She shrugs lightly and offers me a grin. "Annie, this is Beth Lewis. She's from *Country Music* magazine and is running the shoot today. I'm going to find a sweet tea. Want one?"

I grimace. Sweet tea is one of those Southern things I cannot abide. If it wasn't for my love of grits, my dad's side of the family might have questioned his claim on me.

Trina pulls her keys out of a giant designer bag. "Suit yourself."

Beth lets Trina out before peeking into the hallway and calling for a couple of assistants. She then points to the chair. "You. There." I plop down, tucking my grungy satchel between my even grungier Keds. "This is Christian. He'll be doing your hair, and Maria will be fixing up your face."

Christian is tall and slender, wearing a loud scarf even though it's probably a thousand degrees under the hot vanity lights. He sort of reminds me of Lumiere in *Beauty and the Beast,* and I want to be his friend. I feel like you can tell a lot about someone who wears vibrant accessories.

"I love your curls," he gushes, running his fingers through my frizz. "How attached are you to the length? You've got this old-school Taylor thing going on, and I'm picturing you with a pixie."

I shake my head quickly. "Nothing above the shoulders, thanks. I need to be able to pull it out of my eyes when I play."

"No pixie," Beth butts in from the door. I slump in relief. "Carl's vision for this shoot is a modern-day play on Johnny and June. She's gonna need a bouffant."

I inhale sharply and choke on air. "I'm sorry, do you mean Johnny and June Carter Cash?"

Beth scribbles something on her clipboard and then tucks the pen behind her ear. "Good. You know of them? Some kids these days can't see past Blake and Miranda."

I sputter at her offhand tone. "But they are like this epic love story! They're legendary. That's complete sacrilege."

"Easy, Mathers, it's not like we're dressing you up like your parents. That was tossed around, you know."

I whip to face her. "What?"

"Don't get all offended. I talked them out of it."

I swallow hard past the lump growing in my throat. Day one, jumping right in, I guess. "Double-suicide is hardly something to emulate in a publicity shoot."

"Exactly my point. Which is why we are going with Johnny and June." Beth speaks slowly, and I want to smack her upside the head with her stupid clipboard.

Christian places a hand on my shoulder. "Jesus H., Beth."

I shake my head, quickly, and set my jaw. "No, it's fine. Really. Just do the bouffant."

"Good girl. The label is all about image management right now. Clay is country's leading bad boy, and your sweet face is his redemption." She holds up a hand at my protests. "At least that's how they want to sell it. Maria, that means cat eyes and matte red on the lips. There's a mod black frock in the corner that is all you, sweet pea."

With that, Beth slams the door with a loud bang that echoes through the room.

I exhale slowly, my body drooping.

Christian tsks, gathering my hair off my face, and meets my eyes in the mirror. "Welcome to Nashville, Annie."

"Welcome to the Opry, Anna Banana," my dad says in his trademark low growl. He softly propels me forward as we head down the aisles to the very front row. Several times, my father

stops to shakes hands and pat backs. I quit paying attention after the first few and instead stare at the high, arched ceilings, completely taken with the grand architecture and lost in the low murmur of voices. Moments later, my father catches up and settles down next to me on the cushioned bench. The lights flicker a warning that things are about to begin, and I fidget with my dress. It's ruffles upon ruffles. My mom picked it out. "I'll never understand why Stella allows her girls to dress like they're sixteen," she'd said about her publicist, passing me the gown earlier today. "My momma dressed me in ruffles until I was in the ninth grade. Says it's what kept me from getting knocked up before I got my learner's permit." I don't know what a learner's permit is, but as I smooth down the pretty lace flounces on my skirt, I grin. This is a twirling dress, if ever I saw one, and I can't wait to try it out.

A hush falls over the audience as the lights dim, and for the first time, I turn behind me to have a look around. Row upon row of benches are filled all the way up and around a looming balcony. I snap back to the front, my stomach flipping in sudden alarm. I've seen my parents perform more times than I can say, but this feels different.

My patent leather shoes don't quite hit the floor and instead kick out uselessly. My dad places a large, warm hand on my knee to calm me.

"You always get nervous like this when your momma sings?"

I shrug, pinching my lips together. "Sometimes."

"You're so much like her. I bet she's seconds from puking just behind that curtain there." He points to one side, and the corner of my mouth lifts at the comparison.

"Should I say a prayer for her?" I ask.

My dad chuckles low. His face is whiskered and handsome. He has a string tie at his neck and a hat the color of night pulled back on his head. "Sure, Banana. If you think it'll help."

I close my eyes and whisper until I hear the soft rush of heavy *curtains sailing open. My breath catches in my throat. A single beam of light illuminates my mother a few feet in front of me. Her dress falls clear to the floor in heavy sparkles. Her hair floats, soft around her shoulders, and she lowers her gaze to catch my eye and winks once before mouthing "I love you" to my dad.*

She lifts her mic and holds the entire building rapt with her sweet soprano. Sometimes I sing along, spinning in my skirt and clapping my hands. During my favorite song, my mom reaches down to pull me up with her. A burly man dressed in blue offers to help, but before he can reach, my father's hands wrap around my waist and lift me. We sing together, and she twirls me around the stage. The crowd cheers, but I only see the faces of my mom and my dad in the hot lights. I've never felt this way before. As though my entire body were made of glitter and sunlight.

When my dad pulls me down after the songs ends, I whisper in his ear, breathless, "I wanna do this forever, Daddy." He smacks a sandpapery kiss on my cheek and says, "You will, darlin'. You will."

I step out of the dressing room two hours later, my makeup an inch thick and my hair smoothed and shellacked into a style my grandmother would be proud of. I like the dress, at least—a slim-fitting bodice and classy A-line skirt swirling around my knees. Ten years later and I still get a kick out of a twirling dress. Of course, this version is all black to match—

"Clay." His name slips past my lips in an inaudible whisper. It's a damn shame how well this boy fills out a black suit. His brown waves are darkened and slicked off his forehead but for a few artful strands, already escaping to drape across his eyes. Reckless and handsome. As June Carter would say, "A long-legged, guitar-pickin' man." He's got a guitar strap slung over his shoulder and is in a deep discussion as Christian propels me with a gentle shove. I skitter on my ridiculous heels, and Clay turns toward the racket.

I'm happy to report his jaw drops—

—for a split *half* of a half second. I would have straight-up missed it if I hadn't been studying him so intently.

His jaw tightens, and he whirls his guitar around to his front, almost as though it's a barrier to hide behind. I recognize this tactic because my fingers are itching for my own barrier.

"Where's my guitar?" I ask.

"Right here." Trina holds it out. "Kacey sent it along. I planned to give you a prop, but your cousin seemed to think you'd like this better."

I grin my thanks and slip the strap over my shoulder until it settles in its home over my heart. Wall in place, I inhale sharply in an effort to fortify. Yesterday, I was sitting at my grandma's table shelling peas. Now I'm dressed like a legend, standing in front of arguably the biggest country star of the moment, pretending for a camera I'm in love.

5

Clay

Jesus Christ, the set is an old train car.

Do you ever feel like you're hurtling across the continent on one of those high-speed trains?

Next to me, Annie swears under her breath.

I arch a brow down at her. "How's that for irony?"

She shakes her head, walking forward on unsteady heels. She stops and turns to the production assistant, a stuffed shirt named Beth, with her little fists on her hips. Her guitar is slung across her back, and I hide a smile at the picture she makes. I hear the rapid click of a camera behind me. Clearly, I'm not the only one.

"How accurately are we holding to this Johnny-and-June farce?"

Beth looks up from her clipboard. "Why?"

Annie slides her feet out of her pumps and loses at least five inches of height.

More clicking behind me. Beth sighs, long suffering, but doesn't argue.

I move forward, placing a hand on the small of Annie's back and ushering her toward the train car. "That's settled. We have a long afternoon of this, so let's move along."

First, they set us up opposite each other: me leaning casually against one door, her sitting against the other, single bare foot swinging, neither of us looking at each other. Then they had me playing to her, her playing to me, the two of us back to back singing to the heavens. All of it is awkward. We take a break and move over to the food cart so the photographer can rearrange his lighting, and Annie perches on a stool, sipping some kind of green smoothie through a twisty straw. The bottoms of her feet are black, and I can't help but smirk.

My name is called, and the caterer passes me a sandwich on a Styrofoam plate with one of those pickles on a spear. There're no other unoccupied stools, so I stand, balancing the plate in one hand, trying to eat as carefully as possible, but dripping mayo and mustard all over.

Beth claps her hands. "Five more minutes, people."

I chew faster.

"Super-glamorous, right?" Annie says with a wry smile. "I remember my momma running out the door in her curlers more than once when she was late for a shoot. This is the stuff they don't show the enamored masses—dirty feet and mustard in your stubble."

I swipe at my chin with my napkin, but Annie's already hopping down, neatly. She grabs the napkin from my hand and moves in so close I can feel the rustle of her skirt against my knees. She reaches up, still chatting.

"I suppose if they did see it, though, we'd lose our appeal, wouldn't we? Who wants the man behind the curtain when they can have the Wizard?"

She finishes rubbing, lowers her hand, but is still so close. Her eyes find mine, and her lips are parted. Even though they have way too much red lipstick smeared on them, my mouth waters.

Click click click. Annie stutters backward, and I breathe again. Her eyes are wide, and her cheeks are a high pink.

"S-sorry," she says. She's patting down her dress as if looking for something.

"Don't be," the photographer says behind me.

I roll my eyes. "Back at it, then?"

"Change of plans," he says sharply. "Stand together in the middle of the door. *Someone get me a backlight!* We're going to do some silhouette work."

The rest of the shots are face-to-face, our bodies entwined and draped together, the picture of iconic love.

The entire crew is cooing over a particular backlit favorite where I have my guitar strapped to my back and I pick up Annie. Her face is inches from my own, and we look moments from a kiss. In reality, my arms are shaking because this is the tenth time I've lifted her and she's breathless from being squeezed so tightly. Any awkwardness we might have felt at the start of today is nothing. I've learned every inch of this girl's shape in the last two hours. It's like some sort of cruel trust exercise. My restraint has been tested beyond belief, and I'm wrung out and exhausted.

Suddenly it's become very clear to me I didn't have the first damn clue what I was signing up for this summer when I went to Michigan and got her signature.

may
atlanta, georgia

A few mornings later, Fitz bangs on my hotel room door bright and early, and he's not alone.

"Summer Tour Day of Bonding!" he shouts, shoving through the door. I've been awake for a while, making use of the fitness center's weight machines. Even still. I haven't made it through my coffee yet.

Dark-haired Kacey perches on my unmade bed as if she owns the place. She wrinkles her nose. "He needs to shower."

"Yeah, thanks," I say. "And you're here because?"

She grins. "Summer Tour Day of Bonding."

"I heard that part." I turn to Fitz, who's commandeered my Mac. "What does that even mean?"

He doesn't move his eyes from the screen. "Means I got us off the hook from Trina, and we're gonna spend the day getting to know Under the Willows."

"Like zip lines and shit?" I ask. I grab my toothbrush from my case and load it up with toothpaste.

"It's not a corporate retreat, man. It's supposed to be fun."

"I, for one, think zip lines sound amazing," Kacey says.

"Yeah, well, another time. We're going to an amusement park."

"Actually, I haven't been on a roller coaster in years. I'm in."

"Of course you are," Fitz says. "And I just bought us Flash Passes, so it's too late to turn back now."

"Isn't the closest Six Flags, like, over two hours away?"

Kacey pops up. "More like thirty minutes. I'd better go wake Sleeping Beauty."

"You planned this without asking her?"

Kacey shrugs, walking to the door. "If she wanted input, she needed to wake her ass up earlier."

I shake my head, closing the bathroom door. "No love for the headliners, apparently. No big deal. We only pay you."

"I heard that!" Fitz yells through the door.

"Quit listening at the bathroom door, you ingrate!" I yell back before stepping in the steaming water.

Hours later, a sleek black SUV is dropping us off at the entrance. We step out, blearily blinking at the hot sun. Annie shades her eyes while taking in the roller coaster closest to the entrance.

"You don't look excited," I observe in a low tone next to her. After our intense "getting to know you" photo shoot the other day, I've wondered if things would be uncomfortable.

"I'm not," she says, equally quiet. "I get sick on the Tilt-a-Whirl, and escalators make me dizzy. This place is gonna kill me."

I freeze for a second before shaking my head at her. "Why didn't you say something?"

"Oh, Kacey knows, but she's all moony over Fitz in the Jeans, so . . ."

I snicker. "Fitz in the Jeans?"

Annie's cheeks take on color. She lowers her hand and looks at me sheepishly. "Yeah, so if you could forget I said that . . ."

"Not a chance."

She sighs, her small bare shoulders hunching in her simple tank. "Figured not." She winces. "Look, you guys have to know the blue jeans situation in your band is ridiculous."

"So, am I Clay in the Jeans, then?" I ask, trying not to laugh at how uncomfortable she looks. It's such a change from her self-assured stage persona. She glares. It's not very effective.

"I refuse to answer any further questions. You're obviously feeding your ego, and at this point, a bigger head might kill you dead."

"We're in!" Fitz yells. He's waving a bunch of neon bracelets in his hand and starts to pass them out.

"Mathers doesn't need hers. She's afraid of fun," I say.

"Lord give me strength," she mutters, rolling her eyes heavenward. She holds a wrist out to Jason, who obliges with a snort.

"I forgot about that. Remember that one time when you puked up all your cotton candy on the Shaker?" He turns to the rest of us. "Neon-blue vomit everywhere."

Kacey frowns. "I thought that was because you were her date and you doused yourself in Axe beforehand."

"It certainly didn't help," Annie says drolly. "Let's get this over with."

We walk through the gates, hitting every roller coaster at least three times with our quick passes, while Annie watches from the ground. She keeps us fed and offers to wait in the lines for food, which our bracelets do nothing to speed up. At some point, she winds up with a stuffed tiger the size of a small child.

"You pick up a date?" I ask, taking the hot dog she's offering.

She nods. "It's how I like 'em," she says. "Cuddly and silent."

"I want one!" says Kacey. "Let's play some games for a bit. My lunch needs to settle."

We make our way over to an alley of various gaming carts decorated with lurid stuffed animals. Kacey sees the tigers, and we follow. There's a pit in front, filled with baseballs and three impossibly small targets set up in a row along the back wall. Fitz steps up, hands the vendor a five, and grabs a ball. He hits on the first try, but the target doesn't budge.

"Needs a little more oomph," Annie instructs him.

Fitz throws the next two wild.

Jason steps up and taps two, missing the third.

Kacey shakes her head. "I'm afraid of the ball," she offers.

Fitz looks to me with a smirk, and I wave them off. "Naw, it's a waste of money."

"You're rich," Fitz says. "Besides, Annie did it." I want to slug him. Maybe it won't be so bad. I take out a five-dollar bill and pass it to the vendor while picking up a ball. I try to hold it the way I saw the others do, but it's no use. It feels completely foreign in my hands.

I toss the first. It's short. I chuck the second, refusing to look at the others.

Too much oomph. I nearly decapitate the vendor—who is nowhere near the bull's-eyes—or the game, really.

Annie sidles up beside me. "So, Clay in the Jeans was a band geek."

"Oh, I ran track, too," I say, still not looking at her. She takes the ball from my hand, winds up, and pitches it perfectly at the center of the final bull's-eye, punching it to the back of the tent with such force it spins in a circle.

"Winner winner chicken dinner," intones the bored vendor, and he hands her another tiger. She smirks. "All-State Softball Champs three years running. Michigan Pitcher of the Year, both junior and senior year."

I grunt. "So, she sings like an angel, plays like the devil, pitches championships, and slays amusement park games. Is there anything you can't do?"

She passes the tiger to a squealing Kacey. "Yeah. I can't hold my cotton candy."

"We're going to hit a few more rides before dark," Fitz says.

Kacey's looped her arm through his, and they look for all the world like they've been together for their entire lives.

"I'm good for a few more," Jason says around a mouthful of hot dog.

"I think I'll sit the next few out." I look to Annie, who gives me a half smile.

"What about the Ferris wheel?"

I follow her line of sight to the biggest Ferris wheel I've

ever seen. It's one of those ginormous deals that only goes around once because it takes so long.

I shrug. "That sounds okay. Nice and slow."

She grins full on now. "Exactly." We agree to meet back in an hour or so and weave through the vendors and crowds to the Ferris wheel. When we finally make it to the entrance, we both stare straight up.

"No fear of heights?" I check.

"Well . . . I don't actually know. I didn't think so . . . but now . . ."

I grab her hand. "Come on. Don't overthink it."

Annie gives me a wry look.

"What?"

"Nothing. Going to be an interesting summer, is all."

Moments later, an attendant slams the door to our carriage with a loud *click,* and my gut swoops as we lift in the air. Annie watches out the side, and I take in the sight of her frizzed curls whipping in the warm breeze.

"I saw you perform once, a few years back," she says suddenly. She doesn't look at me, still staring determinedly at the scenery.

"Where?"

"Chicago? Young Stars."

That was the last place I'd expected. My face scrunches, and I shift on my bench. The carriage rocks in response, and Annie grips her side tighter, tensing.

"I'm surprised you remember that. I try to forget it myself."

She lets out a soft laugh, still holding on. "I doubt anyone who saw you that day would've forgotten. You left your audience in a puddle of hormones."

I groan, rubbing at my face. "Don't remind me."

She's merciless. "If memory serves, you wore highlights in your hair back then. Sort of Bieber-esque. In fact," she continues, moving closer to the middle of her seat. "Didn't you sing Bieber?"

"Please stop," I beg, but I can't help the grin twitching at my lips at her snark. "For your information, it was Hunter Hayes."

Her blue eyes dance. "My bad. You're right. Hunter Hayes is *much* better. The twelve-year-olds went wild."

I let her have her laugh before raising a brow. "And yet you seem to remember it quite well."

"Naturally." She shrugs. "I was barely older than twelve myself."

I roll my eyes. "Fine, laugh all you want. That's the show that got me the attention of the label."

"Okay, fine. Full disclosure. I was fifteen. And I didn't even see you or the atrocious highlights at first. I remember because I was in the middle of prep on a smaller stage when I heard your singing over the loudspeakers. I missed a step and fell down the stairs. Had this totally embarrassing purple bruise from here to here." She gestures from her knee to her upper thigh. "A medic rushed over, and there was this small crowd of onlookers, but I just plowed through them, bleeding and deranged, trying to get my eyes on the owner of that voice. It was no shock to me when I heard you on the radio last year."

"I don't know if I believe you."

She tilts her head to the side, squinting. "Maybe not. We're our biggest critics, aren't we?" She tugs her shorts up on one side and points to a thin scar about three inches long. "Believe it, man."

I clear my throat. "I heard you before, too. In Michigan, last summer. We were local for our tour, and I like to hit the county fairs on my nights off to scope out new talent . . . or competition, as it were." I nod in her direction, and her mouth drops open comically.

"I didn't think anyone knew we did those. We certainly didn't have scouts turning up and offering us contracts at that point."

"Would you have signed if they had?"

She shakes her head, easing back into her bench. We're nearing the top now, but neither of us are taking in the view. "No."

"Why? You obviously love it. I saw you—not only at the fair but at Lula May's. You're a performer; it's in your blood."

She speaks quietly—so quietly I can barely make it out. "I do love it, more than anything. That's what scares me. I know it's hard to understand, and I don't think I really get it myself, but it's like music is tied to everything happy *and* awful in my life. All my highs *and* my lows. I mean, look at all of them down there." She peeks over the side and gestures at the throngs of people milling around like tiny, faceless insects. "Can you imagine? They don't have to sing and parade around onstage to be happy—to feel whole." She looks back at me, her eyes wide and piercing. "But I do. My parents did, too. To the point that they died for it." She shakes her head. "I tried to do something else—be something else—but I couldn't. I can't shake it."

I'm speechless. Part of me feels what she's saying so hard. The other part of me, the part that throws empty beer bottles at my brother's headstone, doesn't want to hear it. That kind of passion for anything scares the shit out of me. I might die because of country music, but not for it. Inadequacy churns in my stomach, and I want off this ride.

"Yeah, lucky bastards, all of them," I say, looking out the side but not seeing anything.

"What about you?" she asks, shaking herself. "Enough of my dreary backstory. What are you here for?"

"Booze and girls," I reply automatically. I don't bother keeping the sardonic slant from my tone.

"Of course. But, like, besides that. You can get booze and girls in college."

I grin as though the thought hadn't ever occurred to me. "College. Now that's an idea."

She rolls her eyes lightly. "Fine. Play the fool. I get it. I overshared, and now it's your turn to shut down and pretend you're a jerk."

"Maybe I am a jerk, Annie."

She shakes her head, more curls springing out of her pony. "I call bull. But that's fine. Just remember, I've heard your voice, and I'm not some fangirl. You're more than good vocals."

We're finally descending, and I can't get off this thing fast enough. Before I do, though, I turn to Annie. "Look. I'm sorry if I made you feel like you overshared. It's fine. I asked, and you answered. Don't apologize for that. But I really am a jerk. I promise you that." I run a hand through my hair, only realizing I'm wearing a hat. I tug on it uselessly. "That said, your future isn't set in stone. Okay? If you don't want to end up like your parents, then don't."

She doesn't get up—just sits there and finally nods once, slowly, in response. Before I can say anything else stupid, I jump out, leaving her behind.

That night, we all eat together in the hotel lobby before deciding to rent a movie in our room to watch. For the first time in years, I feel my age, and I savor it because I know when I wake up, the feeling will be gone. Sure, touring is fun as hell.

It's a summerlong party. But it's also a grueling job. Shows run late, and then you're on the road to the next location through the night. You wake up in a new city every day. You rehearse, bullshit with radio deejays on their morning shows, make guest appearances, and squeeze in studio time.

At some point during the movie, we'd all piled up on one bed in a mass of pillows and blankets. Fitz and Kacey are sharing a pillow, heads tilted close together. Jason is sprawled across the bed, snoring softly.

"Poor guy's all tuckered out," Annie mocks. I was worried she'd hold this afternoon and the Ferris wheel against me. But again, I'm wrong about her. By the time she'd caught up with the rest of us, nachos in hand, you'd have never been able to tell anything had happened. To the point that I wondered if I'd imagined the tension in the first place.

"I wish we had a Sharpie," I say.

"Oooooh, Trina would kill you." Annie gently rolls to her side and pulls out her purse. She digs around a second and passes me a pink Sharpie.

"Who *are* you, Mary Poppins?" I say, not bothering to keep the awe from my voice. She giggles. "What should I write?"

"Nothing mean. How about facial hair? He's being so annoying about his almost-stubble."

I grin. "Nineties boy band or professional wrestler?"

"Oh. Boy band for sure."

"Pink soul patch it is."

6

Annie

friday, may 24
atlanta, georgia
opening night

"Aren't you nervous?"

Jason glances up from his phone and shrugs. "Yeah. A little, maybe." His fingers return to his tapping.

A huff slips past my glossed lips, and I lean back against the small leather sofa set in my temporary dressing room. We have approximately thirty minutes until lights up. A toilet flushes, and Kacey steps out of the small bathroom, plenty green around the gills. I toss her a complimentary seltzer water, and she cracks the lid with a practiced wrist flick. She takes a small sip and moans.

"Nothing to be nervous about. They're not here to see me," Jason continues, speaking into his lap. "Someone asked me where the mic stands were again."

Jason keeps getting mistaken for a roadie. It's pretty annoying. Well, I'm annoyed; he's . . . resigned. There's not a whole lot of diversity in country music. At least onstage, anyway. We've always lived right near the university, and

Jason's dark skin is barely a blip among all the different cultures in Michigan. In Nashville and on tour, he sticks out. It's a new experience for all of us, but of course, he's the one left managing stereotypes.

"I told you your haircut looked shaggy," I joke.

He looks up from his phone, his dark eyes piercing. "Yeah, that's it."

"I'm sorry. It's nothing to joke about. How about I promise, by the end of summer, every person in the industry will know the name Jason Diaz, mega-genius drummer extraordinaire."

"Sounds good, though, like I said, these crowds aren't here to see Jason Diaz, drummer."

"You're right. Not yet, anyway. This is Clay's tour, and he's got a hell of a following."

Jason throws his phone onto the counter and steals my water, taking a long swig. "Oh no," he says after swallowing and passing it back to me. "Packed house already. They might've bought tickets for Clay, but word's out. Those people out there are here for Annie Mathers."

Kacey sprints for the bathroom again.

I sigh. "Kacey, I'm gonna need you to get ahold of yourself, chickadee. This here's a trio."

A muffled groan and more coughing.

"Knock, knock."

"Come in," Jason replies cheerfully.

"It's just me." Fitz steps through the door, closing it behind him. "Aren't you missing one?"

I nod toward the bathroom. "Kacey's got a case of the pukes."

"Nerves?"

"Thanks to Captain Encouraging over there," I say.

Jason rolls his eyes, fiddling with his ever-present drumsticks. "I'm just being the realist."

I aim a scowl in his general direction. "I'll thank you to sit on your realism. I need my fiddler."

Fitz casts a concerned glance toward the closed door. "I've got something that'll help. Be right back."

A minute later, he returns with a bottle and taps on the bathroom door. Kacey opens it a crack, and he holds the bottle in front of her face, wiggling it in his hands. "Liquid courage. Come on. It's tradition."

"Distribution to minors is a tradition?"

Fitz flashes a grin and waggles his rusty brows. "Only when it's by other so-called minors."

That little nugget gives me pause. "Wait, how old are you?"

Fitz smirks. "I turned the big two zero last week."

"No shit?" Jason asks.

"Yes, *shit*. That's between us, though. Ain't no room for legalism on tour, Annie. That's lesson number one." He quirks a look at Jason. "Write that down, young apprentice."

I smile despite myself and scoot forward on the couch. Fitz pulls a couple of shot glasses out of his back pockets and lays them out on the coffee table in front of us.

"Now," he begins in a serious tone. "One is too few; three is far too many. But for our first night, we have to take queasy stomachs and all-around nervous jitters into account. So we'll do two half shots."

"So one," I say, amused. Kacey is already reaching for hers as he pours.

He protects the glasses with a palm and looks at me. "Lesson number two: Fitz always knows best. I say two half shots, and that's what we'll do." He passes the glasses around, and I see mine reads: *Spring Break Panama City*.

"Wait. Do you travel with these?"

"Lesson three: always be prepared. Drink!"

I watch as my band members drink. Kacey is dainty;

Jason, full of false bravado. Fitz is already pouring the next. He raises a brow at my untouched glass.

"No, thanks."

"Not nervous?"

"Oh, I'm full of butterflies. But I don't drink."

"How do you know?"

I offer him a patient look and point to my throat. "I'm not interested in finding out if golden vocals are all my momma left me."

A dark shadow falls across Fitz's face. "Fair enough. I won't ask again." He turns to Kacey, and Jason and lifts my glass. "For the rest of us, it's best not to wait. To your first night of many. May you change the world with your music."

"Wow, that's lofty—" Jason mutters.

"Lesson number two!" He reminds him loudly. "Drink, apprentice!"

I swallow hard against the itch in my throat as I watch them. I've never so much sipped my grandpa's Budweiser, but that doesn't stop my brain from thinking it might be a good idea to try. I take a long swig of my ice water and shake out my fingers. I meet Kacey's eyes. She's no longer sweaty and green. Now she's flushed, but smiling. "Feeling better?"

"Much." She turns to Fitz with hero worship glowing out of her blue irises. "That was amazing, thank you!"

His face reddens under her attention, and I have to swallow my own grin. "That's nothing. Just a little show biz trick. I always keep some on hand for Clay. He's not technically allowed to pre-drink this tour, but if I don't get a few shots in him, he clams up, and that's *no bueno* for the party tour of the summer."

"Sounds like a banner start to alcoholism."

Fitz smiles, but it doesn't reach his eyes, and he shifts in his seat. "Probably. That's what I'm around for, though. Everyone needs a buddy. Do you all have your tour buddy? Someone to keep you out of trouble?"

I can't help but smile at his antics. I'm grateful for devil-may-care Fitz.

"Let's sing 'Should've Been You' tonight," I say impulsively.

Jason groans. "We can't change the set now; we have ten minutes."

"Why? It's not like we have backup dancers or anything. You know it, Kacey knows it, I know it."

"I thought we agreed to stick to covers tonight," Jason replies, looking anxious.

"Yeah, but I don't want to play it safe. It's on YouTube. It's not totally unheard. Plus, I think it will play well to a young crowd."

"You mean a female crowd."

"You're only hesitant because you know the song's about you," Kacey says with a giggle.

"Come on, Jason. It's got a killer solo for Kacey in it, and if you want to throw in a drum solo, I'm down. Please?"

"Are you going to tell them all it's about me?"

"Probably. Will you hate me for exploiting you?"

Jason purses his lips, considering. "Probably. Unless . . . maybe it can work in my favor. Might make me a heart-breaker."

I give an unladylike snort. "Whatever you have to tell yourself, dude."

Another knock at the door. "Five minutes, Willows. Time to hit the stage."

I inhale sharply, grabbing my guitar. "We'll pray backstage. Let's do this."

"Good evening, Hot-Lanta!" I shout into my mic, adrenaline rushing through my veins and spreading out to my fingertips. I strum a chord on my guitar and still the strings with my palm. "My name's Annie Mathers, and I'm sure glad to be here in front of all your gorgeous faces, kicking off the summer."

A cheer rises up, plastic cups and bottles sloshing into the air, held by tailgaters making a day of the show. No surprise with this tour. Summer concerts are in a league of their own. The sheer number of people calms something inside of me. They turned up. For us. The weather showed up for them. The sweet summer air is glorious and balmy. A group of a half dozen tweens scream out from the front row a few feet away. They're holding a sign with glittery block letters that reads OUR BOOTS ARE MADE FOR WALKIN, and I wink at them in their hot-pink cowboy hats and strum again, nodding at Jason over my shoulder, who takes my cue and strikes the snare.

I can do this. I can play my heart out for this crowd. The rest is biscuits and gravy. Kacey raises her bow and starts to rub out the tempo, and I grin. "This song's for every gal who ever got tired of her guy messing her around." The crowd roars in response, and I give Her Majesty, Loretta Lynn, my best shot.

The next half hour passes in a blur. The best dang blur of my life. By the second song, the stragglers had found their seats, Kacey's fiddle a siren to their sensibilities. I doubt they even realized they'd come in until they had to fetch their next overpriced beer. Just as promised, Jason's heartbreaker status seemed secured after I told the story of our song, and when he tossed his cheap Ray-Ban knockoffs into the crowd, a catfight broke out.

After the lights shut off, I practically skip stage left. I glimpse a ball cap across the stage. Clay lifts the brim in a casual nod before sinking back into the shadows. It takes me a second before I see Fitz had been standing next to him. Had they been in the wings the entire time? Was he watching our performance? It bothers me how much I want to know what he thinks of me.

Sings like an angel, plays like the devil, he'd said. Was he just being flip? Clay's smooth, for sure. Hundreds of people cheer my name, and I still only want to know his opinion.

Since we don't have to leave right after the show, I allow myself a sneak peek from the wings into Clay's performance. If I thought Fitz was charming offstage, his onstage antics are adorable. He's the comic relief to Clay's heady sensuality. It's not that Clay doesn't smile—he does—and Lord, when he *does* . . . but Fitz has a way of making it seem like it's well and truly a party onstage. Clay balances on the precipice of a jagged cliff, and Fitz secures the carabiners just in case. Midway through the performance, Fitz jumps upstage next to Clay, and they play at trying to stump each other with classic hits. It's like *Name That Tune* brought to you by Jack Daniel's. The crowd goes crazy for it, and I have to admit, it looks like a blast. I'm halfway tempted to jump onstage and join them, but I doubt Clay would appreciate my intrusion on his spotlight.

Maybe later in the summer when it's too much of a hassle to replace me. The ladies of country are sorely underrepresented in their shtick. It's about time I mixed things up a bit.

I haven't forgotten what happened between Clay and me on the Ferris wheel. I'm not an idiot; I saw how he watched me afterward, all nerves and guilt. He might say he's a jerk, and I'm inclined to agree, but I don't think that's all there is to him. Something's got him rattled. There's a lot unsaid between Clay and me. Well, there's a lot unsaid by Clay, period. I'm just not sure I'm the one to open that particular can of worms.

Still, I'm drawn to him. Annoyingly drawn. Like a bruised and wayward moth flying into a flickering light bulb.

I skim the set list taped on the side of an equipment trunk and see things are wrapping up. Time for me to head back to my bus. Kacey is singing at the top of her lungs, so I nudge her, and she waves me off. I lost track of Jason a few songs back. He headed off with his nose in his phone screen.

Sneaking out the back way yields a small crowd. There're two ginormous security guards dressed in black, blocking the exit. Shoving through the stage door, I'm hit with some cheering and flashes of light.

"Only me, sorry!" I say with a grin. My smile falters after the flashing continues and I recognize the tweens from earlier. I walk over to where they are standing behind a waist-high metal barrier. "Goodness, have you girls been out here all night? You do realize there's still a show going on!"

A mom speaks up with a knowing grin. "Well, I would have stuck around for Clay, but these girls wanted to make sure they were back here to see you instead."

A sudden rush of emotion has me biting my lip. At once, I'm backstage with my momma after one of her performances. She's all glitter and leather, and her hair floats in a gorgeous, feathery halo around her sleek bare shoulders. "Hold tight, Annie May," she'd whisper to me. "Grab on to my fringe now and don't get lost. This will only take a minute." I would peer from her shadow, amazed at the sheer number of fans who would wait for hours backstage for the chance to see my mom for even a second. She'd beam at them all like they were individually precious to her. As a kid, it'd make me jealous to have to share my mom with the world, but right now, I almost understand it. Maybe she couldn't help herself? The gratitude of another person—a lot of other persons, even—wanting to connect with you over your music?

It's the best kind of overwhelming.

"Girls. You've made my night!" I turn to catch the eye of one of the scary-looking guards watching us curiously. "Can you take our picture?"

The girls let out a collective squeal as the giant, uncomfortable-looking man slowly trudges over to us. I hand him my phone, and the mom hands him hers. Before he can object, I hop over the gate and wrap my arms around the vibrating preteens. "Come on, Momma. You, too," I say with a wink. "Maybe if we're lucky, Clay Coolidge himself will walk through that door." Her face lights up in a full-on beaming grin. "There's the smile!" I tease.

I take my time, signing whatever the girls shove into my hands, and take a few more pictures. "Did you know y'all are my very first fans?" I ask. "I won't forget you ladies."

A light casts over us, and I can tell the back door is opening. I glance out of the corner of my eye. "See? I told you they'd be around." I wave Kacey over, and she skips to my side. Clay and Fitz trail at a slower pace.

"You guys! My first fans!" I say, feeling a little giddy. Fitz gives me a high five while Clay allows himself a small flicker of amusement. I'm positive he's rolling his eyes so hard at me, but I don't care. Even his cool cynicism can't ruin my moment.

Kacey and I pose together with the girls, and then the mom asks if I would take her photo with Clay, who obliges with a kiss on her cheek, and I have to grin at the thought that her life is basically made with his small gesture.

"Can we get one more of you two?" Since the show is

over, the crowd has grown substantially. Now there is plenty of press around, too. The guards are getting edgy, and I know it's about time we hit the buses. I glance up.

"Which two?" I ask, distracted.

"You and Clay."

I shrug, and he moves closer to me, wrapping his arm around my shoulders. I try so hard not to blush, thinking of the mom, but he smells unbelievable. Like cologne and spearmint and man-boy, and I'm dizzy with it.

Flashes break out around us, blinding me. "You guys are my favorite new couple!" someone gushes, and I blink, trying to clear my eyes.

"Oh, well—"

"That's all the time we have for tonight!" Trina announces over the crowd. "These guys have to hit the road. Thank you all for coming out and supporting Clay and Annie!"

My teeth click together, and Clay steers me away before I can say anything. Once we clear the crowd, he drops his hold and hisses under his breath at Trina.

"What the fuck was that? 'Clay and Annie'?"

"For the record, I was all for clarifying," I say.

Trina waves us both off, but Clay rounds her and stops her in her tracks. "This isn't some publicity stunt, Trina. These are our lives we're talking about."

My heart starts thrumming in my ears, and my feet stick to the ground, immobilizing me. I'm taken aback at how livid he is. It shouldn't hurt, but of course it does. This summer is about to be death by a thousand paper cuts.

"Listen, Clay, I can clear it right up. I'll tweet something tonight, and by tomorrow, your groupies will be all lining up again."

He *does* roll his eyes this time. "That's not the problem.

I don't care about that." He narrows his eyes at Trina. "It's one thing to do publicity shoots to garner up press, but the shows are booked. Annie has more than proved her merit tonight. There's a difference in letting the fans make their own assumptions and feeding them a fake relationship."

I'm at a loss for words. He's sticking up for me? Did I hear him say I have merit? It's not a secret Clay's in trouble with the label—that I'm part of Operation Clean Clay's Rep—so his defense of me is all the more stunning.

He huffs at whatever expression is on my face. "Jesus, Annie, don't look so shocked. I'd have to be an idiot to not see you have talent. And I can promise you Trina knows it, too, so *why*"—he turns back to her, and I notice she's leveling him with a calculating glare—"would you use that tone?"

"I don't know what you're talking about."

"She just said, 'Clay and Annie,' Clay; it's not a big—"

"Oh, she knows. Trina does nothing by accident."

Trina smirks. "If you must know, your photo shoot went live this morning. Social media has lit up with speculation. Whether you two play it up or not, the world is convinced your chemistry is what this tour is about. Now." She raises a long-nailed finger. "I'm not saying you need to play up the fake relationship or anything so classless. Clay is right. You both have gobs of talent, and that's enough. I'm just saying, maybe don't deny it. Leave the mystery. The inevitable speculation can only be good for you."

"But . . . it was just a photo shoot. It was all staged. They get that, right? I mean, we haven't even been seen together." I'm unsettled. Seriously uncomfortable. Clay is trouble. He's too smooth and drinks too much. I can hear my gran's voice in the back of my mind—*Cocky cowboy strutting in and taking my little girl away*—can feel the comparison to my mom. Cora Rosewood was a megastar. She held the world rapt with her vocals, but my father held *her* rapt with his charm, at least in the beginning. Too good-looking and far too connected. On their own, they were sparklers in the hands of children on the Fourth of July. Together, they were a house on fire.

Trina gives me a patient look. "Until tonight."

"That wasn't . . . I was just excited. Those girls . . ." I feel like crying. The buzz I felt earlier is now pooling around my feet in a puddle of terrible dread. I've spent years honing my craft, preparing to do this and do it right—*better* than they had. One show in, and I'm tabloid fodder.

"Trina, knock it off," Clay bites out.

"I'm not my mom." My breath catches, and I feel like my vision is tunneling. "This was a mistake. I'm not like her." I'm rambling, and I try to slink away from Trina's wide-eyed assessment. It's embarrassing how quickly I'm unraveling.

"Annie! What happened? Annie. Look at me." Kacey's face swims into view. She takes my cheeks in her warm hands and drags my eyes up to focus on hers. I blink and start to calm down. She leads me in a few calming breaths while speaking in soothing tones. "Annie. It's okay. It's all okay. You aren't like her. I promise. No one thinks that. At all. It was a misunderstanding."

"I know," I say, feeling stupid. I wave my hands in front of my face in a sorry attempt to cool my burning skin. "I overreacted."

I hear Jason somewhere behind her, his voice raised. Suddenly he's there next to Kacey, a candy bar and water bottle in either hand. I take the water and sip, shakily.

"I'm fine," I insist. "Just humiliated."

His lips spread a big goofy grin. "Every rock star has a meltdown at some point. Best to get it out of the way early on."

"Shoulda had that shot," Kacey teases before her face falls serious. "You aren't Cora, you know, but the comparisons are inevitable. This won't be the first time fans show up, and it's not the only time people will make assumptions about you. This business is built on assumptions. You can't let that prevent you from taking what's yours."

"You were great out there tonight," Jason says.

My lips curl. "I had good backup."

"And you'll keep having us. Don't forget that. This isn't just you, even if you are the star of the show."

Jason stands, holding a hand out, and I take it.

Kacey shoots a glare at Trina, who still looks gobsmacked, before wrapping an arm around my shoulders and leading me back to the bus.

"I feel like I should apologize or explain or something." I slump onto a bench seat, dropping my head onto my arms.

"To who? Barely anyone even saw anything."

I raise my head. "Except Clay and Trina."

"And Fitz, but that's okay," Kacey says. "They needed to see it. Everyone needed to get on the same page. To everyone else, Cora and Robbie were a sad song, but to you, they were real life. In the meantime, you killed it tonight and proved to the world—and your headliner, by the way—that you deserve to be on this tour. You're the real deal in your own goddamn right. So drink your water, and then grab your guitar and write your feelings. Jason and I can handle the rest."

There's a knock on the door of the bus, and Jason and Kacey exchange looks. Jason grabs my hand and tugs me up to his wiry chest. "Come on, girl. I'll get you all settled in." I smack his shoulder playfully.

"Don't you try those eyes on me. You know they're wasted."

He flashes a blinding white grin. "Oh, I know. Your taste

in men has evolved in the last few years. You prefer crooners over drummers, I hear."

With anyone else, I would sink into dismay all over again, but with Jason, I can laugh.

"Holy mother, it's gonna be a summer, isn't it?"

7

Clay

After the Meltdown, Fitz went to help console his new
fiddle-playing friend, and that left me in my bus. Alone.
Well, not totally alone. I have my guitar.

I could go out and find some company, but watching
Annie collapse in a trembling heap of tears and grief sort of
killed any urges I might have had.

Not that I blame her. I think we all learned a valuable
lesson tonight. Annie Mathers is not just some eager beaver
starlet. No, sir. She's messed up.

Having my early suspicions from her birthday performance confirmed doesn't change anything. She's still too
talented to stay home. She deserves this place on the tour.
I wasn't bullshitting tonight when I argued with Trina.
Annie's proven her worth. I haven't forgotten how much I
need her here, but I'm starting to wonder if maybe she
needs me.

Which is some first-class tomfoolery, but nonetheless
rings true. If there's one thing I'm good at, it's putting on a
performance. If Annie Mathers is going to survive this tour,
she's gonna need to put the performance first and forget the
rest.

I hear footsteps and voices outside my bus and peek out the blinds. It's that Jason kid. I surge to my feet and throw open the door. "Hey, man, where you headed?"

He stops, raising his brows, confused. "Uh, I'm hungry. Fitz and I were gonna get some pancakes. Wanna come?"

I shake my head. "How's Mathers?"

He shifts on his feet. "Okay. She locked herself in her room to write."

I hop down and stumble a little as I do.

"You're not going over there." He's suddenly right in front of me. "Especially not drunk."

I crack a grin. "Easy, Diaz, it's just water." Now it is, anyway. I spin, and with deliberate care, I place the bottle behind me on the step. I don't know why I have to antagonize this kid, but I do. "What's your deal? Afraid she mightn't be able to resist me?"

Jason's eyes glint in the parking lot light. "The last thing she needs right now is to be connected to you. You saw her tonight. She's not some hookup."

I rub a hand down my face. I've aged ten years since yesterday. "Look, if I were interested in a hookup, I wouldn't be out here talking to you, and I definitely wouldn't be knocking on Annie's door. She's a mess."

"Then what do you want with her?"

"I only wanted to check on her. I'm not a complete dick. I feel somewhat responsible since it was our photo shoot and my tour manager that threw her for a spin." I lean back against the bus, crossing my arms. "You don't know me, but I swear only half the things they say about me are true. I happen to think you guys are pretty good. I wanted to offer some—"

Jason's grin is shit-eating. "Some what? Advice? Yeah, you're clearly one to talk."

I'm annoyed. More annoyed than the situation probably warrants, and that makes it worse. "Know what? Forget it." I shove off the bus and stagger back to the steps, swiping a grab at my bottle. "You're right. What the hell do I know?"

Fitz comes around the corner with the little fiddler, Kacey, in tow. "What's wrong?"

"Nothing," I answer before Jason can. "Abso-fucking-lutely nothing. I was just about to finish *my water* alone because I'm an asshole who doesn't care about anyone. Right, Jason?"

The kid looks uncomfortable but doesn't disagree.

"Right. Enjoy your pancakes." I let the door slam behind me and lock it. Fitz can find somewhere else to sleep tonight.

I wake up to banging on the door.

"We need to leave, Clay! Open the door and let me in!"

I swing it open, relishing the burst of fresh air it brings. The bus smells of staleness and sweat. I don't say anything, just work my way down the windows, sliding them open.

"I slept in the Willows' bus, in case you were wondering. Thanks for that."

I roll my eyes. "I'm sure that must've been terrible for you. Did your fiddler friend lend you some pajamas or offer to take off hers instead?"

Fitz presses his lips together, and for a second, I think he might be mad. "I heard what Jason said to you. It was un-called for. You weren't doing anything wrong. They're just super-protective of Annie."

I shrug and open the minifridge, pulling out the orange juice. I take a long sip right from the carton, and it sloshes in my stomach. "Whatever."

Fitz sits down on a bench, and I hand him the OJ and a

glass. "Not 'whatever,'" he says as he pours his glass. "You aren't a dick, Clay."

Fitz never calls me by my real first name. Never has. He tried to call me Jeff after Danny died, and it never took. In the same way, I never call him Jacoby. It's this unspoken pact we have—a refusal to overstep. Still, when he says it now, it feels like a lie because *Clay* actually *is* a dick sometimes.

"I was drunk. The kid was right."

"That kid is the same age as you. He doesn't know you."

"Knows enough." I look at my hands, picking at my callous.

Fitz sighs, cradling his glass. "Why did you want to see Annie?"

"Honestly? I don't even remember." A lie.

Fitz can tell. He raises a dubious brow.

"Fine. I felt bad for the girl. She looked really shaken up. She's had a bad deal with her parents, and I sort of get it, but she shouldn't quit."

Fitz narrows his eyes. "I don't think she's going to quit."

"Good."

A telling pause.

"You're such a pain in my ass."

He smiles, and I can feel the corners of my lips twitch to match.

"We leave in fifteen." He gets up and pats my shoulder, giving it a familiar squeeze. "You stink, my friend." He starts for the flap of curtain that divides his bedroom and pulls it open. He plops on his bed, kicking off his boots before crossing his legs and placing his hands behind his head.

"Didn't get much sleep last night, huh?"

He readjusts his hat farther down over his eyes. "Stop fishing, junior. I ain't telling you a thing."

8

Annie

We spent the days in between Georgia and Mississippi in the recording studio. Immediately after my panic attack, I was assigned a manager. I suppose it was completely naive of me to think I could get away without one for the duration, but I thought Trina was enough, even if she wasn't technically ours. Thankfully, a quick call out to Patrick Royston saved the day. His lovely wife, Connie, has fifteen years of tour management under her belt after touring with the Dixie Chicks in the '90s and early 2000s.

I hired her on the spot and washed my hands of things. Good riddance. Until she came knocking on my door the next morning, saying she'd scheduled us studio time. Our label decided they wanted to ride the wave of our sudden popularity and needed an album to release by summer's end.

I wouldn't have thought it possible, but it seems Connie is a force to be reckoned with. Behind her sugar-sweet image, she's cut from the very same cloth as Trina. In fact, if I didn't know better, I'd say they were sisters in another life.

I don't mind, really. It's not comparable to the high I get from a live performance, but I've been stockpiling songs for years. While a good number of them are childish or more emo than I care to admit, enough are salvageable for an album. Besides, I would prefer not to have time to think right now. It's as though the Muses heard my cry for distraction and answered posthaste. Between the hours spent in the studio and the hours preparing to be in the studio and the scheduled publicity appearances on various local radio stations, I can barely remember my last name most days (though there is no shortage of people willing to remind me). Thanks to my new manager, however, I now have a ready response to the "Clay Dilemma."

I give a coy smile and a cute little wink. "No comment."

Of course today, Long-Winded Larry with WPK out of Biloxi isn't buying it. He shakes his head. "Oh, now, y'all cain't see this, but the lovely Miss Annie Mathers just gave me a wink worthy of her momma. You ain't getting off that easy, girl. Inquiring minds beg to know; are there any sparks between you and Clay?"

I glance at Kacey, who shrugs helplessly, and bite my lip. The thing is, in show business, only a sliver of the acting is confined to the stage. I let loose my Tennessee roots. "All right, Larry. Let me tell you about Clay Coolidge. That man can sure 'nuff fill out a pair of blue jeans. Whew!" I say, fanning the collar of my button-down before leaning closer to my mic and lowering my voice conspiratorially. "And what you ladies witness onstage, *Lord,* in person it's a thousand times worse. Like staring down the sun. But I'll be honest with y'all . . . Clay's not to be tied down. It would be a disservice to the man to place a claim."

Larry nods in approval. "Fair enough, fair enough. So, Miss Mathers, we like to do a little game with our guests called Twelve-Minute Tunes, where we give our callers a chance to come up with any topic of their choosing and you, our star guest, will have twelve minutes to write a song about that topic and perform it live on the air. How's that sound?"

I squirm in my seat, but otherwise it sounds like a semi-fun challenge. "Can I request a second cup of coffee first, Larry?"

He laughs. "Of course! We want you to be ready."

We got to commercial as Larry and his assistant field a handful of phone calls, choosing a few to air. The first offers the President, the second suggests the World Series hopefuls, and the third obviously was my headliner. They weren't messing around.

"What'll you chose, Annie?"

I take a slow sip of my coffee, the lyrics already clicking into place in my mind. "Well, I'd rather drink paint thinner than offer political insight, and I'm a fair-weather Tigers fan, so I guess that means I'm writing about Clay."

Larry cheers, and Connie gives me a thumbs-up. Kacey pulls out her fiddle—always ready for me, even on the fly.

I reflect on how little I truly know Clay Coolidge so far. From the moment he turned up on my porch, hungover, to his defensiveness after our first show. He's a conundrum, but I doubt many see that. His MO is straight-up Trouble with a capital *T*, but his eyes are full of something more.

Of course, I can't fit all that in, and anyway, Long-Winded Larry and his listeners aren't interested in me waxing poetic about Clay's "something more" on their morning commute. They're only interested in the trouble part and how that bodes for little ol' me.

So that's what I give them.

Larry comes back from a weather/traffic report and I still

my strings, ready to go. I've jotted down a handful of notes on some scratch paper, but I don't need them. When words mix with melodies in my brain, it's nearly impossible to erase them, regardless of nerves.

"All set?" he prompts off mic.

I nod, and he comes back live. "All right, folks, we're back with the lovely Annie Mathers and her fiery fiddle-playing cousin, Kacey. We've challenged her twelve minutes to write up a ditty about her tour headliner, Clay Coolidge. Take it away, Ms. Mathers!"

I start strumming.

"This little tune is gonna have a bit of a Creedence Clear-water Revival feeling to it. I figured y'all might dig that being in the Gulf bayou," I start.

Well, I met me a man in the bayou
His voice gave me shivers and swirls
His last name was so presidential,
His first name was straight from the soil

I sang with this man in the bayou
He swung Levi hips to a beat
All the ladies went nuts in the bayou
All the fellas drank their whiskey neat

I was tempted by this man in the bayou,
Oh Lord, he was sin wrapped in vice
His lips are why kissing's invented
His skin's pure sun-drenched and spice

I met me a man in the bayou
I knew he wasn't to be tied down
Y'all will fall fast for that man in the bayou
But that ain't a road I'll go down

For we all crave the man in the bayou
And his songs will serenade us late
He'll make love to us all in the bayou
But my tour goes through many a state

So I'll leave this here in the bayou
Our memories, we will hold dear.
With Larry and friends in the bayou
Perhaps y'all will call me back next year

I open my eyes as a sparkly-eyed Kacey is wrapping the final pull of her strings. For a half second, it's all silence, and I can feel my face start to heat, but then Larry busts into a full-on belly laugh, and I sink back into my chair. I take my time putting away my guitar, composing myself.

Larry is beaming and wiping at his eyes. "We've had a lot of singers come on our show—young and old, newcomers and industry icons, and"—he turns to his associates, who are all smiling—"I think we can all agree that twelve-minute tune will go down as a favorite."

My face feels hot as the sun, but I laugh. "Aw. I'm so glad. Guess Clay makes for easy subject matter. You'll have to use him again sometime and compare the two."

"I have to address the elephant in the room," Larry says seriously. "You sang that you've been tempted by Clay, leading to even more speculation about you two kids. Are you saying that you'd be interested if you could?"

I decide to toss Larry a bone with some honesty. "It's really impossible to say. I'm too busy having fun of my own. This is my first tour, Larry. I just graduated from high school! These are the best years of my life! I don't want to waste them chasing after a mustang."

Larry's female cohost, Lisa Marie, gives me a fist bump. "Even a mustang as wild as Clay Coolidge?"

"Ain't the chase half the fun, y'all?" I say.

Connie gives me an enthusiastic thumbs-up from outside the booth, and I allow my shoulders to slump the tiniest bit as Larry leads us into a commercial break. I pull off my headphones and shake hands all around. We hit the sunny street a few minutes later, and I stop in the middle of the sidewalk to let the warm rays seep into my skin and give it a chance to darken my freckles.

"Connie," I say, not bothering to open my eyes. "What day is it?"

"Thursday. Show tonight."

"So, no studio time?"

"Not today. You're off until Tuesday." I think I can hear the amusement in her voice. I open one eye to confirm my suspicion.

"So, technically, I don't have to be anywhere until sound check?"

"Technically," she says, sounding wary. "Why?"

I suck in a lungful of humid air and can almost taste the sea salt. I grab Kacey's arm. "I wanna find a piece of coastline and fall asleep with sand in my hair."

Kacey grins, pulling out her phone and tapping at the keys. "I'll let Jason and Fitz know if they want to join us."

"Ask Jason to grab my bathing suit."

Connie sighs, but it's relaxed. A black town car pulls up to the curb. "Let me guess—you aren't coming back with me."

Kacey confirms the guys are coming.

I shoo Connie. "Go. Find your husband. I know I've been cramping your extended honeymoon."

"Fine, but find me when you're back. Southern Belle has called me three times already this morning."

"Not happening, Connie," I reply in a singsong voice.

She purses her lips but slides easily into the back seat

without comment. A tinge of annoyance creeps up my spine. Southern Belle is a record label fronted by Roy Stanton. Who is not only a first-rate douchecanoe—who pimps out his all-lady clientele under the ruse of female empowerment— but also happens to be a former lover of my mom's. So *ew*. I cannot for the life of me understand why Connie insists on pushing this meeting.

I take another deep breath of ocean air and brush it off. Summer is in full bloom on the Gulf, and all I want to do is take off these espadrilles and stick my toes in the surf. I wasn't lying when I told Larry I want to have fun and experience these so-called best days of my life. What good is traveling the country if I don't see any of it except the inside of sound studios or my bus?

Kacey and I duck into a hip little smoothie-and-bagel shop to wait for the guys. Jason walks in as we're finishing our drinks. "Your boyfriends are down at the pier."

We're not quite at the point where we're recognized in public yet. Maybe if I carried around a mic and my guitar, but without music paraphernalia, I'm pretty forgettable. Clay and Fitz? Not so much. They can hide behind shades, but Clay radiates charisma wherever he goes. Not to mention, we all have security shadows. So once we get down to the pier, it takes me no time to find the guys. Jason lets out a shrill whistle, and they pull off the railing they've been leaning against like a couple of Abercrombie models.

I slip into the public restroom and strip off my jeans gratefully. I look at the suit, and my stomach sinks. It's not mine. "Kacey?"

"Yeah?"

"I think I got your suit."

"One of them, probably. I have my other."

I bite back a cussword. I'm a good deal curvier than my pixie-stick cousin. "I am going to kill Jason."

Slipping on the scraps of material, I unlatch the door and step out to where Kacey is gathering her short hair up into two spiky pigtails in the dull mirrors. She raises dual brows and smirks. "If you mean because you're going to give him a coronary, maybe."

"Sweet Jesus," I mutter. "I can't go out into public like this." I try to adjust my cups, but shifting one sends the other off course, and it's a fine line to my very own Nipplegate.

"Don't be so dramatic. You look fantastic. Who knew you had all that going on underneath your T-shirts?"

I huff. "No one. That's sorta the point."

Kacey drops her hands from her hair and turns to me, her smile understanding. "The way I see it, girl, you have two options: embrace or retreat." She holds up her phone. "I can call you a ride and you can spend the afternoon on the bus alone, or you can own what God gave you and show that dweeby ex of yours what he's missing."

I roll my eyes playfully. "Oh, please. Jason doesn't care what I look like."

Kacey pulls the strap of her beach bag over her shoulder and reaches for the door. "Maybe he didn't before, but he sure will now."

I glance once more at my reflection and throw my shoulders back, experimentally, before letting them drop naturally again. I slip on my sunglasses. I really don't want to go back to the tour bus. Logically speaking, this is probably as good as my boobs are ever going to be. I might as well show them off. Besides, I have a feeling Jason thought he could rile me up with this, and I'd hate to give him the satisfaction.

I shove through the door into the streaming sunlight.

Even in the fifteen minutes I've been in the bathroom, I feel like the beach has gained a zillion more people, and every one of them is staring at me. They aren't, of course. That's ridiculous.

One sure is, though. I spot our group down by the water. Jason is tossing a Frisbee back and forth with Fitz in the surf, and Kacey is already laying towels close to the water. Clay might have been getting in on the Frisbee with Fitz and Jason, except he gets nailed in the back of the head because his eyes are locked on me. I nervously fidget with my glasses and keep the course. *Remember what you said this morning, Annie. Wild mustang. You aren't your momma.*

But for some reason, all I can think of is when I said staring at Clay was like staring down the sun. Because it is. I see him and I'm blind to everything and everyone else on this godforsaken coastline.

"Holy hell, Mathers! When'd you grow up?" Jason, the idiot, thankfully interrupts my inner turmoil.

I take a second to catch up and glory in my best friend's slack-jawed expression. Now *that* I can cope with. I even stop my approach to lower my shades and jut out a hip like T. Swift on a runway. "Who, me?"

Kacey snorts from her towel. "Who feels like an asshole now, Diaz?"

Jason mock-tips his hat and lets out a low whistle. "Well played, Mathers. Well played."

I readjust my glasses, careful to avoid Clay even though I can feel his eyes burning a trail down my skin, and make my way to the towels. It feels like the longest walk of my life, though I'm positive it takes less than a minute.

I finally make it to Kacey and drop down beside her. I roll up my bag and tuck it behind my head and lean back immediately, my heart still thudding in my chest.

Kacey grabs my fingers. "You made it," she whispers. "And he couldn't take his eyes off you."

I don't need to ask who. I slowly release the breath in my lungs, trying to calm myself down. "It doesn't matter," I say.

An hour later, a dark shadow falls over us, and it's Fitz trying to cajole my cousin into a swim. Her resistance is futile. He could ask her to go Siberia with him and she'd be down. I plug in my earbuds and listen to some Hailee Steinfeld, feeling my muscles melt deeper into the white sand. I can't keep my hips from swaying slightly and prop up on my elbows, tapping out the backbeat with my fingertips and watching Fitz grab up a screeching Kacey, tossing her in the rolling deep-blue waves. A grin spreads across my lips. Clay saunters up the beach toward me, and I take advantage of my mirrored aviators to study the way the salt water drips and clings to his torso. He reaches down to pick up a spare towel and rubs it stupidly slow down his biceps before ruffling his wet hair and spreading the towel next to me. I pretend to be focused on Kacey and Fitz's antics while surreptitiously turning down the volume on my earbuds. Jason walks up trailing two girls in athletic-looking bikinis. One is holding a volleyball. He says something to Clay, and I watch as the foursome walk off to a net set up in the sand. One of the girls shoves at Clay's shoulder playfully, making it all look so easy. Her fingers graze his sun-warmed skin, and he tilts his head back, laughing.

I reach back for the volume toggle on my phone and turn the music so loud a fighter jet could fly overhead and I wouldn't hear it. Then I close my eyes and sink back into the white sand, ignoring the empty towel next to me.

I shake out my freshly showered hair a few hours later, knowing in this humidity, resistance slash professional elegance is flat-out futile. Not that it matters, I suppose, as Jessica, my newly hired stylist, will just torture it into perfection before I hit the stage anyway. Wardrobe has set out a pair of artfully torn jeans and a black leather vest with gobs of fringe dangling off the edges. It's actually sort of cute. When I was little, I had a favorite suede jacket that was pale pink and covered in rhinestones and fringe. I probably looked like a walking BeDazzler infomercial, but I didn't care. Kacey has a pair of dangling feather earrings that would look perfect with this, but she's MIA, so I set off to find her.

After checking the food trailer and the soundstage, I decide she's probably with Fitz. He's taken it upon himself to teach my bandmates how to play Texas Hold'em. I approach the trailer Clay and Fitz sometimes share with their grizzled, leather-clad drummer, an older man named Jackson Colter.

I make out guitar playing through an open window and slow my approach, sneaking closer to the trailer. Rows of goose bumps pop up on my arms at Clay's voice, but I don't recognize the words. I freeze in place and close my eyes, leaning against the side of the bus, letting his smooth tenor wash over me.

It's so different from his other music. It's like his soul is bared and naked before me. Gone is the bravado of his stage persona. The beer-drinking frat boy ladies' man has been replaced by a tortured boy who speaks of a hurt that wrenches his heart and burns in his gut.

I'm breathless. It's too much. I'm feeling too much. But it's everything. This man has such a gift. Up until this point, his voice has been wasted. This is his life's work right here. I'm shaken and thunderstruck and electrified to the point of jittery. He's a fiery summer storm and I'm in the middle of an open field.

His voice fades, and before I can stop myself, I raise my

hand to knock on the bus-trailer door. I know Kacey isn't in there, and anyway, I can't remember what I wanted her for in the first place. I don't wait for his response, just climb in.

It's dim inside, and Clay is sitting on a sofa in a pair of loose-fitting jeans and a faded T-shirt. His hair is still stiff with ocean spray, and his face glows with too much sun after the beach this morning. I open my mouth, but nothing comes out at first, and I feel my cheeks warm.

What am I doing here?

He drops his hands from his guitar and flips over the paper in front of him as if to hide it. Too late.

"What?"

I swallow, realizing I've spoken out loud. "I said, 'Too late.' I already heard you." His eyes widen slightly, and I gesture to the open window. "Don't worry. Only me. I came by looking for Kacey."

"It's nothing," he says. "I'm just messin'." Clay's from southern Indiana originally, but a year on the road has tightened his accent. Now, however, it's looser—softer, somehow. As though being caught out and exposed has thickened his tongue and sent him south toward the Bible Belt.

I run my fingers through my hair, but my hand sticks in a patch of curls. "Look. I know I don't have your sales or CMAs, but I do know real music. That was not nothing. That was the best damn something I've ever heard. Why're you hiding that?"

Clay blinks, his face a mask of indifference, but I swear I can feel his appreciation. "No one wants to hear that. They come to me for a good time."

"Maybe so, but surely you see you are so much more than a good time."

A shadow passes over his features. "A good time is what pays for this tour and that fancy bus you're riding in and your band, and really, it's paying you for the right to be all high and mighty about what music is real or not real, so forgive me if I don't give a shit about what some internet sensation thinks about my work."

I stumble back, slapped by the sting of his words. He closes his eyes, and the brief moment of camaraderie between us snaps.

"I-I'm sorry. I didn't mean—"

He lays his guitar on the seat beside him and gets to his feet. "No. You did. Don't backpedal now." He's smiling, but it's the cruel kind of smile. "You think you're the only one who can write about something real? You aren't. I've been singing for crowds for a few years now, Annie Mathers, and I know a thing or two. So don't jump on my tour and give me all those gooey-eyed stares like I'm different than you thought. I'm not. This is who I am."

I reach for the door, feeling humiliated. "I'm sorry I bothered you."

Clay turns, swinging his arm and accidentally knocking over a bottle that falls to the floor with a clatter, and I flinch. His eyes widen but then harden. "You did. We aren't friends, Annie. And I'm not your mentor like Patrick Royston or any of those other washed-out stars who fawn over you. And I'm sure as hell not Johnny to your June, so I'll thank you to remember that. You work for me. That's it."

"You're right. I know that. I'll get out of your hair. I shouldn't have come."

As I close the door behind me with a slam, I hear his voice through the open window again. "No. You shouldn't have."

My encounter with Clay rattled, wrung me out, and then spit me out, so hours later, all that's left is pure fury. Rationally, I know he was embarrassed I'd heard him being vulnerable. I get it. Fine. And I probably did sound high-minded approaching a megastar like him and cooing over his private songwriting. But I ain't no newbie. I was raised up by legends in the school of music. To call me an "internet sensation"?

Oh no, he did not just say that.

Call it my stubborn pride, or maybe I'm my father's daughter, but who the hell does he think he is saying I work for him? Like I've ever once looked to him to be my mentor? Or my Johnny? What the actual eff is that about? It wasn't my idea to do that stupid photo shoot, and I'm not the one whose manager is dropping hints at attraction between us.

No, sir. That ain't me.

Maybe I should give Southern Belle a call. Maybe Clay needs a little reality check. Internet sensation. Puh.

My anger carries through to showtime, and when I tape up my revised set list, Kacey and Jason exchange nervous looks.

"Um, Annie, I'm all for being adventurous, but are you sure you wanna do 'Coattails'? It's brand new. The label hasn't given it a pass yet."

I throw him a glare before replacing the giant Gucci sunglasses wardrobe provided for nights when I'm performing facing the sunset. "Whose name is on the top of that paper, Diaz?"

Jason's lips twitch, and he affects a cowboy stance. "Annie Mathers, ma'am."

I grab my guitar and head for backstage. "Don't you forget it."

The crowd in Biloxi is the biggest yet in the week we've been on tour. Connie pulled me aside this afternoon to tell me there would be a film crew taking live footage to incorporate for a music video, and I'm tickled at the turnout. I stride across the stage in my brand-new black Tony Lamas with pale pink scroll, feeling the fringe on my vest swing against my skin. One week in and I'm full-on Nashville. Back in Michigan, I wouldn't have thought it possible, but the fringe and leather feel like home.

"Hey, y'all! My name's Annie, and the gorgeous fiddle player beside me is my cousin, Kacey, and that good-looking goofball on the drums is my best friend, Jason Diaz. We're called Under the Willows, and we're here to show you a good time, so let's get things started!"

We open with a cover, this time Reba's "Fancy." It's part of my personal crusade to introduce these little girls to some music appreciation. Maybe Clay's right about that. Maybe I do have some lofty ideals about country music.

Someone clearly needs to, even if it's just some internet-famous eighteen-year-old with frizzy hair.

After "Fancy," we jump right into "Should've Been You," which has been gathering steam and is the reason for the film crews today. Keeping them in mind, I milk the story of Jason breaking my heart and make sure his biceps get plenty of airtime with a drum solo.

I slow it down for a bit, throwing in my take on Dolly's "Jolene" before pulling out my ace in the hole. My body is literally vibrating with anticipation. I hope he's listening. Of course he's listening. In fact, I glance stage left and see his cap in the shadows next to Fitz. I nod once and turn to my mic.

"Y'all have been fabulous tonight! Truly, you make a girl feel so welcome. I might need to come back to Mississippi when this tour's all wrapped up." A cheer rises up, and I grin. I pull the mic off and start for the front of the stage, adding a little swagger to my step, and I wink at the red light blinking of the video cameras still aimed at my face. Perfect.

"We wanna play one more for you guys tonight before we let the big boys hit the stage. Is that all right?" Another cheer. "This one's brand spanking new. Never heard before, so it's an exclusive for y'all. You don't mind being my tester crowd, do ya?

"I know there's been all sorts of rumors about me and a certain country boy . . ." Cheers erupt, and I smirk. "Well, I'm here to set the record straight. I don't need no ball cap–wearing, Levi-filling, sweet-crooning man in my life. I don't need no 'Coattails'!"

Jason hits his cue with admirable intensity, and I glance at Kacey, whose eyes are twinkling as she raises her bow and gives me a nod of approval. I close my eyes and sing.

You might think I'm here to
Crowd your photo ops or
Dim your glaring spotlight,
Shamelessly name-drop
But I'm too far along now
And I've got my own thing going
Or I'd be damned to follow
Down where your rapids flowin'

You had better check yourself
Cuz, boy, I ain't draggin' on no coattails
Your style just ain't mine
Your drama is too much for me
Your ego's outta line

So fire up those engines
Saddle up your horse
Be ready for this rodeo
I'll be right up front a' course
With my sunshine vocals
And my wild-ass hair
I'll thrill all the locals
You just pull up a chair

You had better check yourself
Cuz, boy, I ain't draggin' on no coattails
Your style just ain't mine
Your drama's too damn much for me
Your ego's outta line

Put those bedroom eyes away, boy,
And hush up that pretty mouth
I ain't got time for your up and down
I ain't got no patience for your pout
I've got my guitar and my pen
My fiddler and my best friend
The sweet Lord up above
And you're just a walkin', talkin' sin

You had better check yourself,
Cuz, boy, I ain't draggin' on no coattails
Your style just ain't mine
Your drama's too damn much for me
Your ego's outta line

At last I'm coming to the part I rewrote just this afternoon. My face flushes hot, and anger spikes in my veins at his audacity to call me out when I was just encouraging him. I lean in even closer to my mic, my lips curling in an ironic smile.

Take some notes,
Jot this down
I'm not here for you
You can't mess me 'round
I don't need this
You ain't no Cash
And I'm not a Carter,

I do just fine on my own
This ain't charity, it's a barter

So you had best check yourself
Cuz, boy, I ain't draggin' on no coattails
Your style just ain't mine
Your drama's too damn much for me
Your ego's outta line

By the end, the crowd is doing a passable job of singing along. I'm holding the mic out to the crowd and clapping for their efforts. A loud cheer rises up, and before I can guess why, I feel a tap on my shoulder. Kacey points her bow stage left. Clay's stepped out of the shadows and is standing on the edge of the stage. I freeze, my adrenaline still pumping in my veins. He removes his cap, his eyes locked on mine, and holds it to his chest bending forward in a small bow. Then he raises his head, an amused smirk lighting his lips. He replaces his cap and gives me a small clap before waving to the crowd and slinking back into the shadows.

I giggle and turn to face the crowd. "Clay Coolidge, everyone!"

I don't know for sure, but I think that means I won this round.

9

Clay

friday, june 7
daytona beach, florida
country 500

Daytona means the first festival of the season. Three days of country's biggest artists playing to seventy-five thousand strong at NASCAR central. It's like the redneck Woodstock of the South. Last year, I was so intimidated, I puked all over the legendary Grant Matthew's boots the first night. His publicist sent me the bill. He still hasn't quit calling me Puker Coolidge every time our paths cross, which is unfortunately often. Country music is like high school. Everyone knows everyone.

This year I've managed to capture the main stage the first night, which means Willows have it before I do. Since it's a festival, people have been camped out all day, drinking and causing a ruckus in the hot sun. By 8:00 P.M., when Willows is prepping to get onstage, the crowd is already at a roar. The stage is giant and centered in the middle of the even larger racetrack. Barely a scrap of grass can be seen, people are so packed in. The label's got to be thrilled. Summer's barely gotten started, and already we've gained momentum.

Not half-bad for a girl who hasn't even cut her first album.

Because, let's face it, Annie's pulled in more than her share. I can reconcile this despite what she might think of me after I drove her out of my trailer. I was angry—still am. Her "Coattails" was smart as hell, and it pisses me off she seems impervious to the boozy industry standards I've been given.

I know I'm not being fair. She knows I'm not being fair. For now, that has to be enough. She still invaded my privacy and butted her nose in my business—still felt it was her place to comment on my music.

I take my spot in the wings, and Fitz does an admirable job of pretending it's not unusual for me to be here, hovering, instead of on the bus, where I spent last summer whenever my opener would take the stage.

"So that's the famous Annie Mathers."

I don't bother looking. I recognize that voice. Been halfway expecting it, even. "That's her."

"I'm not gonna lie, Clay, I kind of hate you for scoring her. Wherever did you find her?"

"Michigan," I say.

Lora Bradley nudges my shoulder with a laugh. "For real? Talk about off the map. Well, she's a doll. What's she doing with the likes of you?"

I shrug. "Stealing the show, I think."

"Aw, now ain't no one gonna replace you and your good-old-boy anthems. You've cornered the market. These summer festivals were practically made for you."

I hold back my eye roll. Lora's almost as good at bullshitting as she is at belting out power ballads. Lora Bradley started off a beauty queen before turning her vocals into a career that easily spans the pop and country music charts.

She's smart as a whip and so ambitious it makes most people uncomfortable. Last summer was both of our firsts at Daytona. We spent the entire weekend together, and I never heard from her again. Until the next time our schedules intersected, anyhow. She's pretty harmless, but Fitz doesn't like her. Or he doesn't much care for our arrangement. He thinks she's using my name.

Believe me, the irony hasn't been lost.

"What do you want, Lora?"

I feel her fingertips trail up the back of my thigh and around. "Same as last year. You up for it, or are you busy lusting after the Tragic Miracle out there?"

My eyes snap to hers, and she smirks knowingly. "It's not like that between us. She's talented."

Lora takes a half step back, leaning against a giant black speaker stand, amusement clear on her pretty face. "I see. We're all talented, Clay."

"I'll be at your trailer around midnight," I say tersely, turning back to the stage.

"Well, aren't you the charmer." Her voice has an edge to it. "I won't beg for it, Clay. I have plenty of other options, even if you are my first choice."

"I'm sorry, okay?" I try to sound like it, but I probably fail.

Lora narrows fine brows before squeezing my hand and letting it drop. "It's fine. This is just for fun, Clay. No strings. No pressure. If you're no longer up for that . . ."

"I am," I insist. "I'll see you after the show."

Lora slinks off, and I return to my watching. Annie's kicked off her boots and is hopping along to her own song, twisting this way and that, making the crowds fall in love with her. I think of the deviously stubborn pride painted across her face when she first sang "Coattails" last weekend. A big old *fuck you* to me after I'd tried to put her in her place in my trailer.

I grin at the memory. As they often do—far more than she realizes, I'm sure—her eyes dart to the wings, where I'm standing in the shadows. I touch the brim of my cap in salute, and she winks, spinning back to the audience lightly.

When the song ends, I realize I'm still grinning like an idiot after her. I swallow my smile, suddenly uncomfortable, and reach around, patting my back pocket where my grandpa's old flask is settled.

I have my own show to get ready for.

Lora was right: I was meant for stadiums in the summertime. We're two birds of a fame feather, Lora and me. She's not one to care for the softer side of music. Give her booze, big hair, and prewritten tracks to work her impressive vocal runs over. She's Vegas country. Carrie Underwood spliced with a Kardashian. She's good for a last-minute hookup, top-shelf liquor, and a pragmatic view of the industry.

We're what stadium tours are all about. Lora wouldn't be caught dead in a tiny little dive bar like Lula May's and would never let me hear the end of it if she ever caught me singing some hills song in my bus. If Annie is the good angel on my shoulder, pushing me to do better, Lora is a heady compromise of all sorts of things I'm not legally old enough to know about. Not bad, necessarily, but probably not good.

That about sums me up. Not bad, but probably not good. Tonight, I happen to be a little inebriated—but if I forget some of my own lyrics, the crowds don't mind. They live for it. We're a stadium full of sinners who desperately want to feel better than we had when we came in.

That's my job, and I'm the fucking best at it.

It's not like I have to sing. They're all chanting the lyrics at the top of their lungs anyway. I just laugh and hold the mic out like I can capture their individual melodies and amplify them over mine.

Fine tanned legs in daisy dukes,
Pretty girl, come on closer, give a scoot
Honey sweet tea glistens on your lips,
Lean in, baby, wanna give you a kiss

Holes in jeans,
Mud on my tires
Fish on my line
Cold beer, hot fire
But ain't nothing compare to you, baby
Nothing in the South can compare to you and your—

Fine tanned legs in daisy dukes,
Pretty girl, come on closer, give a scoot
Honey sweet tea glistens on those lips,
Lean in, baby, wanna give you a kiss

Thankfully my fingers move of their own volition, plucking out the correct chords after more than a year of almost constant play. Even so, by the time we hit the encore set, I toss my guitar to the side and motion for Fitz to take the lead. His nostrils flare for a split second, and he presses his lips together before turning a blinding grin toward the screaming crowd.

This is where I *know* she got to me. Suddenly, after two years on the road, I feel like I have to prove my salt. Which is ridiculous. This crowd, seventy-five thousand strong, should be proof enough.

But it's not. It's like she's created this fissure in my self-worth. As Clay, I sing songs people like. There's never been anything wrong with that. What does she expect from me?

Fitz starts with the steel guitar, and I step up to the mic, cradling the stand between my fingers and closing my eyes to the crowd's intent stares. The words start in my gut, swirling with the burning churn of alcohol and erupting past my gravelly throat and out my curled lips. My boots stomp and hips sway involuntarily, keeping time with the swing of Fitz's chords. My face scrunches as I give the lyrics my screaming all. She might publicly call me out with her words, but I'll tuck my intentions away. I don't feel much like inspecting this seething need inside of me for her approval—to care why impressing her, why winning that shining respect she showed me in the bus the afternoon we fought, is suddenly important to me. Why I can't just be content with Lora and the crowds and the glimpse of happiness they offer? Since the tour began, I've been in the wings, watching Annie. Rooting for her. Admiring her. I doubt she's doing the same, but in case she is, this is for her.

Some nights the whiskey ain't enough—
Nights after days spent with you
Tonight the whiskey ain't gonna be enough—
I only wanna spend my days with you

From here on out, they're all for her.

After we perform, Lora is waiting in our trailer. Guess she got impatient. I bite back a groan; Fitz doesn't hold his back.

"Dang, Lora, you have a tracker on my man here or what?"

She takes a sip of her drink, licking her glossy lips, and flips Fitz the finger. "Don't you have somewhere you can hole up, Fitz? I have big plans for Clay, and they don't include you."

Fitz shoots me a look, and I shrug. "Never mind that we share a bus, Lora. I'll just pitch a tent out front here so you won't be inconvenienced."

She's ignoring him, though, her eyes fixed on me and her fingers already working the buttons on my shirt.

He slams the door behind him in a huff, but I give in easily to the distraction she's offering me tonight. I can always apologize later.

The next morning, Lora's gone. There's a note on the mini-fridge from Fitz that he went on a run with Jackson. I grab a water and a banana from the basket Trina always stocks up for us and open the bus door to sit on the steps. It's early yet, before eight. Usually a hangover and late-night date with Lora wear me down, but I'm restless.

I finish my banana and decide to go for a walk down the coast. I slip inside and grab a thin hoodie that smells like cigarette smoke and perfume. I walk the three blocks to the shore and immediately step off the boardwalk for the packed sand. I start off at a stroll, letting the sun warm my lids, but my lungs itch to burn, so I tighten my laces and move into a sprint.

I pump my legs as hard as I can, hoping to drown out my noisy, senseless thoughts with my heavy breathing. After a quarter mile, I rip off my hoodie, Lora's scent irritating me. It's too . . . something. Usually I love how easy things are with Lora. She's a sure thing. A night of release with someone who knows better. I don't have to send her flowers, and she doesn't have to explain any late-night texts from strangers. She's a big fan of the Clay Coolidge brand. In fact, I don't think she's ever even bothered to ask where I'm from originally or what my real name might be. I know I've never asked her.

I never wanted to know.

Suddenly, I wish someone knew me as Jefferson. The only people who ever called me Jefferson are all dead. Maybe that means Jefferson is dead, too.

Annie would probably be crazy for Jefferson. Christ knows he'd have been over the moon for her.

Even if I am better than Clay, I might still not be good enough. I'm not Annie Mathers. I don't have her guileless charm or last name. That's not fair. Maybe her name grabs attention, but her talent is what's growing the crowds and selling out our shows. Just as many people are coming early for her as are coming to see me. At this point, I'm barely more than an eighteen-year-old working on a drinking problem.

I slow to a walk, scrubbing a hand down my gritty face. God, I'm such a mess. I can smell the alcohol oozing out with the sweat from my pores. I kick at the wet sand, sending it flying into the choppy blue waves lapping at the shore. Here I am, having a pity party on a beach in Daytona. I have one summer. The tickets are already sold. The stands are already filling. Maybe I can do both—have both. The stadiums and the real music. Amber waves of grain and the neon strip. Clay the frat boy and Jefferson the farm kid.

It all starts with a song. Maybe it's time I finish mine.

10

Annie

friday, june 14
atlantic city, new jersey

I wake up in a real bed and stretch languidly, savoring the way I can reach my body in every direction and not run out of mattress. The late-morning sun slants in through wispy drapes, painting my surroundings in a soft buttery yellow. I turn on my side and curl my toes in the cool sheets, reaching for my phone. I flip idly through Twitter, Instagram, Snapchat, and the CMT home page, not really taking in anything but seeing it all nonetheless. My stomach growls low, and my bladder protests my neglect, so I roll out of bed and set my bare feet onto the carpeted flooring of my hotel room. I move first to the bathroom, cleaning up enough that I can be considered presentable, and then make a call to the front desk for room service. I order enough breakfast for three people and then send a quick text to Kacey and Jason before flipping on the TV for background noise.

A few minutes into a Maury Povich rerun, there's a knock at my door. I flip it off before letting Jason in right as our breakfast is rolling down the hall. I lean out, peeking toward

Kacey's room. "I haven't heard from Kacey yet," I say. I hold open the door farther for room service.

Jason snorts. "I imagine not."

I hand the hotel employee a tip and close the door behind them. "What's that supposed to mean?"

Jason pulls the lid off the steaming stack of pancakes and leans forward to inhale. "I saw our sweet Kacey sneaking off with a certain redheaded man last night after sound check."

My eyes widen. "Really? Wow."

"Yeah, wow is right. I'm sort of shocked it took them as long as it did. My guess is the appeal of privacy was too much. They've had weeks of being cooped up on a tour bus. Probably worse for privacy than having a nosy roommate."

I grab tongs and start dishing out some fresh fruit into a glass bowl. "Well, good for them."

Jason squints one eye, regarding me while chewing a mouthful of over-syrupped pancake. He swallows hugely. "Really?"

I narrow my eyes. "Yes, really. Why wouldn't I be happy for them? Fitz is great."

"I was more thinking about your whole 'no rock star hook-ups, waiting for Mr. Perfect' stance."

I roll my eyes and pop a grape in my mouth. "You make me sound like a nun."

Jason doesn't correct me.

I throw at grape at him, and it bounces off his forehead. "I'm not a prude. Just because I wouldn't have sex with *you* doesn't mean I have anything against the practice. I just don't care for the idea of derailing my career over a man." Which is mostly true. I daydream about derailing my career over a certain man a thousand times a day. Doesn't mean I would, though.

"How Susan B. Anthony of you," he says drolly.

"Whatever. Think what you want. Regardless, it's great Kacey and Fitz have hit it off."

"Uh-huh." Jason starts hacking at his stack again, his fork and knife squeaking against his plate and making me cringe. "So does your free-love goodwill extend to the rest of the tour members?"

"Why? Are you about to tell me you're hooking up behind my back, too?"

He shakes his head. "Believe you me, if I were sexing it up, the entire world would know about it." He puts down his silverware and levels me with a serious look, making the orange juice whirl in my stomach. "No, I'm talking about our headliner."

I lower my eyes. "Oh. Right. Well." I shrug easily. "That goes without saying. Clay probably has a girl in every city on this tour."

Jason waits for me to raise my eyes again, and after confirming I'm not in pieces, he shoves more food in his face, talking around his breakfast. "I don't know about that. Maybe? But I did notice his supposed on-and-off-again flame tagged along up the coast."

Hm. That little tidbit seems more serious, but still. "Jason. I have literally zero designs on Clay. It's more than fine." *Mostly* more than fine, anyway. I mean, I really *don't* have any designs on Clay. Daydreams and designs are very different things. Like practically opposites. More like, it's just . . . something undefined swoops in my belly whenever I think of him. And her. Or just him, period.

It's pretty obnoxious.

He holds up a hand. "Okay, okay. I didn't think you did, really. Honestly, I sort of thought *he* had a thing for *you*. Well, at least before you started giving him the vocal smackdown with 'Coattails,' but if he can't hang with a little competition, then he ain't worthy of you."

I grin and hold my glass up in a toast. "Cheers, Jay. That's remarkably sweet-*ish* of you to say. Though completely unnecessary. Lora can have Clay."

Jason smirks. "Ah, so you did notice her hanging around."

"Maybe, maybe not." In truth, it was hard to miss the dark-haired beauty. I would love to easily dismiss her as some typical ex–beauty queen, but honestly, she's cool. Kind, pretty, smart . . . and has a pair of pipes on her I'd murder for. Her rendition of "America the Beautiful" would make professional football players weep. She also thinks my song about Clay is hilarious.

She's clearly got her head on straight.

"It's not serious."

I bite into my bagel with extra cream cheese and take my time chewing. "It's none of our business if it is or isn't."

"The way you two stare at each other, I figured you might want to tuck it away for later. Fitz says they're only fu—"

I cringe. "All right, that's enough. I'm not interested in a show business romance. I'm busy as all get-out, and even if I weren't, Clay Coolidge seems like the exact kind of trouble I should avoid."

"According to Fitz," Jason plows on, "Lora's not really that great for Clay. She's all about his image and not interested in his art. She doesn't challenge him."

I lift a shoulder, dipping my finger into the cream cheese oozing off the edge of my bagel. "He doesn't want to be challenged. He likes his gig, and I can't say I blame him. He's comfortable, he's rich, he's got it all in the palm of his hand."

"Yeah, but he doesn't have someone who really knows or cares about him. He doesn't have support."

I drop my breakfast and wipe my hands on the cloth napkin. "Holy Hannah, Jason! How do you even know this? Fitz? I had no idea you two were such old biddies. I talked to Clay, and he took my head off when I suggested he might be more than booze and barflies. He's not pining for something different. Leave it. *Please*."

"You said that to Clay?" Jason whistles low. "So that's what all of the icy avoidance is about?"

"I don't know what you're talking about. I haven't been avoiding anyone, and neither has he. We don't have to be best friends; we're basically coworkers when it comes down to it." And I mean it. I'm not angry any longer. We both said our piece. Perhaps I overstepped, and maybe he was a jerk. It was weeks ago, and I'm too busy to hold a grudge.

Mostly. Rehashing it in front of thousands with "Coattails" hasn't hurt.

"Okay, then."

I open my mouth to argue before his words sink in. Well. I close my mouth just as there is another knock on the door. Jason stands up to get it, revealing a rumpled-haired Kacey.

"Oh, perfect. I'm starved."

I grin at her as she starts grabbing food and loading her plate. "Yes, I imagine a night of being ravished does that for a girl."

Kacey freezes in her gathering a split second before tilting her head and picking up another croissant. "Indeed, it does." She looks at me out of the corner of her eye. "Do I need to apologize?"

"For what?"

"For being ravished? By a musician out of wedlock?" She shrinks away from me slightly, and I bite back a sigh before throwing a glare at a smirking Jason.

"Jesus. Is that what you guys really think of me? I'm curious. Which part did you think I'd be more offended by—the musician or wedlock part?"

Kacey relaxes a little into her fuzzy robe, nibbling on the edge of her pastry. "Honestly? Depends on the day. You haven't mentioned your stance on purity since starting the tour, but I didn't figure being a country music starlet changed your opinion."

I sit taller, putting down my napkin. "All right, apparently this needs to be said, so I'll just come out with it: Yes, I might have a bit of relationship PTSD after my parents died, and yes, that anxiety infuses essentially all of me. No, I don't expect either of you to feel the same. Should you wait for marriage to have sex? That's between you and Jesus. Bible school said to wait. Bible school also said I shouldn't wear a two-piece bathing suit. I didn't get cast into the fires of hell for my transgressions, so I doubt Kacey boinking a redhead is any worse. Should either of you date someone on our tour?" I raise my hands. "If you can handle things if they go janky in the end, then so can I. It's not my business."

Kacey and Jason stare at me slack-jawed, but I pick up my fork and stab another piece of fruit. After a moment, they do the same.

"Good talk," Jason mutters, and Kacey giggles nervously into her coffee.

I flip Maury back on, and we eat the rest of our breakfast in silence before I get up to shower. I turn the water extra hot and let it relax my shoulders. I'm not upset about my friends having sex lives or, in Jason's case, not yet. We're (mostly) adults now. I would never assume my friends would hold off on love because I'm terrified. I'm sort of sorry I never clarified before. I had no idea they would be afraid to tell me if they cared about someone. That's ludicrous.

No. That's not actually what's bothering me now. So what is it? My belly swoops uncomfortably as I remember what Jason said about Lora being here with us all in Jersey. Maybe that's it. Maybe I'm feeling a little jealous. Maybe I selfishly figured Clay was as lonely as I am. Or maybe I did hope he was pining after me a little. Not realistically, of course, but in a faraway kind of way. Like in the way one might daydream about the popular boy in school who the teacher assigns as your lab partner. Your relationship is purely based on frog spleens and formaldehyde, but sometimes he laughs at your joke and you think . . . maybe. Maybe.

It's the *maybe* I'm mourning. The daydreams, even. That's what I'm all out of sorts about. My lab partner asked someone else to the dance, and I'm left with the uncomfortable realization he was just being polite. In my mind, I see Clay's dark eyes flashing, angry and hard.

Well, maybe *polite* isn't accurate. Maybe *complicated* is more like it.

I turn off the water and wring out my hair, stepping onto the plush bath mat and grabbing a towel to wrap around my chest.

The thing is, my stupid heart likes complicated puzzles, even if I wish it didn't.

11

Annie

The following night, after our show, I slink back to my hotel room, begging off sleep. I sit down at the table with three bottles in front of me. All of them liquor. All of them ridiculously tiny and likely overpriced.

I don't want to drink. I don't want to be like my parents. For eighteen years, I've completely avoided the stuff.

But if you can't drink mini bottles of top-shelf liquor in your hotel room on the fifth anniversary of when you found your parents' dead bodies, when can you? I figure this is just like the free space on a bingo card. Nothing counts as real today. I'm not me today. I'm that girl—the one who felt her mom's icy-cold, stiff, and very dead fingers—the one who can't erase the blood splatter out of her mind, from when her dad put a gun into his mouth and pulled the trigger.

And that girl, the girl I'm *not,* wants a drink.

Tonight, Jason found a pack of groupies who invited him out barhopping after our show. Kacey was dizzy, waiting for Fitz to finish his set, clearly planning to make another night of it with him. Connie saw me back to the hotel, but I knew the *pings* coming from her pocket were Patrick.

Hotels make people horny, apparently. I don't love living

on a bus, but at least I never felt lonely in my box on wheels. Maybe I should be relieved they don't get so inspired in such tight quarters.

Sighing, I lean back against my seat, the wood creaking in protest. I probably shouldn't be alone right now. My therapist back home certainly would have some things to say about me sitting in an empty hotel room in Jersey with three bottles of booze to keep me company.

"Gaaaaaahhhhhh," I groan, rubbing my sweating hands down my jean-clad thighs.

I should have spoken up, but once it was apparent no one else lives their life according to the date my parents killed themselves, I didn't have the heart to ruin anyone else's night. Or worse, what if they tried to talk me out of this?

The real question is this: If a girl gets drunk in her hotel room alone, and no one sees, does it really happen?

Without a thought, I reach out for the first bottle, and with a satisfying crack, the twist cap falls off. "To you, Mom." Her gray features and bloodshot eyes stab behind my eyelids, and I ignore the burn of the tequila as it goes down, finishing the bottle in one quick motion and shuddering at the foreign taste.

I stand and start to pace the room, relishing the warmth in my stomach. My cheeks feel flush and sort of staticky. The more I pace, the heavier my head feels. I turn on the TV and turn it off just as quickly. I find my silenced phone and dock it in the alarm clock station, scrolling to some hip-hop. I turn off one of the lights in my room.

"Mood lighting," I say to myself as my hips slowly sway back and forth to Beyoncé. I walk over to my curtains and pull them open. It's pitch dark, but lights flicker like a zillion stars on land. I squint to see past my reflection to the shore below. I crack open the window. Up here, it only opens a few inches. I smirk darkly at my reflection. *Well, ain't that something. We all know jumping out a window isn't the only way to end your life.*

Sad reality starts to creep in again. I spin for the table and grab the second bottle. This one, whiskey. It burns worse than the tequila. I grimace, and another shudder runs through me for a second, but then I feel lighter. Like I should go somewhere. Do something. Why hide out in my room? I'm young, and I'm a celebrity.

I slip back into my boots and stride to the full-length mirror in the center of my room. My hair is considerably larger than I prefer, so I gather it up on the top of my head in a knot. My eyes look wild. Too wild. I've seen those eyes before. On my father. I pinch my eyes shut and shake my head back and forth.

"So you're just going? Just like that? Forget your kid, forget your wife?"

"Screw you, Cora. I've stayed back three times in the past year playing the doting spouse while you travel all over God's green earth. It's my turn. Or did you forget I had a career, too?"

My mom's laugh is shrill. "Had *a career, Robbie.* Had. *When was the last time you were even in the studio?"*

"Someone has to raise our daughter, or did you forget about her while you've been screwing your way around the continent?"

"No, no, no, no, no." I walk back to the table and crack open the third bottle. How many of these does it take to erase them from my brain? I swig the third, vodka this time, and throw the empty bottle on my bed. I grab my phone from the dock and slip it into my pocket along with some money and my driver's license.

I'll text Jason on the way and see where he's ended up. Maybe I can crash his party.

The elevator doors open, and it's Clay. Alone.

"Hey," he says, stepping past me.

"Hey yourself," I say and stumble slightly in my effort to brush past him to the door.

I make it to the back of the elevator and turn to see his hand shoot out to stop the door. The doors fly open again. "You okay?"

"Fabulous." I slap the lobby button again. He stands there, holding the door a second before exhaling.

"You're drunk."

"Don't be ridiculous. I don't drink." I stand up straighter as if to prove my sobriety.

He grimaces. "I've heard that. But the booze on your breath says otherwise. Annie, you can't go out there drunk. You're underage."

"That's never stopped you from going out."

He presses his lips together and scratches at his stubble. "True. But that's my reputation. You're a role model. Role models don't get arrested in Jersey for underage drinking."

I jab at the button again.

He holds the door with his foot and holds out a hand. "Come on. Please? You can drink all you want right here. I won't tell."

I consider him. Even blurry, he's still stupid-handsome. "Where's Lora?"

It looks like his lips twitch, but in the shadow cast by the brim of his ball cap, it's hard to say. "Probably halfway to Cali right now. I put her on a plane. You coming or what?"

"I drank all my little bottles already," I admit.

He raises his brows. "I have plenty."

"Today's the anniversary," I blurt, feeling like an idiot.

He nods, his hand still outstretched. "I know."

My stomach drops. "How do you know?"

"Come on, Annie. I'm not a complete heathen. I never cared much for your dad, but your momma had the voice of a saint. I was a huge fan. Still am. The day Cora Rosewood died is right up there with Kurt Cobain and John Lennon."

Somewhere between his frank honesty and the knowledge I'm not the only person in the universe who remembers this date, I'm convinced, and my feet move forward. I don't have to be alone, and I don't have to explain myself.

He waits until I'm off the elevator before letting the door go. "I'm down this way."

I follow him to his room, and he swipes the key card with a click. "Sorry for the mess."

I take in the rumpled bed linens and the clothes draped over the chair in the corner. He tosses his card on the table and reaches into his cabinet, pulling out several bottles and two glass tumblers.

"What do you like?"

I tilt my head, thinking. "I tried one of each tonight. Tequila made me want to barf the least."

He laughs, and the hairs on my arms raise. Even his laugh is rich and musical. "Jose Cuervo it is, then." He reaches into his fridge and pulls out a lime. Then he reaches into a take-out bag and tosses some salt packets on the table. "It's pretty redneck, but we're all country singers here, right?"

I grin as he tries to cut the lime with a plastic knife. I point to the pocketknife at his waist and then feel my face get hot as his shirt lifts and exposes his toned middle when he pulls it from his belt. He cuts the lime into wedges and passes me a few.

"First, lick your wrist, like so."

I watch, rapt, as his tongue darts out to wet his wrist. My breath is dangerously close to panting, and I can't help but remember Jason's teasing me about finding my lady parts when I first heard Clay's sound check at the start of the tour.

The damned things are basically humming their approval right now.

He raises a brow, and I quickly imitate him, feeling stupid licking myself.

"Then you shake a little salt on your wrist." He shakes some from one of the packets, and I do the same, spilling more than a little on the table. He pours a shot into my tumbler and passes it to me.

"So lick, drink, suck," he says. I bite my lip and nod. His eyes follow my mouth, and I try not to pass out.

Some part of me—we'll call her Reason—is screaming.

"On my count," he's saying.

Lick, drink, suck.

It's actually sort of delicious. Way better than drinking straight from the bottle. I slam my drink down and almost laugh, but still, I remember. Calling the police in hysterics and forgetting my own address and having to run out in the street to check the mailbox in my bare feet, nearly dropping my phone in the dirt. Throwing up against the giant oak tree in our front yard until my ribs felt like they would crack apart.

"I still see them," I gasp, shaking my head. "I need to do it again. It's not working yet."

Clay nods seriously. "Okay, but I should warn you, if this is your first time, you're dangerously close to getting sick."

"Are you doing this with me or not?" I ask, feeling a little angry at his misplaced rationale. "Because I'll just take this back to my room alone if you're going to preach at me."

Clay watches my face and then pours another glass. "I don't think you should be alone."

I lick my arm without waiting for him this time. "I didn't ask you."

"To outdrinking our demons," he says, holding up his glass.

For a moment, our eyes meet, and it's as though something

long buried inside of me recognizes a similar something long buried inside of him. I open my mouth as though to ask him about his demons or maybe to spill all of mine. It lingers in the air between us, tangible and warm. His hand is still hovering, though, and instead, I clink his glass with mine and pour it back.

This time, the dizziness is real. I slip out of the chair at the table and crawl over to lean against his bed. He grabs the bottle and moves to sit next to me. His long legs stretch out close to mine, and I tap my boot-clad toes together, watching as they blur.

"I was the one who found them," I say slowly. I'm trying not to slur, but my tongue feels thick and tired.

"*Christ.* How old were you? Twelve?"

"Thirteen. It was a few days after I turned thirteen."

"That's plenty messed up."

I snicker humorlessly. "Yep."

We sit in the silence, and my head sinks to his shoulder. He smells so good. I turn my face and inhale. He doesn't say anything.

"I still see them in my head. Lying there, all gray and bloody. I can't . . ." I shake my head back and forth again. "I can't get it out of my brain. I can't unsee it."

"Why are you alone tonight? Where's your cousin?"

"Making sweet fiddler love with Fitz."

He snorts, and my head bounces on his shoulder. I swear I've never felt anything softer than this boy's shoulder in all my life.

"What about Diaz?"

"He found groupies." I inhale again, nuzzling his shirt. "They forgot it was today."

"And you didn't remind them? And then decided to get drunk alone?"

I shrug and lift my head, rolling it back to stare at the ceiling. "If a girl gets drunk in her hotel room alone, and no one sees it, did it really happen?"

"Ah. But I ran into you on the elevator."

"I don't drink."

"You've mentioned that already."

"My parents were junkies. Addicted to each other and to getting high."

"I don't think you're going to turn into a junkie after one night, Annie. In fact," Clay says softly, "I'm pretty sure you'll regret this in the morning."

"I won't regret you," I say. I grab the bottle from him and take another swig. "I've always wanted to drink straight from the bottle like I was in some old western." He chuckles low, and I pull my legs up to my chest and lay my head on my knees. I squint one eye and look at him. My heart squeezes in my chest. "You really are too attractive for your own good."

He takes the bottle from my hand and takes a swig, grimacing. "So are you."

"I'm sorry I eavesdropped on you in your trailer. It was uncalled for, what I said to you."

He leans his head back, rolling it to look at me again. "Maybe, but you were only speaking the truth."

"I shouldn't have written that song about you. It was mean."

He laughs. "No, that was genius. I love that song. You're a clever girl, Annie Mathers, and crazy talented. Don't you ever apologize for that."

My stomach swirls giddily. "Clever *woman*. Even so. I didn't mean to mock you."

"The hell you didn't!" he sputters.

"Okay. Fine. I did." He wraps an arm around me, and I tip my head onto his shoulder again.

"Well, maybe I didn't need to be such a dick."

"Maybe?"

He releases a breath, and my head sinks farther. It's as though my body is melting into his. My eyelids feel heavy, so I let them drop closed.

"Probably, okay. You were right. It's a good song. I should play it."

"For me," I insist tiredly.

"Someday, maybe."

"I like you, Clay."

"You're pretty likeable yourself," he says as I drift off.

12

Clay

Today we're back in Nashville for the CMA Music Festival. It's 9:30 on a Sunday morning and way too early for Trina, if you ask me.

"Where did you say Annie went?" Trina asks, her heels clacking on the tiles as she paces the short lobby of our hotel. I lower the brim of my cap as a small family of tourists enters through the automatic doors, a too-warm morning breeze following them in.

"Church," says Kacey. She's sitting on a sofa next to Fitz, sipping a steaming complimentary coffee.

Trina stops her pacing. "Church?" She rolls her eyes heavenward, and I don't doubt she's having a private conversation with God about his followers messing up her schedule.

"Gran printed off a schedule of churches in every tour stop."

"You guys don't go with her?" I ask, leaning forward and picking up my own cup from the glass coffee table in front of me.

Jason shrugs. He has gray bags under his eyes, and his T-shirt is a rumpled version of the one he wore yesterday.

"Sometimes. Usually back in Michigan I go. She hasn't really been going since we left on tour. She seemed oddly determined this morning, though. Called up Patrick and Connie and asked if she could get a ride. Wonder what lit a fire under her butt to plop it in a pew?" Kacey raises one brow in my direction, but I ignore her, sipping at my coffee. The fact of the matter is I might have something to do with it. But not because of the reasons Kacey and the rest of the world think.

Annie was honest with me. She doesn't drink. It doesn't take a psychologist to know why she avoids the stuff. Instead of cutting her off and tucking her into bed that night, I invited her back to my room and taught her how to do proper tequila shots. If that's not reason enough to go to church, I don't know what is. More than once I've found religion after a hangover.

The following morning, she crept out of my room before the sun came up and we were on a plane most of last Sunday. Point is, I'm not surprised she dug out the church list now.

"Ah, there she is. Morning, Mother Teresa."

Annie blushes, tucking a rogue curl behind her ear. It springs right back. She's wearing a blinding white summer dress and flat sandals and looks too beautiful to be believed. She's casually holding a gigantic bundle of long-stem red roses down at her side, as if she could hide them. "Shush, you." She takes in our haggard group in the lobby. "Were we supposed to meet this morning?"

"Yes, but you didn't know, so don't worry," Trina allows. "We've had a change of plans for tonight's performance at the festival. They've decided they want to feature Willows and Clay together for a live feed that'll be broadcast on XM radio as well as on pay-per-view."

"Wow, that's . . ." Annie's brown eyes flicker to mine.

"Great," I assure her. "More than great."

Trina smiles too brightly. "Glad to hear it. There's a slight catch. You know how the theme this year is 'Take Me Home, Country Road'?"

We all nod.

"Well, it's sort of comical. They must be really feeling this Johnny-and-June thing, because they want you to sing 'It Ain't Me, Babe.'"

"Oh, well . . . ," Annie starts.

I laugh as the idea sinks in. "Actually, it's sort of genius. We get a set of three, right? I'll kick us off with 'Some Guys Do,' and Annie can follow up with 'Coattails,' and we'll wrap with 'It Ain't Me, Babe.' A little back-and-forth to keep their jaws yapping and the papers speculating, right?" I turn to Annie, mindful of her freak-out in Atlanta. "Only as long as you're game?"

She releases a breath, but grins. In the weeks since her panic attack, we've been able to ease more into the media attention. I've heard a few of Annie's interviews, and she fields questions about us like a pro. I figure if the ball is in our court . . . "I can work with that. As long as I can be me onstage and not some dressed-up icon. Imitation makes me uncomfortable."

"Fair enough," Trina agrees, already pulling out her phone. "No bouffant this time. Just Annie Mathers and Clay Coolidge. I'm going to call us a town car." She looks around. "Or two. Grab anything you'll need for rehearsal and meet me down here in fifteen."

Before we can disperse, however, the glass lobby doors swish open once more to reveal Connie and Patrick in deep conversation with a tall man wearing a fitted black suit and a black cowboy hat. The man raises a hand to tip his hat at our group, and Annie gives a small wave back before the trio moves through to the elevators.

I glance back at Annie. She's studiously avoiding Trina's wide-eyed stare, but from my angle, I can see her grip tighten on the roses, still hanging at her side.

"You went to church with Roy Stanton?"

Annie shrugs.

"*The* Roy Stanton?"

"I didn't know he would be there today. He used to be friends with Cora."

"Not Robbie?" I ask, grasping onto the first question that pops into my brain. I'm not sure who this Roy guy is, but Trina is practically radioactive.

Annie's eyes flick to mine. She shifts the roses to her other hand, flexing the first. "No, not Robbie. Robbie hated Roy. Roy is the president of Southern Belle Records, Clay."

I swallow. Holy hell. No wonder Trina's flipping out. Southern Belle is SunCoast's rival in every way. How could I forget? The story is the stuff of Nashville legends. Roy broke off with SunCoast, stealing Cora Rosewood and starting his own label with her as his top act.

It was a gigantic scandal in the late '90s. Completely rocked Nashville, because Stanton decided to base his enterprise on the West Coast. There's still a lot of contention about it.

Lora's with Southern Belle. It's not unheard of to have acts from different labels share a stage, but I doubt SunCoast would be super-happy with me if Annie and Willows jumped ship after the tour wrapped; not after all the trouble they went to in sending me to secure her in the first place.

"Did he talk shop?" Trina asks evenly.

Annie shakes her head. "No, nothing like that. I mean, of course he mentioned it, but I have zero desire to be courted by Roy or his label. I've made it very clear. I've been avoiding his calls, but then there he was, right in the sanctuary, holding a dozen roses." She snorts. "Called it 'divine providence.'"

Trina's shrewd eyes follow the numbers lighting up over the elevator. I'm sure she's replaying the scene in the lobby—the familiar way Connie and Patrick spoke with Roy and then left to talk in their room with him. They were likely old friends as well, but still.

I turn back to Annie in time to catch her shaking her head at some silent entreaty from her cousin.

"So," I say, clearing my throat. "You were calling our cars, Trina?"

Trina shakes herself, clutching her phone in her hand. "Absolutely. Get your things. We have a show to get to."

No one brings up Stanton again, but when we return to the lobby a few minutes later, I notice a bunch of stems sticking out of a trash bin. Annie catches my eye, the corner of her mouth lifting in a half attempt at a grin. "Cora loved roses. I hate 'em."

That night when we perform, the cosmos shifts. I knew it might happen. It's why I haven't offered to share my stage with Willows yet, despite Fitz and Trina mentioning it a thousand times. Once this happened, we couldn't go back.

It's not just chemistry. Lora and I have chemistry. If you're a good-enough performer, you can create believable chemistry with anyone. Even in still photographs, Annie and I have chemistry that leaps off the page.

No, what we have is something more; we have magnetism. Chemistry is give-and-take; magnetism sucks you in like a black hole. Annie sucked me into her universe back at the fairgrounds last summer, and her hold has yet to release me. And I'm not being cocky when I say I have a similar effect, albeit on a smaller scale.

So putting us together singing a classic for all the world to see? I knew we'd never come back from that. Still, I couldn't refuse. For as much as everyone else wanted to see what would happen, I needed to feel it for myself. To confirm what I already suspected.

I've never been able to turn down a dare.

As planned, I start in with "Some Guys Do." Annie creeps onstage about halfway through, and I don't have to see her to know the exact moment she's there. Barefoot and dancing to my song. She doesn't have a mic and doesn't plan to sing along. She's just there to dance and be a fan, and I've never wanted to sing so well in my entire life. She and Kacey are bobbing along, mouthing the lyrics and laughing as if they were in the front row and not standing alongside Fitz.

Goddamn.

At the end, I pass off my mic, and Kacey takes her fiddle from a stagehand. Jason kick-starts into "Coattails," and while I don't take off my boots and dance like Annie did, I don't leave the stage either. In fact, I take a second mic on a stand from a stagehand, and when she gets to the line about not being a Carter to (my) Cash, I give Fitz a nod. We start low and quiet, leading into an overlay of music we planned backstage as a surprise: a little taste of Johnny's "Walk the Line."

Annie's so caught off guard, she cuts off midsentence. I round my mic, strumming my guitar in a steady rhythm and humming the start. Annie begins to laugh—full-bellied and high-pitched—as I hoped she would. She's shaking her head and swaying her hips, and I recite the first lines. We don't get far, though, before she cuts me off to skip straight into "It Ain't Me, Babe." It's the best kind of battle of the bands, and I'm having the time of my life under the lights. She takes on Johnny's smoky lines, and I harmonize with June's half in a falsetto, which adds to the crowd's amusement. If they're of the generation who came up with Johnny and June, they'll appreciate our back-and-forth. If they're too young to recognize it, they'll still find the open flirting to be fun to watch.

I've never been able to pull off anything like this with anyone else, but that's because I didn't know Annie. She's the darling of the country music world for a reason, and blessedly, she's taking me along for the ride. We close out our set to uproarious applause. Annie grabs my hand to bow, but I step to the side, holding out both of my arms to her. This was her debut, if you ask me. A handoff of epic proportions. I'm not sure what I've witnessed tonight, but I'm positive it wasn't *my* star shooting into the stratosphere.

The question now is whether I hang on for all I'm worth or let go so I don't drag her down.

13

Annie

monday, june 24
nashville, tennessee

This summer was a terrible idea. Or maybe the best idea in the history of ever. I go back and forth. I'm doing exactly what I've always wanted to do. Since I was a little girl watching my parents perform under the hot lights to screaming fans, I've wanted to do the same.

Just not the same way.

We perform "It Ain't Me, Babe," and it's a resounding success. I'm riding high. I'm feeling more *me* than ever before and I swear, *I swear,* I could do literally anything at this moment.

So naturally, when we return to our hotel after the performance and the subsequent after-party and it's 3:00 A.M. and I should just go to bed because I'm wrung out and my mascara's probably streaked to my earlobes, I knock on *his* door instead.

And he opens it.

He leans a hip against the jamb and folds his arms across

his chest. My eyeballs seem to get hung up on his tanned forearms before I drag them north to his down-turned lips.

"I'm not going to be your booze hookup, Mathers."

At first, all I hear is *hookup*, but then my dizzy brain snags on the rest, and I'm indignant. "I'm not looking for tequila, Coolidge. I have some in my own room." I think. Probably. To be honest, I haven't looked. Last weekend's hangover is still mighty fresh in my memory.

He raises his brows, expectation painted across his face. "It's late, Annie. We leave early for Milwaukee."

"I know that. I only wanted to come by and say I had fun singing with you tonight." I hear a door slam within his room behind him. Fitz's bronze hair flashes over Clay's shoulder, his toothbrush dangling between his teeth. He waves and gives a salute. Clay rolls his eyes and pulls the door shut behind him, stepping out into the hall in his socks. He leans back against his door.

"Me, too. I was thinking, maybe we should incorporate it into the show from here on out . . . you guys come onstage with us for a song or two."

He seems so genuine, it gives me all sorts of warm fuzzies. "Really? That would be great. I mean"—I try to play it cool—"as long as we can keep the fiddlers off each other. We have to think of the tweens."

He barks out a laugh, and I glow at the sound. Making this boy laugh might be more rewarding than performing.

"I'll have a talk with Fitz about appropriate touching."

"I'm not worried about the appropriate kind," I say without thought, and his eyes darken. I swallow hard, resisting the urge to backtrack. Holy hell, did I just hit on Clay Coolidge? My words could have been innocuous enough, but the suggestive tone . . . did I have a suggestive tone? Do I even know what that is?

"Are you hitting on me, Mathers?"

I grimace and cover my face with my hands, walking back until I hit my door. I drop my fingers and stare at the ceiling, taking a deep breath. "Yes. I don't know. *Maybe*. Why? Is it working?"

Suddenly he's in front of me, his hands on either side of my head. "Annie, I'm not the kind of guy you should be hitting on." Even as he speaks, his body betrays him. I can feel the heat radiate from his skin. It's as though there's a magnet charging between us, drawing us closer and closer.

I lick my lips experimentally and thrill as his intense eyes follow the motion.

"I'm not a good guy," he protests weakly.

I reach up and brush a soft wave off his forehead, dragging my fingertips down the side of his stubbly cheek and tracing down to his collar, skimming the blazing skin peeking out of the top of his V-neck T-shirt. "I know who you are. You're Clay." I press forward and pull him toward me at the same time. He gives easily, and suddenly every soft part of me is overcome by the hard planes of him. His lips are pliable and soft against mine until I sigh and his warm tongue pushes past my open lips and starts to dance with mine. My fingers twirl themselves in his hair, and I tug lightly when his hot hands tease up my sides. I don't know when my hips started grinding into his, but it's obvious he doesn't hate it, and my heart is in my throat. Am I doing this?

Are *we* doing this?

He pulls back with a groan, and I know without a doubt we *aren't* doing this.

His face is pained, and he runs his hands through his mussed hair. His mouth is the exact shade of my lipstick. He licks his lower lip and then wipes a hand across his mouth as if to erase me.

"Annie, you're—" He swallows. "You have so much . . .

I'm not—" He stops, taking another step back and curses to himself.

"Did I do something wrong?" I ask and then immediately feel stupid. The heat slips from my face. Of course I did. "Oh my gosh. I totally forgot about Lora."

He looks up at me. "Who?"

"Your girlfriend, Clay. *Jesus*."

He lifts a shoulder. "Lora's not my girlfriend. She's . . . an old friend. I get lonely on the road, I guess, and we have a history. We aren't anything, really. No. You did nothing wrong, Annie. Kissing you, that was . . . it was a lot of things. Good things, but also bad because I'm wrong for you and you don't want to be like me. You're so much better than a tour piece. I mean, *Jesus*, Annie. You went to church this morning."

I clasp my hands behind me to keep from reaching out and lean back against my door again. "So?"

His eyes widen. "So? So you're a good person. A good g—"

I raise my hand. "Don't say it."

He slumps. "Well, you are!"

"I'm eighteen, Clay."

"Can you please stop calling me that? Clay isn't my real name. It's Jefferson. I can't—" He struggles with himself, waving his hands around uselessly as though hoping to catch on a word. "I'm trying not to be Clay Coolidge right now. Okay? I'm trying to do the right thing."

I don't know how to respond. This feels bigger than I am, but I can't figure out how. "Okay, fine. I'm eighteen, *Jefferson*."

"Are you a virgin?"

Suddenly I'm very aware we are in public. "Maybe we should talk in my room."

"No!" He catches himself and lowers his voice. "No. That's my point. I can't go in there with you. I can't be alone with you right now."

I roll my eyes and slump against the door again. "I don't see what my virginity has to do with anything."

He rolls his eyes right back, but his face is relaxed. "It has everything to do with everything."

I exhale loudly. "So that's that, then. You don't want me."

"Oh, I want you. Never doubt that. But now isn't the right time. So I'm going to turn around, walk through that door"—the corner of his mouth twitches—"and pretend to sleep while replaying that kiss until I give up and drown myself in a cold shower."

My cheeks heat, and despite my annoyance, I smile, feeling bolder with his confession. "Save some cold water for me." I tug my key card from my pocket and turn to my door, leaning my forehead on the cool, painted metal. At the click, I turn to see him watching me, still standing in the hallway. "Night, Jefferson."

His eyes darken, but he seems pleased, and that's enough for me.

saturday, july 6
columbus, ohio

Kacey and I sit in our bus trailer, dipping homemade gingersnaps into a tub of Cool Whip while our gran fusses at the tiny stove, warming up some vegetable soup she brought from home. She and Pop came up last night and are sharing a hotel room with Kacey's mom in town. I figured I wouldn't see any of them until tonight, since travel is hard, but Gran and a far more reluctant Pop showed up at our door bright and early this morning with a picnic feast planned. Aunt Carla begged off with a headache we'll call "Pop's Back Seat Driving" and promised to catch up with Kacey after the show.

"Gran, it's a hundred degrees out," Kacey says. She licks

her Cool Whip before double dipping her cookie in the plastic container of fluff.

"You look jaundiced. You need more vitamins in your diet. This is the quickest way to get veggies."

I snicker, and Kacey shoots me a daggered glare. "I don't have scurvy, Gran. I eat my veggies. I'm just suntanned."

My grandma grunts to herself, stirring once and tapping her wooden spoon on the side of the pot before laying it on top of a folded paper towel on the counter. The screen door opens, streaming yellow light before closing with a smack. Jason hops up the stairs in one bound and sniffs loudly.

"Is that the famous Rosewood family recipe I smell?"

My gran preens under his flattery, and Jason leans over to kiss her cheeks. "Grab yourself a place setting, young man, and I'll bring this outside for you kids to enjoy at the picnic table."

A timer dings, and she pulls a sheet of hot rolls from the pocket-sized oven.

Kacey whispers, "I didn't even know that thing worked." I didn't either. Not that I would've taken the initiative to check. My culinary skills reach as far as buttered toast and memorized Chipotle orders.

"Grab the cold meat tray out of the icebox, Kacey. Annie, make yourself useful and grab the jar of sweet pickles I packed. I think it's in my handbag." Only my gran would unashamedly admit to carrying pickles in her purse. In short order, we're all sitting out in the sun with a full homemade Sunday picnic, looking for all the world like it's just a typical summer weekend, which I guess it is.

"This is the most at home I've felt in ages, Mrs. Rosewood," Fitz says, ladling himself another serving of soup. Kacey grins at him, all smitten kitten.

I glance around at the table, sipping my unsweetened iced tea. Clay—I mean Jefferson—is engaged in some conversation with my grandpa about woodworking, while Jason and Ever-Silent Jackson are leaning over Patrick's iPad watching the Tigers lose against the White Sox. Connie is talking my gran's ear off about some sermon we heard at the megachurch in Nashville.

My cousin leans in. "Sorta weird how a month ago we barely knew these guys, right?"

I lower my eyes to where I know she and Fitz are holding hands under the table. "No kidding."

Her cheeks turn a happy, glowing kind of pink. "How about our headliner talking shop with Pops? Never saw that coming."

I glance back over, a crazy flutter in my stomach. "Me neither, but he fits, doesn't he?"

"Did I hear you calling him Jefferson?"

I nod and lower my voice. "It seems to be a touchy subject. I wonder if he's changing his image or something."

Kacey narrows her eyes. "You do realize that it's only *you* he wants to call him Jefferson, right?"

"What?" I ask loudly. The guys watching the game startle and look my way. I sip my tea, waving them off. Kacey nudges Fitz.

He pulls a reluctant face and motions for me to move closer after checking Clay and Pops are still talking. "All I said was that since his open mic days, Clay's always been Clay. His brother and his grandpa called him Jefferson. Both died a few years back. Then I heard you calling him Jefferson, and he seems pleased as punch." Fitz shrugs, perplexed. "Maybe it's some identity crisis. He's been sort of weird since Nashville."

This time, I'm the one flushing. I wave my hand. "Whew, soup in July. Scurvy or not, I'm gonna need to find some ice cream."

Kacey's eyes widen. "I'm coming with."

I open my mouth to protest, but she's already at the door. Fitz shakes his head, chuckling to himself as I stand, untangling my legs from the fixed picnic bench.

"Ugh." I open the trailer to find her perched on the tiny counter, holding the ice cream hostage.

She hands me a spoon. "What happened in Nashville?"

"Nothing. We sang Johnny and June. It was a hit. He asked if we wanted to collaborate the remainder of the tour."

Kacey opens a pint and scoops a bite without removing her glare.

I sigh, reaching with my spoon, but she pulls the container back. "Not a chance."

I throw my arms wide, brushing against either wall of the tiny tour bus. "What do you want me to say? That we had a hot make-out session in the hotel hallway? That I offered myself on a silver platter and he flat-out rejected me, even though I swear he wanted me, too?"

Hot tears sting the corners of my eyes, and Kacey's mouth drops open. She plops the tub of ice cream on the counter behind her before hopping down and pulling me close. "Shit, Annie."

I sniff, accepting her embrace. "It was not my shining moment."

She pulls back, confused. "But you said it was hot and he clearly wanted you?"

I nod. "I thought so. He *said* so." At the root of everything is boiling humiliation. My pride took a massive hit. I offered myself to a rock star, and he turned me down. Forget the details; I'd been rejected. "He's apparently got this idea I don't know my own mind and it would be a mistake. He's being honorable or something."

Kacey bites her lip, considering. "And this is when he told you to call him Jefferson?"

I pull the Ben & Jerry's toward me. "Yeah. He got all mad and said to stop calling him Clay because he was trying not to be Clay around me."

Kacey's hand stills in midair, and she points her spoon at me. "Bear with me here. What comes to mind when you think of Clay Coolidge?"

"Levi's," I blurt before thinking.

She laughs. "Okay. My bad. This isn't a word association thing. I mean, what would your average female say about Clay?"

"Sex appeal, boozehound, makes love to the mic, rock star, stadium filler."

My cousin grins. "Yes. All of that. Now what do they think of Jefferson Coolidge?"

I blink. "I don't think anyone even knows that's his real name."

"Exactly. He doesn't want to be Clay the megastar booze-hound around you. He wants you to see Jefferson. Just you." She shrugs lightly. "I can't pretend to know what's happening in his mind, Annie, and I know rejection hurts, but maybe it's not so cut-and-dried as you think."

I put my unused spoon in the sink, suddenly not hungry. Kacey grabs a handful of fresh spoons, and I help her carry plastic bowls to the picnic table. I return to my seat and my iced tea and meet Jefferson's eyes. He's still talking to Pop, but he gives me a small, friendly smile. A real smile.

And for the first time, I realize it's a Jefferson smile.

"A very good evening to you, Columbus!" I shield my eyes from the spotlight and find the section of the stadium where my grandparents' tickets are. I imagine I can make out my gran's proud smile, but in reality, it's impossible. I blow a kiss in their direction, anyway. "This is a special night, y'all.

My gran and pop are here in the audience, along with Kacey's momma, Carla. In honor of them making the long drive out here to see us, we wanted to play one of my gran's old favorites."

The crowd shouts their approval, and I wave offstage. "And to play this oldie, I brought along some of my good friends to help. Clay Coolidge and Fitz Jacoby, everyone!" The stadium turns thunderous, and I have to laugh. The guys join us in the center of the stage. Fitz, carrying his fiddle, faces Kacey as if to challenge her to a fiddle duel. Or eyeball sex. It could go either way.

Jefferson accepts a mic from a stagehand and flashes his award-winning smile at the cheering thousands. He's Clay right now, except for the tiny wink he flashes just for me. That's Jefferson.

A girl could get whiplash trying to keep up.

I turn to the crowd, lifting my glittery mic. "We're all friends here, right?" I move to the edge of the stage. "Because I have a confession, y'all. I think I've lost my immunity to Southern boys." I fan my face theatrically as every female in the audience cheers their approval.

"And I'm finding I'm a bit partial to those Northern girls myself," Clay says. *Lord,* this boy. I don't know how to respond, so I punch his arm. He grunts into his mic and rubs his arm. "Your gran approve of that sass, Mathers?"

I grin and place my hand on my hip. "Who do you think taught me?"

He barks out a laugh and concedes, lifting his mic. "Okay, fair enough. I don't want to make Gran angry at me." He motions to Jason. "As Annie said, this is an oldie but a goodie. In fact, it's an old favorite of my granddad's as well. So, without further ado, 'We've Got Tonight' by Kenny Rogers and the stunning Dolly Parton."

I'm selfishly thrilled that I don't have to jump in until the second verse, because it means I get to sit back and watch Clay at work. It's hard not to imagine if he's feeling these lyrics as strongly as I am. A song about a man convincing his lover to stay with him for one more night . . .

Well, it hits a bit close to home, doesn't it? That's the glorious thing about music. It speaks to the very heart of things in the most absolute and obtrusive way. When I asked my gran for requests this afternoon and she answered with a twinkle in her eye, I knew I was doomed. My gran has a massive, decades-long crush on Kenny Rogers, and despite her reservations about Clay being too charming for his own good, he's one of the few in the industry who can pull off Kenny's signature coarse tenor. Which is really unfortunate for me.

Clay stands, legs spread at the hips, knees bending as if to absorb the force of his powerful voice. He growls into his mic a few lines before softening his plea so that it sends chills dancing down my spine. I'm so stunned at the stark appeal in his eyes when he turns to face me, I almost miss my cue.

I step off my stool, slowly making my way over to him. It takes a line to find myself again, but by the time I'm returning his staged advances with my own longing for love, my words strike home, and I can feel every eye of the audience painting us in sincerity. He reaches out his hand for mine, and I grasp his fingers in a squeeze, punctuating the meaning in my words. We come to the crescendo of the song where he's supposed to beg his case, and hell if he doesn't do a stand-up job. If the tabloids weren't speculating about our feelings before, duets like this one will seal the deal.

He sings to me that he knows my plans don't include him, but it's a lie. They do. I don't want them to, but that hardly matters. We wrap the song, and as the fiddles fade out, he pulls me close with a friendly, brotherly hug to his side, and without overthinking it, I raise on my tiptoes and kiss his stubbly cheek.

Because, fine. He doesn't feel like "Clay" deserves me. He's wild and reckless and a bit of a slut, if we're honest. And I'm careful and sheltered and damaged. Okay, then. We don't jump into bed together. I can handle that. I need to handle that, because I'm not sure I'm ready to be jumping into bed with anyone.

Instead, I'll take what he's offering me. This Jefferson—who I get the feeling is the truth behind the persona. The person he wants to be. The voice from the trailer the afternoon we fought.

And the man I could easily fall hopelessly in love with, but we won't worry about that right now. For now, we'll sing.

14

It's not long after we return to our buses that night that there's a knock on the door. Fitz props it open, letting Annie, Kacey, and Jason in. Kacey and Annie are holding hoodies and flashlights. Jason holds up a plastic grocery bag.

"We're gonna go find some shoreline and build a bonfire. Interested?"

Annie beams. "It's not too far out of town, and Aunt Carla said we could borrow her car as long as we brought it back before morning!"

It's after midnight, but their enthusiasm is catching. "I haven't had s'mores in years. Got any chocolate?"

"Duh." Kacey shrugs. Her eyes dart to Fitz. "Coming?"

Fitz is already tying on tennis shoes.

Within minutes, we're nearing a state park. Instead of turning in the main entrance, Jason continues down the highway another quarter mile and pulls down an unmarked dirt road.

"Should I ask how you knew that would be there?"

"Band camp," the drummer mutters, concentrating his efforts on navigating the rutted road in the dark.

"I'm sorry?"

"Went to band camp a little ways from here. Found this spot a few summers ago . . ." He swerves us around a particularly deep rut and pulls off to the side in a patch of tall grass before parking and shutting off the lights.

We climb out of the small car, and Jason pops the trunk. Annie flicks on her flashlight, and everyone takes turns pulling out blankets and a cooler. The moon is plenty bright out here so far from the lights of the city, and we don't even need the flashlights to find our way to the shore. Lake Erie is in its full glory this evening, freshwater waves crashing and washing along the quiet, rocky beach. The wind whips the humidity right out of the air, and I'm glad I brought a sweatshirt, even though it's July. Annie and Fitz spread a quilt on the ground, and Jason drops an armful of kindling on the sand. I follow him back to the edge of the woods and start collecting larger driftwood pieces that should burn hot and long. By the time we're back, Fitz already has a small, smoky fire started, and Kacey's passing out bottles.

She holds one out to me. "Just soda, Coolidge."

I take it, pressing the twist cap to my forearm, not removing my gaze, and crack it open without using my fingers. She smirks and holds out her bottle to clink with mine.

"Nice party trick."

"Lest you think I can't do anything but sing . . ."

"Wouldn't dream of it."

"He can also do a mad Hula-Hoop."

I groan, tipping back my head. "Damn it, Fitz, you know these hips don't lie." And I roll them once in an exaggerated circle as if I can't prevent it.

Annie giggles, and I turn to see her sitting cross-legged on the blanket, plucking leaves from a few roasting sticks.

"Quiet, you. I'm sure these two have plenty of dirt they'd be willing to share."

I move to join her on the blanket, taking one of the sticks

from her hands and pulling the pocketknife from my belt. I flip it open and slide it along the tip, cleaning it.

Annie leans back, meditating on the cozy fire, and lifts her bottle to her lips, taking a sip before saying, "Not bad for a bunch of Nashville stars, eh?"

I grin. "If you think about it, in all seriousness, we're barely a step above camping trailers in our buses. Of course, I didn't grow up with a silver spoon, like some people, Little Miss Country Music Royalty."

Annie flinches slightly at the title but recovers quickly, slugging me in the arm. "Please. You saw my grandparents' farm. You're the rock star."

I pluck a marshmallow out of the plastic bag and stab it on the end of my stick. Annie passes me another, and I raise a brow.

"Sensuous," she says, smirking.

I choke. "Excuse me?"

"*Since you was* already roasting . . ."

I snort. "Haven't heard that one before. I'll have to remember it."

"Jason," she says as if that explains everything. Which it does.

I hold out the stick to the fire. Kacey and Fitz are dipping their toes in the surf a few yards in front of us. "Speaking of your ex . . ."

Annie rolls her eyes. "Lord. Barely. We dated for, like, a month."

"Long enough to write a song about it."

"Yeah, well, that's nothing. As you very well know, I can write a song outta nothing more than a glance. It's called artistic license."

I roll the stick between my fingers, evening out the heat. "Silly me, I thought that was called exaggerating."

Annie gets a couple of crackers ready and reaches for the

Hershey bars. "Potato-potahtoe, my friend. 'Sides, it's not like y'all are complaining when my so-called exaggerations make you heartthrobs."

I pull back on the stick, tapping the gooey mess with my finger and licking it. Annie's eyes follow the movement, and I can't help but remember our kiss from the other night. I know I said we couldn't do it again. Shouldn't do it again.

But, fuck, I really want to do it again.

I clear my throat and hold out the stick. She takes the crackers and deftly tugs off the marshmallow mess between, keeping her fingers clean. She repeats it for mine, and I lean the stick against the pile of waiting driftwood.

"Are you implying we weren't already heartthrobs?"

Annie's tongue darts out to capture some of the melted chocolate on her top lip, and I take another swig of my Diet Coke, washing down the graham cracker suddenly dry in my throat.

Who knew s'mores could be so hot? Hell, a thousand songs written about dancing in taillights and drinking home-made wine, and not a one about marshmallows. It's a damn disservice to the industry.

"So if Jefferson is your first name, is Clay your middle name?"

I nod.

"If you don't mind me asking, why'd you decide to go by it?"

I brush off my fingers, settling back on my elbows. "I don't know," I hedge. "I mean, *Jefferson* is pretty lofty, isn't it?"

"Maybe, but it fits you." Something in me warms at that.

"I guess, it's like when I go by *Clay,* I can be Clay. Like, to the rest of the world."

"Like, an alter ego?"

"More like a persona I can adopt when I'm onstage. Or being interviewed. Or on a date, even."

Jason walks up, dropping another log on the fire, and I watch as the orange embers drift high in lazy spirals and flicker out. Annie passes him a stick and the bag of marshmallows. It's not nearly as fun to watch him molest his s'more. Annie shakes her head next to me.

"Holy hell, Jay. How you manage to put your shoes on the right feet mystifies me."

He rubs at his face, then grins hugely, cheeks puffed out with marshmallows and graham cracker coating his teeth in the moonlight.

"Gross."

"How'd you know of this place again, Diaz?" I ask, changing the subject.

His face falls, and he looks around, his eyes distant as they scan the coastline. "A friend."

"A female friend?" Kacey asks, walking up with Fitz.

"Yeah, right," Annie teases.

Jason winks, regaining some of his humor. He leans back, folding his hands behind his head. "You never know," he drawls out theatrically. "Maybe you're sitting in the very spot I lost my flower underneath the stars."

"Ew. Tell me you're joking."

"All right, then. I'm joking."

In the firelight, I watch as Kacey's eyes narrow shrewdly. "I don't know. I'm not sure you *are* kidding."

Fitz pulls Kacey back to his chest. "Easy, girl."

Kacey settles back and hand-feeds Fitz. They forgo the crackers altogether, and Fitz makes a show of licking Kacey's finger clean.

Annie surges to her feet next to me, brushing at the backs of her thighs. "I'm gonna explore the beach a little bit."

"Me, too." The words are out before I can change my mind, and I get to my feet. Jason's busy roasting another row of marshmallows; otherwise, based on his look of disgust at the fiddling fiddlers, he'd tag along.

Annie and I take off down the beach. Within moments, I feel the absence of our small bonfire on my exposed skin. Annie zips up her hoodie with a shiver.

"Wanna go back by the fire?" I check, hoping she doesn't.

"Nah, I'll get used to it in a sec. I don't think it's actually that cool."

We walk in silence awhile, and Annie shakes her head suddenly. "Seriously, do you think Jason had sex with some girl on this beach?"

I shrug. "You know him better than I do. But, it's sort of, uh, a romantic spot? I guess?"

Annie's face is puckered in thought, and her hair dances around her features like it's trying to fly away. "I guess. But is Jason romantic? And, I mean, band camp? That was two years ago. He was sixteen."

A discussion of Diaz's sex life is not exactly what I had planned on when I jumped up to follow this girl.

"That's pretty average. I think. Sixteen."

Annie exhales loudly.

I bump her with my shoulder. "Listen, that's no judgment on you. I was almost eighteen myself."

"Aren't you eighteen now?" Annie asks quietly.

"I am."

"So . . ."

"Uh-uh," I say, shaking my head. "That's all you're getting from me tonight. Point is, it doesn't really matter. Sixteen, eighteen, twenty-five, forty. Ain't no thang."

She grins in the moonlight, and my chest aches. It's stupid how much I want to make this girl smile.

I cough, kicking at the sand. "Also, you have nothing to be embarrassed about. You aren't old. You're perfect. And you'll continue to get better the older you are, so if you chose to wait until your wedding night, your husband will be a very lucky man."

"Wow," she says. "That's . . . probably the nicest thing anyone has ever said to me."

I lift a shoulder and continue walking. "I'm not bullshitting you. That night at the hotel? I didn't want to stop kissing you, Annie. You know that, right? I could've easily kissed you right there in that hallway all night."

Annie fans herself in that cute way that reminds me she's been raised by her grandma. "Jesus H., Jefferson, you're too charming for your own good."

My head swells. "Only for you."

She stops and looks out at the sparkling water. Then peers past me to the tiny flickering light of the bonfire. We're quite a way from our friends by now, but I'm okay with it. Christ only knows the shit Fitz would give me hearing the words coming out of my mouth under the influence of Annie Mathers. Not that any of it's a lie.

Hell, I mean every single word. Which, I realize, is real rich considering the open invitation Lora Bradley has to my bed.

Maybe I need to—

And Annie's soft lips are pressed to mine. All sticky marshmallow and cream soda. Her tongue slips past my lips, and I don't hold back my moan as I tug her body against mine. We're all hands and heat. I don't even bother with her sweatshirt, my fingers tracing a searing path along her hips and back to dip below the waistband of her jeans. She sighs into my mouth, and I don't even realize I've lifted her clear off her feet until she wraps her legs around my hips.

I groan at the sensation of her pressed against me. A distant part of me realizes this can't end well. I respect her waiting. I respect her . . .

Slowly, so painfully slow, she slips back to standing on the rocky ground. I'm panting and dizzy, and I ache.

Everything in me aches for this girl.

But she doesn't stop kissing me. Her fingers wind themselves in my hair and yank gently, pulling me closer and closer. I take her face in between my hands and slow things down. Tasting her. Savoring her. Memorizing her. I don't usually try so hard, but hell if I don't want to make this count.

I've kissed a lot of girls. I've slept with a few of them. But I've never in my life kissed someone like this. Felt like this. Wanted like this. It's as though we're one person. Like my soul found its fucking other half and I don't even know what to do with that except I can't ever stop this. I will die happily with her on my lips.

The water rushes over our feet, and it's like a shock to my system. I hadn't realized we traveled so close to the lake. We pull away from each other, and Annie laughs, smiling all the way to her eyes, aglow in moonlight and hormones, and I feel a stirring of pride in my gut that I had something to do with that.

"Maybe this beach is a little romantic," she concedes.

15

Annie

The morning after the beach, I wake up too early with a song in my head. Kacey's and Jason's snores echo around me, and so, after brushing my teeth and making a cup of coffee, I grab my guitar and head out into the summer sunshine.

I don't know what I'm doing.

I mean, this isn't for real. This thing between Clay, or Jefferson, and me. He's beautiful and dangerous and not at all committed.

So, like, I'd be stupid to believe any of it meant anything. He's 100 percent playing me, and that's cool. I'm here, and Lora isn't.

I'll just take this for what it is. Temptation in blue jeans and all that. Nothing to it. People have casual relationships all the time. I mean, that's basically what college is all about, right?

Except my summer fling is a gorgeous megastar country singer. And last night didn't feel casual.

But no big deal. Totally cool. I can do this.

Even if I might be a teeny-tiny bit at risk of falling for him.

It's fine. I might get hurt, but . . . I think of his calloused hands dragging along my rib cage slipping north . . . and *whatever. Worth it.*

I'm not my mom. I can do "no strings attached." He's not gonna derail me.

Clay's trouble, but who's to say I have to walk away? I can handle it.

The silent question of *what if he's not—what if he's more?—* well, that's not something I care to think on right now.

Because, seriously, we're only eighteen.

I sing about playing casual and heat and passion and need, and it's all so foreign and gorgeous and thrilling, but it also rings a little . . . I don't know . . . hollow.

As though it's not . . . *me.* It's someone else.

And I want to throw up because it *has* to be me. That's what this has to be. I can do this. People do this every day all over the world.

I can't fall for him.

After lunch, he finds me. Sheepish and almost shy, he knocks on my door. I'm sitting on my bunk with a book that I'm not reading. That I couldn't possibly read because all I can think about is him, him, him.

"Wanna go for a walk?"

"Right now?" I ask dumbly.

"It's gorgeous out, and we hit the road again in a few hours. Come on."

As if I could resist him. Like ever.

We're trekking down a pretty little river walk toward downtown. He's in his ball cap and jeans and is holding my hand.

Holding hands doesn't feel super-conducive to my "casual" MO, but damn if it doesn't feel really nice. Like warm chocolate cookies and knit cashmere and hot tea during a snow-storm.

I'm so super-screwed.

"My brother used to call me Jefferson. My grandpa, too," he says after we cross a busy street into the entrance of a city park. We end up settling on a picnic table.

I don't play dumb. I remember how he easily evaded my question last night. "Used to?"

"They both died. First grandpa when I was fifteen and then my brother a year later."

I suddenly remember Fitz mentioning them dying. Damn. "I'm so sorry—"

He cuts me off. "Anyway, whatever, it's why I go by Clay."

I scramble, trying to think of something to say. The closed expression on his face doesn't really offer more. I can't decide if I'm supposed to press for details—give him the chance to open up—or share something of my own? A give-and-take? I'm not great at this kind of thing. After a pause, I blurt, "I won't sing her songs."

He turns to face me, dark eyes burrowing into mine. He doesn't ask who I mean. Just says, "I wondered about that."

I sigh, tracing some graffiti long ago carved into the table with my fingernail. "It's not like I can pretend to not be connected to them. Everyone knows. But it's this tiny bit of control I can maintain. I can't change my DNA, but I can change my set list. I refuse to honor them after what they did to me."

"They didn't die to hurt you, though. You know that, right?"

"Actually, I don't. And anyway, they certainly didn't live for me."

He grows quiet, and I feel my cheeks heat, and I realize how damaged I must sound. Bitter and ungrateful and angry.

It's a carefully hidden part of me. One reserved for Kacey and Jason.

"You're right," he says in a low voice.

My throat catches, and I risk a glance up at him.

He's determined. "They didn't live for you. You're right."

"That's it?"

He shrugs. "Do you need more? Because if you do, I'm hardly the one to talk about unhealthy hang-ups."

"No, I guess I don't. So we're in a park."

Jefferson glances around, his lips pulling into a smile. "We are. I'm not real familiar with Ohio. You?"

"Definitely not. I didn't even know they had beaches until last night."

He sits up straighter, placing his hands on his knees and half rising. "I have an idea." He holds out a hand, and I grasp on to it. Tugging me along, he pulls us across a busy street and onto the sidewalk entrance to what appears to be a jewelry store. There's a sign that reads, MINE TOURS INSIDE.

I raise a skeptical brow at the storefront. "How is there a mine in this place?"

"No idea," Jefferson says. "But I think we have to check it out. I've never been to a cave inside a store."

We walk in, and it's exactly as advertised: your typical jewelry store. Behind the glittering counter sits a harried young woman who looks up at us from the glass display case.

"We're here for the mine tour," Jefferson says as if it's the most obvious thing ever.

She points a thumb to the back of the store, where the wall has been painted in a janky-looking mural that must be the "cave" entrance. There's a cardboard cutout of an old-timey miner who I'm pretty sure is just a knockoff of Yosemite Sam, holding a pickax in front of the doorway. The little word bubble over his head reads, MOTHER (OR FATHER) LODE $5, LITTLE NIPPERS $2.50.

I snicker. "Wait, you have to pay for this?"

"I take offense at 'Little Nipper,'" Jefferson says under his breath, and I can't stop giggling.

"I don't have cash," I whisper.

"What the hell kind of country star are you?" he whispers back, pulling out his wallet.

"The kind who uses debit, apparently."

Jefferson walks over to the clerk. "Do we pay you for the tour here?"

"Seriously?" she asks, and Jefferson's blinding smile falters.

"Uh, yes?"

"Are you students?" she asks.

"Well, we aren't Mother and Father Lodes, if that's what you're asking."

"Little Nippers are under ten," she says.

It's incredible to see how the mask of Clay washes over Jefferson's face. He's taller somehow and charismatic. Gone is the uncertain teenage boy. "Tell me, Denise," he says, glancing down at her name badge. "Is this tour worth five dollars apiece? Is there even a tour guide?"

"Not really," she admits. "It's little more than a light show."

Jefferson pauses, considering. Then, "Is it romantic?" he stage-whispers, "We're on our first date."

Two can turn on the charm. I take a stab at putting on my stage persona. "If this is a first date, why are you being so dang cheap?"

Jefferson straightens. "Fair point. What the lady wants, the lady gets. Two Mother Lode tickets, please."

He slides her a twenty, and she goes to give us cash back, but he's already leading me toward the "entrance." "Keep the change, Denise."

He hurries me inside, and it's basically a tunnel of what looks like black papier-mâché inlaid with tiny twinkle lights. The floors have glow-in-the-dark strips of tape that we follow around a bend. It's cooler in here, and there is a recording playing through the speakers that sounds like drips echoing off a cave floor.

"A-plus for ambiance," I muse.

"Watch out for stalagmites," Jefferson whispers. "In fact, you should probably take my hand."

I snort in the dark. "Don't you mean stalactites?" I ask.

"I don't know. I never graduated high school," he says.

"They didn't make you take the GED?" I ask.

Silence.

"I just rolled my eyes at you, but you didn't see it," he says. "*Of course* I got my GED. But seriously, who actually knows the difference between stalactites and stalagmites?"

"Fair point."

"I was just trying to be smooth, Mathers. Way to mess up my game."

I snicker louder.

We round the corner—and by *the*, I mean the only corner, because I can already see the glowing red exit light on the wall—and enter into a small room that, to their credit, does sort of resemble a cavern. Twinkle lights are fashioned in broad swirls that look almost like phosphorescence has been painted on the walls. Blue lights accent glittery seams, and the ground is uneven and feels legitimately close to a real cave floor. In the center is a display case of different gems and a key showing us where to find them in their "natural" state, scattered around the cavern's crevices.

"Let's split up and make a game out of this," he says. "Whoever finds the most gems wins."

His enthusiasm is catching and I ask, "What's the prize?"

"Bragging rights?"

"You're on," I say.

We split up, and I read the inscription under the first gemstone. Fool's gold, or pyrite. I skim the bottom of the "cave floor," dragging my fingers through a bin of stones that I'm positive are not found together in nature. From the clattering of rocks against cardboard, I know that Jefferson is doing the same.

"This is impossible in the dark," I mutter.

"You just know you're going to lose."

"I'm pretty sure all the real gems have been stolen already," I complain, picking at another black-colored rock-type object that feels suspiciously like plastic.

"I think I got one!" he yells triumphantly, running toward the only bit of light in the room, emitting from the gem display.

"Nuh-uh," I say, dropping the stones at my feet and walking over to see.

"I did. It's called . . ." He leans closer, and I follow. Suddenly, he drops the rock with a click, and his hands are holding the sides of my face. "It's called 'I just wanted to kiss you again, and Denise is running a scam.'"

"I've never heard of that one," I say, leaning in.

"Oh, really? It's become my new favorite," he says before capturing my lips between his own in a way that doesn't feel casual in the slightest.

16

Clay

friday, july 12
indianapolis, indiana

The first time I played in my hometown after hitting the big time was surreal. It was when "Clay" really took over. I couldn't drive down my streets, sing to my old classmates, in a venue where I used to listen to all my favorites, while still being "Jefferson." It didn't work. I had to create someone they'd never met. Someone I'd never met, even. It wasn't hard. My brother had recently died, and I'd already lost track of who I used to be by that point.

Beer chased the memories, and a solid buzz made Clay easier for me to stomach until I barely had to think about it. The girls helped in their way. I wasn't always such a bastard. In the beginning, I remembered their names and kissed them on their mouths and paid for their drinks. But it quickly became apparent they didn't care either way. None of the girls camping out backstage wanted a relationship. They weren't looking for clumsy efforts at romance. They wanted bragging rights and an incriminating selfie for their Instagram.

So that's what I gave them. When that got too exhausting, I would text Lora. She was even more effortless than the strangers. Or she would text me. Like she did today.

WHERE ARE YOU AT THIS WEEKEND?

I type INDY and wait.

If I'm expecting her to catch the significance of me being back in my hometown, I'm disappointed. Lora has no clue.

After a minute, she responds:

DAMN. NYC FOR THE WEEKEND. CATCH YOU IN VEGAS IN SEP?

I send her a thumbs-up and click the app shut. Probably for the best. Lora in Indy feels a little too real for comfort.

Fitz leans over my shoulder, tapping my screen where her kissing emoji response is still lit up.

I swat his hand half-heartedly. "Do you mind?"

He turns for the fridge, grabbing out a root beer and twisting the cap against his forearm to open.

"I thought you were done with Lora."

"I am."

He raises one brow, swallowing.

"I am done. It's . . . well . . . coming back here. This stop always makes me edgy as fuck."

"So does Lora, lately."

"Yeah, well, she's out of town anyway, so it's a moot point."

Fitz picks at the label on his bottle. The small window air-conditioning unit cycles on with a hum.

"Spit it out, Fitz."

"I'm just trying to understand why you would even cater to the notion of another meaningless hookup with Lora when you've got Annie making doe eyes at you."

"I'm not catering to anything. And she doesn't make doe eyes at me."

"So you told Lora to fuck off?"

I don't answer.

Fitz nods. "I see. So you're keeping her around just in case Annie rejects you."

"The fuck?" I say.

"Classic Clay. Keep a flask in your pocket if things get too heavy and a girl on the line just the same."

"It's not like that with Annie."

Fitz raises his brows. "Really. Indulge me. What's it like, then?"

"I don't know!" I shout, impatient. "It's not like anything. We've just kissed a few times is all. She's cool. I like spending time with her. I can be me around her. Jesus, why does it have to be more than that?"

Fitz stares at me a long minute before saying, "Because anything less than that isn't enough."

I blink, feeling shaken.

"I'm going to visit Danny tomorrow." Fitz is changing gears, and I'm spinning to catch up.

"I'll come with."

He nods, not meeting my eyes.

"What?"

"You know that Mags throws a party every year at Taps in his memory?"

"Vaguely. She emailed me last year, but we were on tour."

Fitz clears his throat. "She checked with me this year. Emailed a few months back to let her know once we got our tour schedule. Wanted to make sure you could make it this time."

My stomach clenches painfully like a punch in the gut. My hands sweat, and I stand up to grab a bottle out of the cabinet.

"I can't go back there, Fitz." My voice cracks, and I feel thirteen all over again.

"It's been two years, Clay. They need to see you."

"If I'm there, it turns into a publicity stunt. Danny'd hate that. He died honorably, and I'd make it a joke."

Fitz shakes his head, disbelief widening his eyes. "Why on earth would you think that? He would be crazy proud of everything you've accomplished. He loved listening to you play. He'd get such a kick out of your fame."

"He'd get a kick out of Annie's fame. He'd tolerate mine."

Fitz throws his bottle in the trash with a loud *clang*. "What the hell, man? What's wrong with you?"

I surge to my feet, feeling miserable and wanting more than anything to let everyone know. And by everyone, I mean Fitz. Because let's face it, he's the only person who will listen. "What's wrong with me? I'm a washout at eighteen, Fitz. I know booze and girls. I sing songs people drink to. I'm being overshadowed in my own tour. I'm borderline alcoholic with barely enough talent to scrape by."

Fitz holds his hand up. "You know what? Fine. I'm not going to sit here and blow smoke up your butt. Those drinking songs have made you wealthy enough to retire by twenty. Those girls deserve better. And Annie works her ass off and is the most unpretentious, talented person I've ever met in this industry. She overshadows ever-loving Garth Brooks. That's nothing to be ashamed of."

Fitz moves forward, his face inches from my own, lowering his voice. "And if you're crying out for help, then I'm here for you. We can walk away today. I'll get you in a rehab program and hold your hand and whatever else you need. *If.* Because all I hear is a bratty show business kid feeling sorry for himself. If I believed for one millisecond you wanted to get dry, I would drive you myself."

I don't say anything, and he backs up with a humorless chuckle. "That's what I thought. We have sound check in thirty. I'll tell Mags we'll be there."

The following afternoon, Fitz finds me propped against the white marble headstone that marks Danny's resting place.

"I thought we were coming together."

"I needed to talk to my big brother alone."

Fitz reaches down and picks up the empty glass bottle at my feet.

"We argued," I say by way of explanation. "Said some things we didn't mean."

Fitz sighs heavily and drops down next to me, picking up the little American flag presumably stuck in my brother's plot over the holiday. "I shouldn't have said what I did yesterday. If you want to get clean, you know I'm here for it."

I lean my head back against the hard, smooth stone, the hot sun a giant, glaring spot in the sky. "No, you were right. I'm not ready to face this sober."

"Danny wouldn't even ask. He'd have dragged you to a clinic months ago." Fitz's voice has lost its lightness. He sounds as defeated as I feel. "I'm fucking this up."

"Yeah, well, Danny chose his way to die. Maybe I'm choosing mine."

Fitz laughs, shaking his head. "Christ, you're melodramatic."

The longer we sit here, the more I need to sleep. Stay here in the sun forever. I'd lied when I'd told Fitz I'd argued with my brother. More like I'd told him about Annie, and then that voice in the back of my mind that has the exact timbre of my brother's told me I was a selfish prick and to quit considering whatever it was that I was considering.

There was no back-and-forth. There never was with Danny. It's what made him such a powerful soldier. His bullet always struck true. He never wavered. His faith was honed at my grandfather's knee, and it's as though God himself whispered in his ear. Our parents were never really together. Dad left after I was born, and he never came back. Mom worked three jobs until the cancer leached every last bit of her spirit. We had the exact same upbringing, but somehow the adversity made Danny decisive and solid and . . . *good*. He was so damn good all the time. Even to me, his mess of a kid brother.

"I should have died, not him," I say.

"He'd disagree. He'd say you have a purpose that keeps you on this earth."

Music. Danny called music my purpose. *My* service. *You make people feel things, Jefferson*. He'd come to hear me play at Taps the night before he left for the desert. It was the only thing I could give my brother. We weren't affectionate growing up. Instead, I dedicated a song to him and paid for his beer.

I grunt as I clamber to my feet, using the stone to steady myself. "Did you drive?"

Fitz shakes his head. "Kacey dropped me off. I figured I'd hitch a ride."

Or he'd assumed I wouldn't be able to drive myself home. This isn't our first rodeo. I don't ask, just toss him my keys and turn for the long walk to my truck, giving him privacy. I lost my brother, but in all honesty, Fitz and Danny were closer than we were.

A few minutes later, Fitz circles the truck to the driver's seat, red eyes hidden behind frames. He throws my old clunker Ford into drive and kicks up gravel as he pulls away from the side of the cemetery gates.

We're silent the entire drive back to my grandpa's farm. He left it to both Danny and me in his will, but really Danny took care of it. He sold off the decent farming soil and kept the house and the woodshed for me. He kept the truck for himself.

But in the end, it all came to me anyway. I could barely drive. When the news came that a roadside bomb had attacked Danny's unit, I'd only had my license a week. That day, it was raining in icy sheets. Fitz found me in Danny's truck, shivering and soaked to the bone. I hadn't bothered to roll up the windows—just sat there, unfeeling and practically comatose. Fitz tells me I didn't speak for three days afterward. I threw out all of Danny's things in a fit of rage. I got into my grandfather's liquor cabinet and drank my way through until Fitz showed up and started pouring it all down the drain.

I never cried. I'd grown used to being alone, so Danny's death was just one more.

In the end, everyone leaves.

Fitz pulls up the drive, and I see his newer-model F-150 parked in front of the barn.

"You told her where I live?"

Fitz sighs impatiently in response and slams his door.

I follow him out, taking a split-second to let the light-headed feeling pass. "You had no right. This is my home."

Kacey swings open the door and steps out onto the porch with a glass of tea in her hand like la-di-da. Fitz grabs hold of my arm in a painful squeeze. "Don't you dare take it out on her. It was this or they were gonna wait at the cemetery. I figured you didn't need an audience."

"They?" I sputter. It's only then I realize Annie has been sitting in the swing the entire time. I meet her eyes as something like pity passes over her face. And something more. It's the pity that grates, though. A frustrated growl starts in my chest. Fitz's hold tightens.

"Clay's just gonna get cleaned up for the party at Taps. I'll be right out to drive you ladies back to your hotel so you can get freshened up to join us."

"Oh, we don't—"

Fitz does an about-face, jabbing a finger at Annie. In mock sternness, he says, "You don't want to finish that. This is our town, Annie. Let us take you out and show you around our home field. I expect the same treatment when we hit Michigan next month."

Annie looks like she wants to protest, but Kacey takes a cue from her boyfriend and grabs her hand, dragging her up from the swing. Annie shakes off her hold and steps to the doorway, blocking our entrance. She glares at Fitz, who huffs and mutters, "Stubborn Yank," and releases my arm, heading inside with a slam of the screen door. Ten to one he's listening right out of sight to make sure I behave.

It rankles something awful. Apparently, his pep talk with Danny included a renewal of his taking over my care.

"That's my grandma's swing. No one's sat in it since she passed," I say bluntly.

Annie turns bright red and starts to stutter an apology.

I cut her off. "Christ. It's fine. You didn't know. I guess it doesn't matter. No one else around but me to care."

I hear the truck door slam and know Kacey is giving us privacy. Annie scratches at her arm, distracted. I follow her fingertips. She's wearing her customary tank top, but this one's more casual. Not stage casual, but real-life casual.

"Guess you know the whole sorry truth now," I say. "Poor Clay Coolidge, brother of a fallen soldier," I say mockingly.

"I'm sorry for your loss, Jefferson."

"Yeah, thanks."

"I mean it. I had no idea your brother was a soldier killed in the line of duty."

"Yeah, well. I prefer it that way. He doesn't need his sloppy kid brother dishonoring his sacrifice."

Annie's blue eyes grow wide. "Is that really what you think?"

I shrug. "Yeah."

Annie just nods in her quiet way. Thinking. She's always thinking. She looks out over my farm, taking it in.

I sway slightly.

"I can see why you might. But someone once told me if I didn't want to end up a certain way, to just don't."

"Just don't," I repeat.

Her gaze flickers back to me, studying my face. "Yes, Jefferson. If I don't want to be like my parents, I just need to not be like my parents. If you don't want to dishonor your brother's sacrifice, then don't. I'll admit, it's a work in progress, but perhaps you ought to give it a shot." I stare at her, and she clears her throat, tucking a wayward curl behind her ear. "Anyway, I wanted to tell you how sorry I am about your brother. I didn't know where Fitz was going this afternoon when I offered to come along. I only wanted to see around town. I . . . we never meant to impose on your personal life."

I crack a smile at her awkwardness. Just like that, she's managed to disarm me. It's like some Annie voodoo. I forget my misery, always—even if only for a minute—around this girl.

"You'd be the very first."

"First what?"

"The first to not want to impose on my personal life."

She grins sheepishly. "Even so, I'm sorry."

I move to lean against the doorjamb and miss. I recover in time to catch her half grin.

"I should get going. We're apparently meeting you guys at some bar tonight?"

"Taps," I say with a salute.

"Right. That one."

She hops down the porch steps, and my eyes follow her to the truck. She turns to face me once more, gives me a weak wave, and gets in. Fitz opens the screen door.

"All right, *Jefferson*," he says with a knowing smirk. "Let's get you in the shower before you sober up and realize what an idiot you've made of yourself."

"You say *idiot;* I call it *charm*," I say, following him up the creaky old stairs and managing to miss the first step.

Fitz snickers under his breath. "It doesn't matter what you call it, friend; it matters what she'd call it."

I grin to myself in the mirror, closing the bathroom door on Fitz. "Then definitely charm."

17

Annie

saturday, july 13
indianapolis, indiana

We're late, mostly because our driver takes us the long way down Meridian.

Taps is nowhere near the touristy bar scene. Taps is barely within the city limits. Once you run out of stoplights, all you see are cornfields and wind turbines in every direction. Then, seemingly in the middle of one of those endless fields, a few short miles from the dusty dirt road Jefferson calls home, is Taps. Which is just as well, as none of us is legal and I'm not interested in hitting up any location TMZ might stake out with the right tip-off.

There's no cover, but they are taking a donation at the door on behalf of the Wounded Warrior Project, and all three of us dig into our pockets to contribute. A burly bouncer barely gives us a glance as we pass through the dark, propped-open doorway. Through the haze of cigarette smoke, I make out a large wooden plank dance floor where multiple couples, young and old, stomp around in circles. There is a neon-lit bar with two bustling bartenders and a few worn pool tables behind them. When we walk in, things feel hushed at once. I take a step back, but Kacey pulls me along, leading me straight to the bar. I try not to cast my eyes around too much, despite the clear fact we're not locals. Jason comes up behind me and leans over the bar holding out a bill. One of the bartenders floats over, and he flashes her a winning smile.

"Six shots of your best Cuervo, señorita."

I roll my eyes so hard, I probably pull a muscle.

Jason catches it and shrugs impishly. "What? The ladies love when I charm them with my *español*."

"Puh-lease," I say. "Kindergartners know more Spanish than you. You were better off carrying around your drumsticks in your back pocket."

The bartender pushes the shot glasses toward us. I hold out a hand. "None for me, thanks."

Jason raises a brow and pulls them all toward him. "Obviously, I wasn't ordering for you. Especially if you're going to make fun of my *muy bueno* skills."

"Grandma Angelica is rolling in her grave." The bartender turns to me, expectant. "Just a ginger ale," I say.

Kacey lets out a squeal. Fitz has found us. He's followed by a curvy woman who looks to be in her forties.

"Maggie, this is our friend—"

She cuts him off in exasperation. "I know who Annie Mathers is, Fitz." She holds out a hand, and I shake it. She looks me up and down with a knowing grin. "So you're the one changing Clay's religion."

Jason spews tequila all over us like one of those fire breathers. A glance at the bartender and she tosses me a rag, which I immediately apply to the floorboards.

"Hey!" Jason protests, and so I toss it in his face.

"I'm not worried about you, ya ingrate." I turn back to Maggie. "I'm so sorry about that."

Maggie waves me off. "I've raised three boys of my own; I've grown used to dirty floors."

"Wow, three? I never had a brother." I feel my cheeks heat when she nods, grinning. Of course she knows. Everyone knows. Ignoring the twinge, I jab a thumb over my shoulder at Jason. "This one's as close as I get."

Maggie laughs. "I have a daughter, too." She points at one of the bartenders, the petite auburn-haired, younger woman who passes me my ginger ale. I smile wide in greeting.

She wipes her hands on a fresh rag and offers one. "Lindy Parsons. I'm a huge fan, Ms. Mathers. Of both your mom and you."

Maggie smiles fondly. "It's true. She's been a fan since the womb. I used to plug in headphones to my Discman and play Cora's greatest hits over my belly."

Usually talk of my parents makes me uneasy, but it's impossible to feel uncomfortable around Maggie. She has this maternal vibe that makes you want her to brush your hair while you talk about your crushes.

"Well, we should probably be friends, then, because that's how I became a fan as well," I say to Lindy.

A slow song comes over the jukebox, and Fitz leads a giddy Kacey in a twirl of her peasant skirt around the floor. Jason starts chatting with a couple of young women in matching straw hats at the bar, and I hop on a stool with my ginger ale. Things pick up behind the bar, and Maggie jumps back to help. Soon it's surpassing even her.

"Is it usually this busy?" I ask as Lindy refills my soda.

She nods her topknot toward a banner off to the side I hadn't noticed. It reads, *Thank you for your sacrifice, Sgt. Daniel Coolidge,* underneath the words, *We'll never forget. Semper Fi.*

My stomach drops, and without meaning to, my eyes seek

out Jefferson, who's been conspicuously absent since I'd arrived. I finally spot him in a dark corner, surrounded by a group of girls, double-fisting longnecks.

Lindy blows her bangs out of her eyes. "They've had him cornered for the past hour at least."

I shrug. "Same story, different town."

Lindy tips her head, deftly pouring three shots with one hand. "I thought I heard a rumor things might be heating up with you two on tour."

I take a dainty sip from my straw, playing for time. "That's show business for you. Those rumors are highly exaggerated, and Jefferson is complicated."

She raises a brow. "Since when? I've known Clay since diapers. He's always seemed pretty cut and dry to me."

"Maybe since his brother died? I'm not sure." Sometimes I feel like I know nothing about Jefferson. Others, I wonder if I'm the only one who knows anything.

Lindy freezes. "I wasn't under the impression Clay was too bothered about Danny being gone. He sure as hell didn't stick around to mourn."

"Wasn't he, like, sixteen? I don't know," I say, poking at the ice with my straw. I'm defensive—on Jefferson's behalf and my own. "My parents died when I was thirteen, and I haven't visited their graves once."

"Well, aren't you two a well-adjusted pair."

My shoulders tense, but I force them back down. "Maybe. I own a closet full of high-end boots I won't ever wear. Jefferson spent the afternoon getting drunk in a cemetery."

Lindy presses her lips together, her eyes suspiciously shiny. She swipes under her eye quickly. "Shit," she murmurs. She rips a taped-up paper from under the bar and places it in front of me. It's one of those department store portrait shots of a little girl with sandy curls and blue eyes. "I've been bitter. This is my girl, Layla. She's mine and Danny's, so Clay's niece. Danny died before he even met her, and I tried to force Clay to be her family. I've been pushing it for years. He can hardly stand to be around her for an entire afternoon without running."

My stomach clenches at her pronouncement. For all of them. For the effed-up situation. Yesterday, Jefferson was just a boozehound. Today has been an abundance of complicated layers peeling back, flipping all my assumptions on their heads. Yesterday, I savored memories of all his kisses, hoping for more, more, more.

Today? Today is *bad*. Today is what happens when your sweet little sandbox is revealed to have been filled with quicksand. Today has *should have known better* written all over it.

"I'm so sorry. I didn't realize."

She gives me a watery, sad sort of smile. She pulls the photo back, taking a long look at it before tucking it away. "It never occurred to me he was grieving. What with the tours and appearances and everything."

"We all have our secrets." Oh, just *how*. "Maybe he's not coming home because it's hard for him to be somewhere Danny isn't. I secretly sold my parents' home the moment I turned eighteen. Didn't even bother to have a look around with the Realtor. Just sent my wishes via my manager, Connie, and washed my hands of the entire business. That Jefferson hasn't done the same is a good thing. Maybe someday he'll be able to be there for you and Layla."

"You're awful nice, Annie Mathers." Lindy dries a row of glasses, one after another, laying them out. "And very real."

"Thanks, I think."

"It was definitely a compliment. I hope you come back here after your tour. You're good for him."

"I'm not much good for anyone these days," I hedge. "But I'd love to visit again."

Lindy passes me a fresh ginger ale, this one with a bunch of maraschino cherries floating in the ice. I dig one out and tug it off the stem with my teeth.

Lindy shakes her head. "I feel terrible I never knew how hard Clay was taking it."

I take my time chewing another cherry, letting the sweetness coat my tongue before swallowing. "I don't know that Jefferson even realizes it, to be honest, so don't beat yourself up."

"Jefferson realizes what?"

I spin on my stool, sloshing my drink over the bar. Jefferson leans on the bar from behind me, his body pressing against my side. He smells way too good. A mix of laundry detergent and beer that shouldn't be as appealing as it is. His hair flops forward on his forehead, his ball cap tucked into his back pocket. He's wearing a western-style plaid shirt, but the sleeves are rolled up to reveal the dusting of blond hair on his tanned forearms.

I narrow my eyes at his unfortunate handsomeness. "Realizes there are other people in this bar who came out to see the hometown boy besides those three cute chickadees in the corner."

Jefferson is unfazed, flashing a toothy grin. "You jealous, Mathers?"

I snort into my drink, picking out another cherry.

He watches me pop it in my mouth, his eyes darkening, and I feel my breath hitch.

"What's that you're drinking? No shots?"

My cheeks heat. "Nope. Not tonight."

The sound of bagpipes plays over the jukebox, and Lindy shakes her head, cleaning a glass. "That's for you, Coolidge."

We glance over at the dance floor. Fitz is in the middle of a mob, stamping his boots and waving at us.

Jefferson throws back the last of his beer, slamming it on the bar. "My people await."

Lindy leans forward. "Girls were like moth to the flame when Fitz and the Coolidge boys would get on the line for 'Copperhead Road.' It's how that little miracle came about." She points at the photo again, smiling fondly. I suddenly wish I had gotten to meet this Sergeant Daniel Coolidge.

"Really?" I turn in my seat to get a clearer view. "I haven't seen a proper line dance in ages, but I don't remember thinking much of it as a kid."

"That's because you never saw it like this."

Dancing would've been okay. I could have survived a dancing cowboy. I could have even survived a stomping Clay Coolidge, country singer.

But holy Hannah, I won't survive Jefferson Coolidge, farm boy.

Even under the dimmed lights, I can spot him clearly, his thumbs hooked in his belt loops. Clay doesn't usually wear the stereotypical cowboy boots offstage; in fact, he usually wears something sturdier like Doc Martens. But tonight, his high-end black boots are polished beneath his tailored jeans. It's all a bunch of tapping and stomping and hopping, but I can't look away. His hips swing sinuously. His ball cap drawing my attention to his backside.

I'm taken.

I'm a cliché.

I don't even care.

Suddenly Jefferson is sauntering over to me, and I put down my drink so as not to spill it. He holds out a hand, and I hop down like an obedient puppy. He raises my hand high in the air. "Annie Mathers, everyone!" A few people crane to see me in the crowd, curious. Even here, in the middle of nowhere, my dad's name carries recognition.

I seriously wish I had taken a shot earlier. Lindy gives me

a wink, laughing from behind the bar. I glare at her, though I doubt she can see in the dark.

Jefferson keeps hold of my hand, leading me through the repetitive steps. Whenever we need to turn, he grabs my hips and helps me along. The first time, I stutter in my steps, but after a full rotation, I have a grasp of the movements.

After another, I feel confident enough to look up and meet Kacey's eyes. She and Jason cheer, and I beam in response, a little surprised to see them out there. I hadn't even realized they were in the mob. I only had eyes for Jefferson's hips.

Speaking of. Jefferson is behind me and then next to me, and I turn early, catching him watching my rear. He waggles his brows, and I shove his shoulder. He careens into a guy next to him with a laugh. He points to me and mouths, "Her fault."

By the end, I'm chanting and clapping with the rest of the dancers and having the time of my life. The song ends, and everyone scatters. There's a slow song on and before I can get back to my seat, Jefferson snatches my hand and pulls me back.

"One more?"

I bite my lip, considering. If line dancing has me this wrung out, I don't know that I'll ever recover after pressing my body up against his.

But still, I can't say no. I don't want to. Something deep down inside me knows this is the last time. The only time I can let this happen. *Just one . . . last . . . hit.*

This music has more of a sway, and I gulp as Jefferson takes my arms, draping them over his shoulders, before taking a firm grip of my waist.

Please, Jesus.

His heart thuds steadily under mine, and he lowers his head to rest it on the top of my own. His chest rumbles as he sings along quietly. I smile to myself. Can't even stop himself from performing when it's an audience of one.

He pulls back a little, taking one of my hands in his before spinning me out and back again. I laugh as he sings louder, spinning me once more. His eyes are crinkled up as they find mine, and my heart clenches. It's just so . . . real. I almost want to shake myself because it *can't* be real between us. That Jefferson smile can't mean anything.

I can't be the one to make him feel that way. It's too much pressure. Too much . . . everything. I close my eyes, tucking myself in under his chin once more, squeezing him tightly against me. Hiding myself from his piercing eyes. His happy, teasing, easy smile.

My smile.

Because it's become abundantly clear in the last twenty-four hours that Jefferson isn't just some frat boy country star. He's more than kissing in the dark and filled-out denim. He's just as damaged as I am. He's got heartache and grief and loneliness, and if I can't survive him, he sure as hell can't survive me.

I don't deserve that smile. I'd break him the way my parents broke each other, and that's not acceptable.

The song finishes, and before he can talk me into another, I release him gently. "I need to use the ladies'."

I hightail it for the bathroom and shut the door behind me, checking for others before locking it with a click. I turn the faucet to ice cold and pull my hair back with the tie I always have around my wrist. Then I cup the water, splashing my face over and over and over. His smile is burned into my mind. My heart aches painfully in my chest, and still I splash as if I could wash away the feel of him.

"I'm not Cora," I say into the mirror. "I won't drag him down with me. I won't be the one to push him over the edge."

I splash more water, washing away any tears that would betray me. Turning off the faucet with a *creak*, I pat at my face with a brown paper towel. From my back pocket, I retrieve a tube of ruby lip gloss Kacey asked me to carry for her because *boho chic doesn't do pockets.*

Spreading it over my lips, I'm pleased with the result. The shimmer pulls attention away from my wild eyes toward shiny lips. Blotting once, I toss the towel in the trash and unlock the door, throwing it open as another woman is reaching for it.

I tug my hair tie out, freeing my curls with a shake, and pass her by.

Lindy is busy behind the bar again, and I don't think I can stomach another ginger ale, so I hop the bar to help.

"You know how to mix drinks?" she asks over the din of clattering glasses and music.

I shrug. "I can pop a cap off a beer and make change."

She grins widely and passes me two bottles, nodding at an older couple at the end of the bar. "Works for me."

18

Clay

The last thing I clearly remember before waking up in this cold jail cell was Annie leaving Taps.

Sometime around midnight, between Annie walking out and Jason buying another round, I lost my head. It was inevitable. From the moment Fitz told me he'd be going to see Danny and I stupidly offered to come along.

It was inevitable.

I hate this place. This town, the people, the memories. The looks of pity and understanding make me want to scream or punch a wall or drink until I can't remember my own name and thankyoujesus because who the fuck wants to be fucking *Clay Coolidge*.

Annie left, and it's like all my composure, my will to be better, do better, left with her. I saw the look on her face. It's seared into my brain. We danced and there was something real between us, and then she walked away, and when she came back from the bathroom, it was gone.

My mask is Clay and hers is Annie Mathers, daughter of Cora and Robbie.

I should have left after she did. Fitz and Kacey invited me home with them, but I'd have to be an idiot not to pick up on the cues Fitz was sending my way. Instead, I convinced Fitz I was in good hands with Diaz as my new wingman. Or maybe I was his. Either way, I'm sure Fitz is being stupid and beating himself up over it.

The report says I swung first. Unprovoked or whatever. And if what Jason says is true, then that sounds coldly accurate. He says some shithead was waxing poetic about what a waste my brother's sacrifice had been. Started ranting about war and politics and things he knew nothing about.

Thing is, *I* can say Danny's sacrifice was a waste. He's my brother, and I hate that he chose the Marines over me.

But fuck if someone else is going to say that. He died because he believed so hard in people like that fucker getting to spout off whatever they want. He died because he was so good, so undeniably decent and noble. The world isn't worthy of him.

So I lost it on the guy.

Or at least that's what Diaz tells me. My swollen and split knuckles are all the verification I need. And the massive hangover. And waking up in a jail cell where they left us to sleep it off. Both of us, Jason and me. Jason was picked up earlier by an irate-looking Connie.

I've been left here to stew. Bitter resentment churns in my hollow stomach. Resentment at who? I can't decide. Everyone. Every person I've ever known.

Trina picks me up.

"Where's Fitz?" I ask.

Trina's silence is deadly. She doesn't answer any of my questions until they've passed me back my wallet and pocketknife and she's burst through the doors out into the misting rain.

"Fitz is on his way to Boston with the rest of the tour. Left first thing this morning."

I chew on that for a bit, wincing as I try to slide my wallet into my back pocket. I flex my fingers and school my features when I see Trina watching me. With a *beep beep*, her car's unlocked, and I slide into the passenger side. She doesn't put the keys in the ignition, instead taking a deep breath.

I'm expecting screaming. Instead, she exhales with a shudder.

"Trina, I—"

She holds up a finger and removes her glasses with her other hand, revealing puffy, red-ringed eyes. I swallow hard. Shit. I've never seen her look so *not* put-together. The world could shrivel in a nuclear strike and Trina Hamilton's makeup wouldn't dare smudge.

"First, I need to tell you that your mug shot is all over the news this morning. Second, while Annie, Fitz, and Kacey left early enough, the fact that Willows' underage drummer, Jason Diaz, was with you and intoxicated has dragged their name into this shit show. Third, out of respect for your brother, the officer on duty managed to slant the story to keep Maggie and Taps out of the news and out of the courtroom for serving minors. I was able to assure them you had started drinking long before you arrived and long after you left.

"Which means," she continues in a tired recitation, her voice wavering, "the damage has been *mostly* contained to your own livelihood. Of course, Connie's been called in to deal with Diaz and that mess. But, as it's his first indiscretion and you were there to be a terrible influence, I suspect he won't face too much media repercussion."

I slump against the car seat, leaning my head back, my eyes closing. "Trina—" I try again.

She clears her throat, cutting me off. "Nothing you could say to me right now will fix this, Clay. You are eighteen years old. That's too young to be legally allowed to do anything you were doing last night and too old to feed me your bullshit excuses."

She sticks her keys in the ignition but turns to me before starting the car, exhaling again. Her bottom lip quivers, and she bites down hard, turning it white, before trying to speak. "As you know, I don't have kids. I have you and Fitz and even the Willows. I realize my exterior is all business, but I *do* care, Clay. I am very sorry for what they said about your brother. That wasn't right. In fact, the only thing I'm not blaming you for is punching that kid for what he said."

I don't have words. All my resentment from earlier falls flat at my manager's loss of composure. It's impossible to hold on to your edge in the face of Trina Hamilton crying.

I'm sick to death of being me, but a faraway part of me realizes the futility of being anyone else. I swallow against the vomit creeping up the back of my throat.

"Where are we going now?"

"We have a month left. Tickets are paid for, and for now, the label wants the tour to go on."

"So we're going to Boston."

Acid swells again, burning my sinuses. How much longer can I do this?

And worse, how many more people will I hurt before I can wash my hands of this tour?

19

Annie

saturday, july 20
boston, massachusetts

Things change after Indiana. After my visit to Jefferson's hometown. The cemetery. Taps. All of it plays out in my brain on a loop. We return to our tour, we're back onstage, and I'm in the studio just as before, but everything is different.

Because I'm different. All the possibility and potential I'd secretly harbored have been locked away far below the surface, where they'll stay. It can keep that tiny bit of admiration I cling to for my parents' company in the Land of Unwanted and Dangerous Emotions.

I'm also locking away my lady parts. Their objection is fierce, but what can I do? They're clearly working against me. Stupid magic Levi's.

Onstage, all will be the same as it ever was. I'll play my part even if it kills me. It's what professionals do. But off-stage, I've been pulling away. No more late-night drinks shared in hotel rooms. No more band bonding or home visits for this girl. I have a month left, and I intend to make it out alive.

I'm crouched on a carpeted step inside a soundproof room in Boston at a satellite studio my label has procured for me last minute. Kacey and Jason are inside the booth, but I can't see them behind the one-way glass.

"This is something new I've written," I say simply, strumming. I wrote it this week. It's the first time I've played it for anyone. In all honesty, the album is done. We have enough tracks to be getting on with, but I have a feeling about this song. Sometimes you write something you know is meant to be shared. It's something I can't possibly say, but something that must be said anyway.

I close my eyes as my fingers find the right chords. In my mind, there he stands: his airy smile, his sensual hips, his whiskey voice.

The lyrics pour out of me in one painful lurch after another.

He was her bleeding heart,
Her soul, her whole life
Her shady hollow
Her beg, steal, and borrow
He was her best friend
Her downfall, her untimely end
He was her too-handsome man
Without a plan
Her railcar screaming off the line
And if I wanted, you'd be mine

My glittering dawn
My twilight con
My overflowing cup
Of whiskey and wrong

My sweet release
My most, my least
My aching everything
My forbidden retreat

But if I close my eyes
And wish it all away
Pretend I'm someone else,
Pretend I'm here to stay
Gave us half a chance,
Let my stupid heart decide
There's no doubt in my mind,
You'd be mine

She was his pedestal
Her voice, his siren's call
She was his beauty queen idol,
His Southern belle of the ball
She was his grass is always green,
His never in-between
His burning house
His no way out
His everything's fine
And you'd be mine

My glittering dawn
My twilight con
My overflowing cup
Of whiskey and wrong

My sweet release
My most, my least
My aching everything
My forbidden retreat

But if I close my eyes
And wish it all away
Pretend I'm someone else,
Pretend I'm here to stay
Gave us half a chance,
Let my stupid heart decide
There's no doubt in my mind,
You'd be mine

They were coasting, clutching, screeching through life
Eyes and hands only for each other
But they forgot,
Or maybe never cared
About me
The three
The end of their flaming family tree
There's always a casualty
And, God, I hate myself for
Wishing
And lyin'
And thinking that maybe
You'd want to be mine

I still the vibrating strings with my palm and open my
eyes, not at all surprised to feel the damp on my cheeks.
Songwriting's always a soul search for me. Often, I don't
know how I even feel about something until the words are
on the page.

This time, though, there's no mistaking how I feel. My
pathetic heart couldn't be clearer on the issue of Jefferson.
This song is a confession and a condemnation in one; re-
gretting something that was over before it even began. But
I know, I *know*, it would have been big. It would have been
real and true and sappy as hell. We would have been a love

story for the ages. Just like my mom and dad. He would become my all-consuming addiction, and in return, I would be his final ruin.

Part of me doesn't care.

I see the future play out, but even still, my imagination has other plans. She sees a time when Jefferson is clean and whole, and I am unafraid and out of my parents' tragic shadow. And who knows, maybe that would be us one day . . . but maybe it wouldn't.

I would be a first-class idiot to jeopardize everything right now because of *maybe*. Maybe we'd blow up like a house fire and take everyone we love down with us. As if hearing my thoughts, the heavy studio door opens, and Kacey and Jason step in, closing it behind them.

"One track," my cousin says, her eyes red-rimmed. "It's laid down in one. Don't you dare change a thing. If you want, I can layer some strings over it later."

I glance at the one-way glass of the booth, and Jason shakes his head. "I sent the sounds guys out for coffee."

I snicker. "And they listened?"

He lifts a shoulder and regards me with a serious expression. "Annie, was that . . . I mean, when did you write that?"

I drag my thumb along the beveled scroll on my guitar, watching its progress. "Oh. Bits here and there. Why?"

I catch Jason shooting a pleading look to Kacey. She presses her lips together. "I'll be blunt. Is it about our headliner?"

"Why?" I repeat.

That seems to confirm it for Kacey, who glances nervously at the one-way glass. "Are you going to incorporate it into the show?"

I'm shaking my head before she even gets the words out. "No way. It's too new."

My cousin nods her dark head, her hair falling to dance just at her bare shoulders. "You really should play it for him."

"I don't think so. Not now. He won't understand."

Jason makes an exasperated noise, shooting another pointed look at Kacey. "I'm going to find the coffee."

As the door closes behind him, Kacey leans back against the step next to me, stretching out her legs next to mine.

"I think he might understand more than you think."

"Fine." I huff out an impatient breath. "He'd understand. Doesn't mean it's a good idea. I'll break him, and he'll break me. We're way too volatile."

"You're barely eighteen, Annie. What on earth do you know about volatile?"

"I was raised on volatile."

Kacey blinks. "Fine."

"This isn't like a movie, Kace. This is real life. He's really grieving over his brother. He's really got a drinking problem. He's really into hiding both of those things by sleeping with lots of women around the country, including his ex. He really just got himself arrested for battery. I'm really a mess of a girl who can't even close her eyes without seeing her parents' dead bodies and can't kiss a boy without thinking she's going to kill him. That's real life," I say. "That's volatile."

"You still see their bodies, Anne? I didn't know that."

"Every single night."

"It's easy to forget all that when you watch you two on-stage," Kacey says quietly.

A harsh chuckle erupts in the back of my throat. "Don't I know it."

"Do you think you might already be in love with him?"

The word chokes in my throat, so instead, I nod once, slowly.

Kacey wraps her arm around my shoulders, pulling me in. "Well, hell."

I tilt my head onto her shoulder. *Hell* about sums it up.

That night, we perform at Fenway under the lights. It's the quintessential summer concert experience. I heard last weekend Sir Paul McCartney filled this stadium, and it gives me the worst case of jitters I've had all summer. Boston is stifling. Midnineties at dusk and only the barest tease of a breeze off the coast. We're inland quite a way, though, so it feels more like a vacuum onstage. I've talked wardrobe into letting me wear a loose-fitting, white cotton sundress with my dark brown Tony Lamas, which I promptly kick off once onstage.

I throw my carefully styled curls up in a topknot as I greet the crowd. As has been typical most of the summer, the seats are filled, even for us. Or maybe not just *even*. I suppose at this point, I can confidently say these people aren't here by accident. This crowd came early for us.

"Whew!" I start. "Y'all, it's hot out here! You folks don't mind my bare toes, right?" I point down to my painted toenails and the crowd cheers. "We're all friends here. You just go right ahead and take off yours if you want. I won't tell a soul," I promise, making a little cross over my heart.

This time, when we play the opening chords to "Coattails," the crowd goes wild, and every female under the age of seventy breaks out in a dance with Kacey and me. When I sing "Should've Been You," the crowd sings the chorus on their own.

It's like watching all of my dreams play out in front of me, and I'm overwhelmed with gratitude toward the fans, Kacey and Jason, Jefferson and Fitz; toward God above. I'm so blessed. My heart still aches and my memories bruise, but I'm a lucky girl because I get to do what I love.

The crowd chants, "Cash! Cash! Cash!" and I'm so grateful for Trina's unerring instincts. After my live performance with Clay, she secured the rights to "It Ain't Me, Babe" from the label, knowing people would come out in droves to see us perform it for themselves.

"All right, all right, y'all wore me down. Let me just check in the back here . . . ," I say as I jog lightly offstage and pull a "resistant" Clay Coolidge onstage with me.

I snort at his theatrics. "Don't let Clay fool you. He's been dying to jump in on my stage all night. He knows I have the best crowd!"

This garners more cheers, and Clay gives a good-natured shrug as he accepts a mic from a stagehand. Fitz lines up next to Kacey, this time holding a couple of silly-looking egg shakers.

I start to strum the opening chords as Clay pretends to flip up his collar and slick back his hair. He approaches the mic stand as Jason taps out the beat. The females are all screaming a little louder for those two tonight. The fact that they were underage drinking seems to have been lost in the whole "fistfight in defense of his dead brother" thing. Not that I blame them. After hearing Jason's side, I was ready to hunt down the punk and punch him all over again.

Point is, the fans don't seem fazed. The label, on the other hand . . .

This song was written by Bob Dylan, who was a big fan of Johnny. They used to cover each other's work, so it's no surprise Cash chose to record his version with June Carter Cash. As with most of their songs, it's one making an almost mockery of their devotion. Onstage, Johnny and June had this very harried Southern charm about them.

The irony is the lyrics are absolutely spot-on for Jefferson

and me, no performance necessary. Talk about mockery—
the joke is clearly on us. To our credit, though, we are professionals, so he waggles his eyebrows and I roll my eyes and
pout my lips, and we pretend it's cute even as it's breaking
my heart.

I wonder if it's breaking his.

The song ends, and we take our bow as Clay and Fitz
wave at the crowd and I retake center stage. I paste a smile
on my face, knowing damn well I chose this. I chose singing over me and him. Whether he would have chosen the
same or if it was ever even on the table for him doesn't
matter. I. Chose. This.

I wrap with one of our new hits, "Never Mind," that's
gaining traction these past few weeks and finish off with the
crowd favorite of "Jolene." When the lights dim, I feel myself slump in exhaustion. Whether it's the heat or the emo-
tional breakdown in the studio earlier, or playing Cash, I'm
beat. The lights come on once more, and I hitch a beaming
grin back on my face, waving wildly at a crowd growing by
the minute. I blow double kisses and take a bow before exit-
ing stage left and accepting a giant bottle of Evian.

"I'm pooped," I say to Trina. "I'm gonna hit some air-
conditioning."

"Of course," she says, stashing her phone in her pocket
and giving me a hard look. "You want me to tell Clay he's
on his own tonight?" I must look more terrible than I'd realized for her to offer.

I consider it. It would be easy to go and hide in my bus
for the rest of the night, begging off with a headache. But I
don't. I'm not hiding from my own choices.

"Nah. Just send someone for me once his set starts. We're
doing 'One of the Guys'?"

She gives me a brief nod as I take a sip. "Is that okay?"

I flash another smile, one I know doesn't meet my eyes,

but I did tell her I was tired. "Yup. I'll be there. Let Kacey and Jason know where I am?"

"Of course." She's already pulling her phone back out of her pocket before I'm past her. Busy little paper wasp that she is.

I make it to my bus and close the door behind me, sitting in the cool semidarkness. I place the bottle on the back of my neck and close my eyes. My phone vibrates, and I grab it out of my pocket. Three missed texts.

NICE JOB THIS MORNING. THE NEW CUT IS GORGEOUS. DEF MADE ALBUM. I'LL SEND A CAR FOR YOU AROUND 8:15 FOR SB MTG IN AM. BRING K&J.

I sigh in exasperation. I love Connie, I do, but she is really pushing this Southern Belle deal. I already explained my aversion to Stanton, but she's insisting on a meeting as a "professional courtesy."

ANNIE, THIS IS SUSANNA DE LA GARZA, PROFESSIONAL ASST TO ROY STANTON. JUST TOUCHING BASE. WANTED TO GIVE YOU A HEADS-UP ABOUT THE VENUE AND MENU TO-MORROW FOR YOUR 8:30 MTG. LINK ATTACHED.

I close without bothering to click on the link. Cora liked swanky. If I had to guess, jeans and flip-flops will not be ap-propriate attire at this so-called professional meeting. Which probably means Jason's out, which maybe'd be best, all things considered.

I crack open the water bottle with a flick and sip slowly. Forty-five minutes still until I need to be onstage. I tap on the last message from Patrick.

HEY ANNA BANANA! CONNIE TOLD ME THE BIG NEWS! SB IS A GREAT LABEL. DON'T LET HISTORY DEFINE YOUR CHOICES. WE'RE ALL HERE FOR YOU WHATEVER YOU DECIDE!

I tap my phone off and toss it on the bench across from me. The thing is, I know I shouldn't let history dictate my life like Patrick says. I know. I'm a grown woman with my own career, and I need to make my own way. I cut my album with SunCoast because that's who I'm contractually obligated to right now, and you don't turn down a record deal when you're making the numbers I am. That's just smart business. Southern Belle swooping in after the tour and the money and the album are all complete just to cash in on the profits? That seems shady to me.

It just does. Yeah, I know the music business isn't clean, but . . .

So it's not *just* about Roy and my mom. That's a factor, though. A real one. I mean, it's gross. Super icky. And the fact that my parents killed themselves . . .

That makes this a gray area. In fact, my entire life is a gray area right now.

There's a tap on the door, and I stand up with a groan. "Come in!" I say, even though I'm already on my feet. I pull open the door with a *snap* and see Lora Bradley standing at the bottom of my steps. Her eyes widen as she jumps back.

"Oh God, I'm sorry. I thought this was Clay's trailer."

"Nope, mine. Clay's probably about to get onstage."

"Oh. Right. I'm early."

I cross my arms over my chest, feeling a throb building in the back of my skull. "You can probably get backstage and watch from the wings."

"Of course. Maybe I'll just surprise him."

"He doesn't know you're here?" I ask, hating myself for the slight note of hope in my voice. I don't get to care about this.

"Oh, he does. I didn't think I'd make it early enough to see him sing. Caught an earlier flight."

"Sure. Well, his bus is the next one." I start to close the door.

"Wait! Annie!"

I bite back a sigh, holding the door. "Yep."

"I saw a bit of your show. You're really great, you know? I'd love to sing together sometime. I was a huge fan of your mom's. I looked up to her so much as a kid."

She's only being nice. I know this. She's actually a sweet person. But she's going to sleep with Clay tonight. He called her the second I made myself unavailable. And I'm just . . . done. Done with Connie. Done with Roy Stanton. Done with Lora. Done with Jefferson, Clay who-the-hell-ever.

"Well, you shouldn't have. She was a terrible role model, shooting up with her daughter in the other room. I'm sorry. I have a headache and have to be back onstage in thirty minutes, and you're making it worse."

I slam the door in her face and promptly start crying.

20

Clay

Only a few weeks left of the tour, and I don't know. It feels like the end. It's like the last time I saw my brother alive. I woke up early to have coffee with him before he flew out. We sat in the dark kitchen, with only the stove light on, his giant green duffel at the door. He was antsy, like he always was before he had to fly. The guy faced down enemy fire for a living, but he always puked before, during, and after getting on a plane. It was the one thing I had on him. I've always been just as comfortable in the air as on the ground.

I can still see his long, camo-clad legs stretched out from my grandpa's old wooden chair. I remember checking the clock, counting down the minutes until I could go back to sleep. He didn't say anything wise or heavy. Just asked me to make sure I changed the oil in his truck and kept an eye on Lindy for him. A couple of the guys around Taps liked to close in whenever Danny was out of town. It was my job to be the Coolidge presence, even if I was only sixteen. I used to wash dishes for Maggie on the weekends to make extra money. I'd hang around the bar, hoping there would be a no-show and I'd get a chance to play. Danny knew, encouraged it. That morning, he asked me to send him any new songs. He liked to play them for his guys, he said. Lifted morale to hear songs that reminded them of being young and back at home.

I don't know what it was about that morning. Of course, in his line of work, there was always the possibility he wouldn't come back, but to be honest, Danny was different. He always seemed invincible to me, but I stayed with him until his ride came. When he stood to leave, I embraced him. We weren't huggers, and he laughed in my ear.

"Whoa there, Jefferson. You going soft on me?"

I didn't even defend myself, just shrugged. "It's only the two of us now."

Danny's lips lifted in a sad smile. "I love you, little brother. Keep an eye on Fitz and Lindy for me, okay?"

I remember my throat closing. Like it wouldn't work. As if the words had been strangled and I couldn't say anything back.

He left, and I never went back to sleep. Instead, I wrote a song and sent it to him. They found it in his pack when he died and sent it back to me with his body. I've never sung it at any of my shows or on any of my records. It died with him.

That day, when my brother walked out, I felt like it was for forever. I knew it in my gut. He wasn't coming back. He wouldn't ever know if I checked his oil. He wouldn't see the guys come around to hit on his girl. He'd never meet his daughter.

That's the feeling I have now. Things are ending. Not only the tour but everything.

———

"What was that?"

I look up from my guitar and paper. Lora stands shadowed in the doorway. She'd gone down to the bar with Fitz and Trina earlier, and I hadn't realized she was back already.

"Just something I'm working on."

Something like forced patience flickers across Lora's face. I put down my guitar.

"It sounds pretty . . . rustic?"

"It's a first draft."

"I meant the tune of it. It's not your usual flash." I wonder how long Lora had stood there before she'd bothered announcing herself. How much she'd heard.

"I thought I'd try something different."

She comes over to me, sitting on the couch, putting the guitar gently on the ground and straddling my hips. I can smell the alcohol on her breath. She leans forward, pressing herself against me and kissing me deeply. My mind is still in my lyrics, though, and I can't flip that switch off, so I don't kiss her back. She leans back, her expression annoyed.

"I'm tired of catering to the label and singing whatever radio-friendly song comes along."

"But you're good at it."

"You used to think I was good at songwriting, too."

She moves off my lap to stand, putting blessed space between us. "You used to be a barely out-of-high-school kid with a dream. We both were. Face it, Clay, some people are songwriters and some are singers. You have the face of a singer. There's nothing wrong with that. People would kill for the measure of success you've landed."

I bite back an irritated growl. "I'm more than just some singing face, Lora."

"Sure you are, baby. I know that, but no one wants to listen to a sad sap song from the hills."

"Lots of people—"

She cuts me off. "Sung by you, I mean."

I close my mouth, and Lora softens her expression slightly as if to cushion a blow.

"I don't get you, Clay. Why the change of heart? You were fine being the record label's lackey last summer. Had the time of your life, touring on their dime. What changed?"

I know what's changed, but I don't feel like telling Lora about it. My brother died. I mean, he died before any of this, but it's only hitting me just now. Booze doesn't fix things anymore. I don't like singing about hookups anymore. I don't like *me* anymore. Maybe I never really did. Or maybe I was okay with the old me because I didn't know any better. I've had a glimpse of better, and now I can't go back.

And then there's Annie. Annie who won't even look at me unless we're onstage together.

"What's wrong with wanting more, Lora?"

"Why change what's not broken, Clay?"

"Christ," I mutter, standing. "It's just a song."

Lora levels me with a look. "It's not just a song. It's consuming you. You've been fiddling with it all weekend. Hours that could have been spent with me. Or at the very least, spent focusing on your performance. Annie Mathers is breathing down your neck, Clay. Word is she's about to drop her album, and you're going to be a has-been by this time next month if you don't salvage the rest of your tour."

I drop my hands. "What are you talking about? This is *my* tour."

"Clay. Be serious. It hasn't been your tour since Daytona."

I'm irritated at her tone. Everyone, lately, is either talking to me like I'm an idiot or a head case, and I'm about done. "Get the hell out of here, Lora. I was here before Annie came around, and I'll be here after she's gone."

"Don't be so sure about that."

"What do you know?"

"I know you haven't signed your contract yet."

I shrug and pick up my guitar, strumming it loudly, avoiding her gaze. "That's not a secret. It's tied up in legal."

"And I know that a certain Miss Tragic Miracle is being heavily courted by Southern Belle."

I huff. "That's old news. Annie told us Roy had tried to talk to her, but she wasn't interested. Something about some dark family history with Cora and Roy."

Lora moves to the couch and scoots closer to me. My grip tightens on my guitar pick.

"Well, that's not what I heard. I heard he's being very persistent and backing it up with some major coin."

"Annie doesn't care about money."

Lora lifts her tanned shoulder and leans back, crossing her long legs slowly. "Maybe not, but Roy's a hard man to resist, and I'm sure she'd love to get out of Nashville and away from her past."

That part does sound like Annie. Still, though. "So what if she does? Tour wraps in a few weeks. It's nothing to do with me."

"So, while Annie's been cutting albums and courting label execs and growing a fan base, you've been drinking beer, getting arrested, acting sullen, and writing sappy songs. That's what."

I blink.

Lora's smile is far too understanding. "You got a shit deal, Clay. We were all crazy jealous when we heard you scored Mathers this summer, but I've got to tell you I feel like I dodged a bullet. I doubt even her legendary mama could have survived sharing her stage."

I wish she would just leave already. "What the hell do you even care?"

"Someone should care about you. Is it so hard to believe I would?" Her smile is self-deprecating, but the sadness in her eyes is a punch to the gut. She really does care. It doesn't matter that she doesn't care about the right version of me—she *cares*. "Anyway, I have something for you. Maybe it will help you get out of your funk." She stands and walks across the room to where she's left her purse. "I've been carrying these around for a bit. After your text asking me to come early, I thought maybe you needed something. It's from my personal stash, but I have a contact if you need more."

She pulls out a bottle, and I hear pills rattling inside. She holds it up, crossing the room toward me.

"I'm not sick."

"And these aren't medicinal. Physically you might be fine, but even you have to admit you're a bit of a mess. Your brand is *fun*, Clay. Careless, immature, drunken, reckless fun. So get your act together and show the label you're still plenty capable of providing what they pay you for: butts in the seats with full cups and high social media presence. Save yourself."

I shake my head, anger surging, smacking the pills out of her hand with a clatter. They smack against the far wall and fall uselessly on the floor. "I don't want your drugs."

She laughs at me, shaking her head, her dark hair swirling behind her shoulders. Lifting her purse strap higher on her arm and turning for the door, she says, "Jesus, Clay, it's not heroin. They're just some pills. They'll loosen you up a little. I'm trying to help. Get your shit together, or you're going to throw it all away."

The door closes behind her with a slam, and after a minute, I walk over to where the bottle is sitting on the floor. I don't pick it up, instead tapping it with my foot like it's a yappy dog or a poisonous snake. I should throw it away, and I'm just about indignant enough to do it. Toss the bottle and return to my old-school hills song. To my grandfather's wood-shop. To my roots.

It's not the first time someone's tried to give me drugs. I've been around for about a year and have had plenty of offers from industry insiders. Uppers to keep you peppy on-stage, downers to help you sleep when you're too exhausted. It's the first time Lora has given me something, though. The cynical part of me wonders who put her up to it. Stanton at Southern Belle? Is this some attempt at sabotage? Or was it Trina? Someone on my side, looking to save their career? I know Fitz wouldn't stoop that low, but he's pretty much as far as my trust extends.

I've never taken them. Always thrown them away without a second thought.

Someone should care about you, she'd said. Like I'm an orphan lost on the streets. Like someone needs to take re-sponsibility for my care. Like I can't do anything for myself. Same shit, different day. Someone always trying to run my life. I pick up the pills, and this time I don't throw them away.

21

Clay

sunday, july 28
cleveland, ohio

The pills haunt me. I know they're safe in my room, and logically I know that days ago I didn't need or want them—that I've never wanted them. That my brother would kick my ass if he (were alive, of course, and) knew I didn't throw them away the second I got them. That my grandfather would blister my backside. I promise myself I'll flush them when I get back. I wish I could flush them now. I wish I had made Lora take them with her when she left.

I don't want them.

But I can't stop thinking about them. I feel like hell. I don't remember not feeling like hell. I'm wrung out and dried up and tired. So tired. Everything hurts. My hangover is permanent these days.

Annie's been avoiding me since Indiana.

Lora left town.

My brother is dead. My grandfather is dead. My mother is dead.

Everyone leaves me in the end.

What if the pills do make me feel different? Better? Up to this point, drugs felt . . . I don't know . . . too much. Too far. They crossed a line I haven't been willing to cross. But Christ knows the booze doesn't do anything anymore. I'm reminded of Annie that night a month ago in my hotel room. "I can still see them," she said. "It's not working."

It's not working.

Thinking of Annie fills me with an irrational anger. Lora's reminder that Annie is eclipsing me was unnecessary. It's not like I haven't spent the summer with her. I'd have to be blind and stupid to not have seen what was happening. To be honest, I've been expecting it since I was recruited to get her signature all those months ago in Michigan.

But I still don't have a contract, and Willows definitely went missing for a few hours two mornings ago. Fitz wouldn't tell Trina where they were, which in and of itself was a shining, blinking *fuck you* to our blond road manager. She's back to sneaking cigarettes and glaring at everyone.

I didn't ask. Lora wouldn't lie to me about Southern Belle homing in on Willows. The question is what I'm going to do about it. If Annie goes with Southern Belle, my label may never forgive me my transgressions. Suddenly, I'm back on the Ferris wheel feeling inadequate in the face of Annie's drive and passion for music. These days, I'm finding it difficult to muster up much of anything.

I'm senseless and bored and, to be honest, pretty blitzed. The goddamn pills burn a hole in my conscience. Lora's condescension recycles round and round in my brain. Annie's unassuming talent. And grace. And beauty. And everything about her is irritating me right now because I'm not good enough for any of it. I thought I could be Jefferson, but Jefferson doesn't get record deals.

And it shouldn't matter. We weren't anything more than kissing on a beach. I got more action from Lora this summer.

But somehow, it does matter, and fuck if I know why.

When we invite Willows onstage to perform with us, I go off script. I don't bother checking in with Fitz. I already know how he's going to react. He's soft over Kacey and thinks I'm a better person than I am. He's hopeful I'm taking after Danny. That my demons are a phase I'm about to conquer.

They aren't, and I'm not. Not tonight anyway.

"We've got the lovely ladies from Under the Willows here tonight." I laugh. "And Jason. I guess he's good-looking if you like drummers." A few cheers erupt, and Jason narrows his eyes at me. "I'm sure you've all realized by now just how talented Ms. Mathers is, but did you know she could shake it, too? Come on, Annie. Turn around and give the crowd a little shake."

Annie's chin juts so quickly, her bemused brown eyes jumping to mine, that her hair yanks out of its clasp. Kacey freezes next to her. Fitz grabs a mic. "Aw, Clay. Let's just get to the song."

"We will, we will," I reassure him, proud my words sound crisp, not slurred. "Come on, Annie. Have some fun with us."

Annie recovers herself and pastes a good effort at a smile on her face. "Oh, I don't think so. These folks are here to see Clay Coolidge shake it. I'm just here to sing." She turns to me, her eyes steely as a knife's edge, her tone cool. "So let's sing."

Fitz starts to count us off for "Some Guys Do" as previously discussed, but I cut in with my guitar. "We're gonna sing one of my favorites from my debut. Is that all right?"

The crowd cheers as the opening chords start. Annie grimaces and leans in. "What the hell, Jefferson? I don't know this one."

I know I told her to use that name, but tonight, right now, the reminder rankles. "Then I guess you'll just have to shake it instead," I say on mic.

Her lips press together, and she's mutinous and gorgeous, and I know she's weighing the damage she'd cause by walking off the stage. She's the consummate professional, though, so she stays.

I can see Fitz fuming out of the corner of my eye, lifting his bow and dragging it across the strings with a furious screech. Jason is glaring daggers at me as someone hands him some prop sticks. He says something to Annie, who shakes her head, her smile still hitched in place. I laugh humorlessly at how much I've rattled them all. I'm the star, after all. I get to choose, and I choose this.

The backbeat begins, and Annie claps along as though everything is fine. This is one of my more popular songs, but it's super sexist so I rarely sing it anymore. It was my breakout hit, and once I had some say, I dropped it. I haven't played it once this tour because of Annie, and for some reason I don't feel like examining, that pisses me off.

I make it worse out of spite. Anger and alcohol race through my veins and fuel my adrenaline. The rush of self-destruction. I belt out lyrics about legs and hips and dropping low and feeling high and curves and bedroom eyes. Lips and little cutoffs and sexy boots and every awful word is made all the worse when I step close behind Annie and grind my hips into her back. She wiggles seductively for a second before turning to face me. The hurt in her eyes catches in my throat. She pushes me lightly, all showmanship gone and replaced with something else.

I'm furious. She *wanted* this. Earlier in the summer, she was throwing herself at me. All that kissing we did in dark places. I was plenty good enough for her in secret. Then she saw how damaged I was, and she decided I wasn't worth it. Her career skyrocketed, and she left me behind. Now she has the nerve to look like I've disappointed her? I step back and finish the song as if nothing happened. The crowd loves the show. They think we're acting, and I let them believe it. We wrap up with a slower song, and I exit the stage with a wave and flick of my guitar pick, following the rest of my bandmates.

Fitz doesn't bother to wait for me. Annie is waiting backstage, standing next to Trina. She drags my arm and pulls me farther into darkened wings.

"What was that, Jefferson?"

"I don't know what you're talking about."

"The hell you don't!" Annie has both of her small hands pressed to her temples.

"It's one of my biggest hits, and I haven't played it all summer," I say.

Annie raises her eyes, searching mine for truth. "Maybe. But why would you set me up like that?"

"I don't know what you think happened, Annie. I played one of my hits. It's my tour; I can do that. If you can't keep up—"

"Can't keep up? Jefferson—"

I snap. "Don't call me that."

She looks like I've slapped her.

I *feel* like I've slapped her. I swallow it back. "What?"

I brush past her. I can't look at her face right now. See the pain there. I don't regret putting this distance between us. *I don't.*

She did it first.

22

Annie

That night, after the show, Fitz and Kacey walk me back to my hotel room, and Fitz says he's still planning to throw a small party in his room for Kacey's nineteenth birthday. I want to turn in early but decide I won't let Jefferson—sorry, *Clay*—take me away from my best friend's party. He humiliated me in front of thousands of people, and I can't even begin to unravel why. I don't know what he's gained from objectifying me. Maybe it's a delayed sense of retribution after introducing "Coattails." Maybe Lora got under his skin and he's taking it out on me. Maybe I misread things between us. Part of me wants to get my guitar and write a revenge song.

But the thought of writing something about him reminds me I've gotten confirmation from the label that "You'd Be Mine" made the cut and will be featured first for radio play. The timing couldn't be more ludicrous or devastating, and I'm just too overwrought over Jefferson Clay Coolidge to see the tree for the forest in front of me.

So I beg off to my suite to get cleaned up and shower off the stage sweat and the feel of Jefferson on my skin. I'm the last to arrive. Fitz answers the door at my knock, his face so pale his freckles stand out like tiny polka dots across the bridge of his nose.

"Ah," he says, not bothering to open the door all the way.

"Do I have the wrong room? I thought this was a birthday party," I tease, peeking curiously over his shoulder. He closes the door farther, but not before I hear shouting.

I push past. "What the hell? Is that Jason?"

To his credit, Fitz doesn't fight me as I press through. Tiny Kacey has a bottle in one hand and another straining against Jason's chest as he's shouting. He's red-faced and snarling, veins throbbing in his neck. On the floor, across from him, blood dripping down his face, is Jefferson.

I scramble in but stop short of the two men, my loyalties painfully torn. Not like Jason notices, his fury laser-focused on Jefferson.

"What's going on?"

Jason still refuses to look at me, but he shakes off Kacey's hands, straightening his shirt. "Ask *Jefferson*," he says in a mocking tone.

A humorless chuckle rumbles from the floor as Jefferson gets to his knees, still bent over. It takes him two tries, as he's intoxicated beyond belief. Eventually, he crawls over to the pullout sofa and collapses there.

"I'm waiting."

"Never mind," Jason spits. "He's high as a fucking kite. He can't talk."

My breath ices over in my chest. I turn to Fitz for confirmation. "Is that true?"

He winces. "I swear I have no idea where he got the pills or how long he's been taking them."

"Jes tah-day," Jefferson slurs slowly.

I'm at his side in a flash. "How many did you take? Where are they? What are they? Holy shit, Jefferson. What were you thinking?"

His eyes are glassed over and dilated and nothing like him at all. Drunk Jefferson is one thing, but he's stoned out of his mind. He slumps over, and my heart throbs painfully until he starts laughing again. It's like watching a slow-motion version of him. Even his shaking shoulders look heavy. My nails dig tiny grooves into my palms. "Where are the pills, Jefferson?" I ask more slowly this time, each word dragged from my throat even as the walls seem to be closing in on me.

"I ate them all."

My heart stutters. "How many were there?" I turn to Fitz, who's even paler than before. He starts digging through the trash and ripping through the suitcases sitting by the door.

Kacey lifts an empty brown bottle. "Is this it? It says, *Shit, you asshole, Clay.*" She keeps muttering, and I snap.

"Focus, Kacey! Don't you sleep, Jefferson," I say, slapping at his face. "Just give me the bottle." Kacey hands it to me. They're pain pills, hydrocodone, but the name on them reads *Lora Bradley*. "Where's Lora, Jefferson?"

He shrugs and smiles at me sleepily. "I sen' her 'way."

"Did she give these to you?" I ask, registering that Fitz is on the phone with someone, probably Trina, in the background.

"She didn't like meh hillsss ssssong."

Jesus Christ. "How *many* were there, Jefferson? I need to know if I need to call an ambulance."

He holds up five fingers.

"Five?" I inhale deeply. That's better than an entire bottle. Still, mixed with alcohol? I relay the information to Trina, who is going to contact the tour doctor. Within minutes, there's a knock at the door. I relent my spot next to Jefferson to Fitz and slump against the wall in the hallway next to Jason.

"He doesn't deserve you," Jason says.

I sigh. "Not that it's any of your business, but he doesn't have me, Jason. We aren't together. You know this."

Jason shakes his head. "You forget, Annie, I know *you*. I heard your song. You can't pull that with me."

"Seriously? Because I wrote a song—"

"You love him, and he only loves himself."

"You heard him, Jason. He's a mess. Not only that, but you saw the shit he pulled with me tonight. Give me a little credit. I don't need protecting." He makes a noise that's obviously disbelieving, and I slug his arm. "Why'd you punch him?"

"He said some things."

My throat aches. "Like what?"

"Like things I won't repeat, so don't ask. Believe me. He deserved it."

"About me?"

Jason shakes his head. "Not in the way you think. Just . . . don't worry about that part."

The thing is, that's impossible. Everyone else heard. Maybe I'll coax it out of Kacey later. The door opens, and the doctor is walking out.

"He's fine. You can go in now. He'll be asleep for some time."

I release a slow breath and get to my feet, holding out a hand for Jason, who shakes his head. "I'm done for. I'm going to bed."

I grab him up in a hug. "For what it's worth, thank you for being noble."

Jason looks like he wants to say more, but I reach up and kiss his cheek and turn for the door before he can. I close the door behind me and wait to hear Jason's door slam before stepping back out in to the hall. I call Trina and Connie first, and then home.

"Hey, Gran, it's me. Change of plans. We're coming back."

Fitz is crouched against the couch, Kacey standing over him, both keeping vigil over a sleeping Jefferson. I walk over to them, placing a hand on Fitz's shoulder. He doesn't look at me; instead, he grabs my hand and squeezes. "I'm such an idiot. He said he needed help weeks ago, and I laughed at him. I didn't take him seriously."

"This?" I say. "This was half-hearted at best. He's still working toward rock bottom, Fitz."

"How can you be so calm?"

My shoulder lifts weakly even though none of them see it. "I'm not. Inside, I'm mad as hell. But anger isn't going to help anyone but us. He needs love and friends, and most of all, Fitz, he needs to get the hell off this tour. I've already got a phone call in to Connie and Trina. We're calling off Kentucky. Jefferson needs some time."

I give Jefferson one more look. Lean down and kiss his bruised cheek. "I'm going to bed. Get packed. We're going to Michigan in the morning. You boys are expected at the farm."

Fitz's head shoots up. "Annie, that's—" He looks to Kacey, who smiles sadly. "You don't have to do that. I know how you—I can take him out of here. We'll go back to Indy."

I grimace. "Wow. He must have said something pretty terrible about me." I raise my hand as he opens his mouth.

"Please. I thought I wanted to know, but I've changed my mind. It's better I don't. Just . . . I'm expecting you both. My gran is, too. Ride to the airport leaves at 8:00 A.M. sharp. Be there."

23

Annie

I leave, my steps heavier than ever as I make my way down the hall to my room. I take out my earrings and change into pajamas, removing all my makeup with a wipe. I refold my clothes, noticing Jefferson's blood on my shirt from earlier. I don't even try to clean it; I just fold that, too, inside out.

I pack everything carefully. Silently. Intentionally. I lay out my clothes for the morning. I place a call to the desk to wake me up. I preorder my breakfast.

But through all of this, I'm thirteen and I've just come home from school. I use my own key to open the door. The house is dark, though it's only late afternoon. All the curtains are still shut. My parents came home late last night. Mom recently wrapped up a three-week tour. Dad's been in town working on his next album. He promised me we'd all go out to dinner to celebrate my birthday once Mom was back.

I run up the stairs calling for my mom. She'd sworn to pick me up something special on the road while in California. I think it's probably the designer cowboy boots I saw last time we were out there. They didn't have my size at the time. She promised to double-check now that I was old enough to fit into women's sizes.

I fling open the door to my bedroom, but it looks exactly the same as when I'd left this morning. No boxes, bed messy, my pajamas puddled on the floor next to my soggy towel.

I slam the door again, running back down the stairs, still yelling. No response. I head for the kitchen, seeing nothing but a few dirty dishes from this morning. I see a slant of light from the den. Of course. My dad spends all of his time in his den, writing. When they're both home, I'll sometimes find her asleep on the leather couch in there. He'd put his finger to his lips to quiet me.

"Shhh, Anna Banana. Ain't your momma beautiful when she sleeps?"

Of course, as I get older, it's hard to miss the empty bottles and stray needles about when my mom is sleeping. Even at thirteen, I understand what's really going on. It's part of their line of work, though. Lots of parents come home and have a beer after a long day. My parents' jobs are extra stressful, so a beer doesn't cut it. At least that's what my dad tells me.

I creep over to the doorway, pushing it open. In retrospect, I realize things were different that day. For one, it was completely silent. No heavy breathing indicative of deep sleep, no strumming or soft singing, no lowered voices or even whispered accusations. Nothing. Eerily calm quiet. The kind of silence that feels more like a void of sound, rather than a hush.

The door opened into my nightmare. I saw my mother first, her sofa directly across from the entrance. She was barely on the couch. A gray, bone-thin arm draped to the floor, the back of her fingers tracing the plush carpet. A scream froze in my lungs. Her eyes were wide, terrified, burst bloody capillaries dotting the whites. Crusted-over vomit trailed from the corner of her mouth and puddled on the floor. Foam coated her shocking blue lips. I didn't need to touch her to know, but I couldn't stop myself for reaching for her one hand, still draped across the back of the couch. It was stiff and curled into the leather, as if she'd tried to pull herself up but couldn't manage the effort.

It was then that I saw my dad. I don't know which was worse: she clearly fought harder, but his death was so violent. He was slumped forward on his desk, blood splattered in a giant burst on the wall and window behind him, pooled underneath his handsome, whiskered face. His silver revolver still clutched in his hand. His eyes were squeezed shut as though he didn't want to see what his fingers were about to do.

Their deaths were later classified as a double suicide. My dad paid for the heroin that killed my mom. It was his welcome-home gift for her. When he'd found her overdosed and laid out in his den, he'd shot himself in the mouth.

My parents loved each other. Madly. And somewhere inside of me, I hope they loved me, too. They sort of seemed to, in a distant, farther-down-the-line-kind of way. But Cora loved Robbie and she loved her music, and she was a slave to her drugs.

And Robbie loved Cora. Full stop.

I've wondered at times, when I really want to torture myself, why my dad didn't even consider living for me. He had to know I would be the one to find him. Find them. What kind of person does that to their child?

Even worse, what if he hadn't thought of me at all?

I never sing my parents' songs. I never talk about them in interviews, and I never, ever visit their graves. Yet I follow in their footsteps every single time I pick up my guitar and step onstage.

Every time I close my eyes and allow myself to dream of Jefferson.

Am I just completing the circle? I knew I was going to agree to this tour the second I opened the screen door at my grandparents' and saw Clay Coolidge on my porch.

I knew I was going to fall for him the second I overheard his soft, tortured singing in his trailer.

I knew I would never love anyone half as much as him the moment he asked me—*pleaded* with me—to call him by his real name.

And I know as long as I live, I will never, ever forget the image of him lying on the floor, pale, bleeding, and still as the grave. I've done everything I can to delay when I will have to close my eyes tonight, because for the first time in years, it won't be my parents' dead bodies I see behind my lids.

It will be his.

24

Clay

thursday, august 1
michigan

Those first few days in Michigan are some of the darkest of my life. I don't remember waking up or the plane ride or anything about the morning after my dance with pills. We arrive at Annie's grandparents' farm, and I'm ushered into a tiny guest room on the second floor at the end of a hallway. The curtains are drawn shut, and I don't bother to remedy that. I slump onto the bed and stay there, under heavy covers despite it being summer.

Food arrives at regular intervals during the day, but it makes my stomach turn and I don't bother to touch it. In another life, I know I'm being selfish, but I can't force myself to care.

No one comes to see me. It seems I've finally driven everyone away.

If nothing else, this should make me happy, but of course it doesn't.

On the third night, I leave my room. It's after midnight, and the house is dark. I plan to go outside but instead find myself standing at a closed door next to the kitchen. I don't remember seeing it before. The door opens easily, revealing a moonlit library. Three walls are covered in floor-to-ceiling bookshelves. There's a modest piano in the center and a wall of windows bisected by a window seat. On the piano rests three dozen bouquets of roses. Their fragrance is heady, and I don't need to pluck the card out to see who they're from.

But I do anyway.

These aren't half as lovely as you. Got a sneak preview of your new song and can't help but wonder where you've been all my life. You're bigger than Nashville. California is waiting!—Roy

A smug grin quirks at the corner of my mouth. "Too bad she hates roses, Roy," I whisper into the dark.

In the far corner, I find an old desk. It looks largely unused. Resting on top is an old bottle of something brown and a set of decorative glasses. My mouth waters, and I round the desk, itching for a drink. But before I can crack the bottle open, I'm distracted by a grouping of picture frames that adorn the desk's polished surface. The first is of Annie and her grandparents. It's recent; she's in a graduation cap and gown, and her curls are long. Another frame shows a preteen Annie and Kacey, sunburned arms flung around each other's shoulders as they stand together on a shoreline. A third photograph shows Annie and her parents. Cora and Robbie could be timeless, but Annie is barely a toddler. The three of them are sitting on a porch swing. Annie's feet dangle in the air between her parents' legs.

The final photo is older still. Cora Rosewood looks to be the same age Annie is now. Maybe eighteen. She's clear-eyed and hamming it up for the camera. She looks airy and happy. Her guitar rests in her lap, a natural extension of her limbs. Across from her sits Robbie Mathers. She faces the camera, but he's facing her. His entire body cued in her direction, like she's his sun and it's all he can do to orbit her.

This is the Cora and Robbie the world didn't see. They were famous for their lusty love—all jealous rages and reckless abandon. But this almost looks tender. Sweet. Innocent. Before the drugs and rock and roll.

My gut twists, and suddenly, a drink is the very last thing in the world I want. That I'll ever want. Because I know the ending to this story. I've seen the fallout. I never met Robbie and Cora, of course, but I know Annie. I watched her fall to pieces after our first show, trembling and spiraling when Trina tried to tie our names together.

I'm not my mom, she'd said. Which can only mean she saw *me* as Robbie.

The realization is a knife to my chest. I stumble over to the windowsill, missing the seat and sliding down the wall to the floor. I bury my face in my shaking hands and tug on the ends of my greasy hair until it hurts.

All this time, without even meaning to, I've seen Annie as my salvation. My light at the end of this fucked-up tunnel. Her name would save my reputation. Her passion would inspire my music.

Her love would fix me.

And all this time, she's seen me as her downfall. Her inevitable conclusion. I would break her, and she was going to let me.

Or we could have been like that. But we won't be because now I know. I'm going to do what Robbie didn't. I'm cutting her off at the start. She can't be my sun. We'd never survive that. I crawl to my feet and stand, feeling resolute. Tomorrow is day one of the rest of my life.

And the rest of hers.

———

I wake up the next morning, the sun already high in the sky. The house is quiet again, and I cringe, wondering how late it is. I've been so rude. My granddad would tan my hide if he could see me.

I throw on some shorts and a T-shirt and slip down the creaky wooden stairs for some coffee. I find a fresh pot brewing. Annie's grandmother putters in behind me, followed by Annie. I want to continue out the door. My late-night resolve is being tested early, and being in the same room with her—sharing the same air—feels like a violation. But it's too late; they've already seen me.

Annie walks past me in silence to the cupboard and pulls out two mugs, lifting the carafe and pouring dual steaming cups, passing me one.

"Thank you," I mutter, taking a long draw. I'm twitchy and uncomfortable, caught somewhere between sheepish and hurt. For all my earlier bravado, the thought of separating myself from this girl feels like amputation, and I'm innately selfish.

She smiles, close-lipped. I'm not the only one in pain. I think of our last show and the disgusting way I treated her. My spine stiffens. Annie takes a sip of her own coffee and moves to the table. I follow, feeling awkward.

"I didn't mean to sleep so late," I say. "I thought I set my alarm."

Annie waves me off, passing a covered wooden bowl of something that smells like freshly baked muffins. Blueberry. "You did. I asked Fitz to turn it off. He and Kacey left early with Jason this morning. I stayed behind to help Gran, so we thought we'd let you sleep in." Before I can open my mouth to protest, Annie continues, "Nope. That's why you're here,

Jefferson. So you can rest up. So we all can. Touring is grueling work. A week of sleeping in will do us all good."

I can't look at her right now, can't face her for being so understanding, so I turn my gaze out the open window. I need to get away from this place.

"Maybe I can help around the farm. I grew up doing farmwork. How can I help?"

Annie's grandma shakes her head at the sink. "It's not a working farm, Jefferson." My throat grows thick at the sound of my real name coming from her lips. This woman who has watched this story all play out before but still allows me a spot at her table. "Hasn't been for years. You might wanna check down at Carla's, about quarter of a mile down the road. But they hire on summer workers every year to help them with planting. I doubt they could use you."

"What about the mowing, Gran?" Annie turns to me, and this time I have to look at her. Her face is luminous in the soft natural light. Across her nose are a spattering of freckles. Her curls are all gathered up on top of her head, leaving her long neck bare. "My pop usually mows, but he could use the week off, I bet."

I nod, liking the idea. A few days sweating on a tractor sounds good.

And so I mow. Up one row and down another. I talk to myself. I talk to Danny. I curse at God. I sing.

I think about my brother. A lot. I talk to him about his daughter. I imagine his disappointment in me for not knowing more about her. It's so real at times, I can feel him alongside me.

I remember going camping when I was ten. Danny was fourteen, and Fitz was there between, a tagalong as always. My granddad took us to the Smokies for two whole weeks. We wandered until we got lost, but my granddad always found us. He'd light these giant fires every night, and we'd roast hot dogs on sticks we'd gathered that day. We'd poke at the flames so much our clothes were speckled with burn holes.

My granddad would talk to us about everything under the sun, and on those nights, we were a captive audience. He'd tell us about a loving God and how to treat women like queens and how to carve little figurines out of sticks.

He'd speak in parables and ghost stories and old mountain tales.

Sometimes, he'd pass me his guitar and ask me to play. I could barely write my cursive letters, but I was born strumming strings. Fitz would pull out his fiddle, and we'd play for the stars. The sky was an inky blue, and the wind smelled sweet as heaven whirling through the tall pines.

If I close my eyes, I can still see the crackling sparks twist and flicker in the funnel of dark smoke creeping to the treetops. I can hear my granddad's sloping baritone. I can see Fitz and Danny, heads bent together in the firelight, snickering like two peas in a pod.

It was the happiest time of my entire life.

When I was fifteen and my granddad was sick, I got into trouble with a couple of no-accounts at school. We were cutting class and smoking pot behind the auto garage, and when the principal called home, he got Danny, fresh home from basic training.

I'll never forget sitting on the bench outside the office when my big brother showed up. He was in civilian clothes, but it didn't matter. He was different from his head clear down to his toes—as though he were somehow taller and bore the world on his shoulders. His jaw was set, and his eyes were steely as he approached, but he barely spared me a glance before striding into the office, closing the door behind him. Less than a minute later, he was in front of me. He picked up my bag and slung it over his shoulder. Danny was halfway down the hall before I realized I was supposed to follow him.

He remained silent as he got in his truck. In dead quiet, he pulled out of the lot and drove us through town. I reached for the radio, and he smacked my hand.

By the time we pulled into our driveway, I was ready to make a run for it, convinced he was gonna kick my ass with his newly honed Marine skills. He turned off the ignition and stared straight ahead. That's when I saw it: the tic in his jaw, the twitch in his whiskered cheek.

Then I heard the snort.

My stupid brother was laughing at me. Red-faced and clutching at his gut. He was howling and sputtering. "Your face!" was all he said.

I tried to punch him in the arm, but there was nothing in it. I was just so relieved he wasn't going to kill me. Soon I was laughing just as hard.

When he died down, he turned to me, his eyes still full of mirth. "Did I ever tell you about the time Fitz and I got caught drinking Granddad's old scotch behind Autos?"

My eyes were saucers.

Danny smiled at the memory. "Drunk as two skunks. Diana Foster had just turned *both* of us down for prom, and so I snuck home at lunch and broke into the liquor cabinet."

"You guys asked the same girl to prom?"

Danny grinned. "It was a bet. We both lost."

"And scotch?"

He grimaced then. "Yeah, it was disgusting. We got caught because Fitz couldn't stop puking. I thought he was dying."

I started snickering now. "You turned yourselves in?"

"I thought he was dying!" he repeats. "And I was three

sheets to the wind. There was no convincing me otherwise. I ran straight for the dean and begged him to call 911. Thank God he didn't. He followed me out behind the Autos and force-fed us day-old sub sandwiches from the cafeteria."

"You didn't get into trouble?"

Danny shrugged. "He figured we had scared the living daylights out of ourselves and the hangover was punishment enough. Then he warned if we weren't early for school the next morning, we'd be suspended."

"Man," I said. "He was ready to suspend me, and I wasn't even drunk."

"Nah, he wasn't gonna suspend you. I knew once he saw I was back, he'd relent."

"What are you gonna do?" I scoffed. "You'll be leaving again soon."

This time, Danny turned to me fully. "You need to cut the shit, Jefferson. You can't be smoking drugs."

"Watch me," I mumbled.

"Granddad is dying, and I'm leaving, as you helpfully pointed out. I have to. We need the money, and being a soldier is all I've ever been good for. But you? Damn it, Jeff. *You* can do better. Get the fuck out of here. You're special. Don't waste your life away in this town. Those guys you were caught with? They will die here having accomplished and contributed nothing. Don't be them. You've got a gift."

I rolled my eyes. "No one makes a living playing guitar, Danny."

"You will," he told me seriously. "You make people feel things with your music. Don't you dare take that for granted."

It's Friday, and I'm revving up the John Deere once again when Annie's grandfather comes up behind me with a slight tap on my shoulder. He holds out an older model, slim iPod between his fingers attached to a set of large headphones.

"It belongs to Annie. I offered to bring it out so I could talk to you."

I swallow and nod, taking the small, outdated device.

"She thinks you're worth saving. Are you?"

The air gushes out of my lungs at his frank question. I shake my head but look him in the eyes. "I want to be, sir."

His stare softens, just barely. "My Cora was intoxicated with fame. She didn't want to be saved. She wanted to dance with the devil."

I wait him out.

"Everyone thinks I don't see things because I'm old and I don't run off at the mouth every chance I get. But I watched you and my granddaughter onstage. I know she's afraid of following her momma's path, but there's a difference. Annie won't dance with the devil. Annie wants to save his soul."

I don't know what to say. I'm not sure I like what he's alluding to. "I don't want to be the devil in this scenario or any scenario, sir."

Pops puts one gnarled hand on my shoulder and squeezes with a surprising amount of strength. "Good. Don't be."

A humorless chuckle erupts from the back of my throat, and my head is shaking again. As if it could shake the messed-up grief and rage right out of my brain. "I don't know who I am anymore. I used to be a grandson and a brother and a son and a singer, and now I'm just a fuckup. Excuse me." I rush to apologize, remembering my audience.

Pops squeezes impossibly harder and the pain sharpens, and I feel something inside of me wake up. I can grasp on to the ache. It's tangible and real. Grounding.

"You are still those things, boy. Just because my Cora died doesn't mean I'm not a father. Just because your family is gone doesn't mean that you are. Your identity is tied to who they made you into, not who they were. The way I see it, you can honor them by becoming the best possible version of who you are meant to be, or you can wither away to nothing with no one to remember you."

"Hell."

"Yes." He releases my shoulder and points to the music still grasped in my fingers. "No one but the best possible version of you is worthy of my granddaughter, so you'd better figure that out."

"I'm not—"

He waves a hand over his shoulder. "Sure you aren't."

I stretch the headset over my ears and tuck the iPod into my pocket before climbing onto the tractor's deck and settling down into the molded yellow seat. When I turn to check, Annie's grandfather has already lumbered halfway back to the house. I watch him head up the front porch steps before I tug the iPod back out. Apparently, Annie's already cued it up for me. I scroll to the first song and let it play.

It's twangy and sweet over the low rumble of the mower. I circle the drive and cut a clear swath across the perimeter of yard acreage. It takes me two and a half songs before I notice the trend in the playlist she's chosen for me. Redemption. Grace. Forgiveness.

I almost laugh. That's such an Annie thing to do. She's not going to hit me over the head with her beliefs. Instead, she slyly hands me music. It's our common ground, our language. *Music.*

A small part of me feels rebellious and wants to switch it off to spite her. That same part of me that threw back the pills and washed them down with a bottle of hard liquor. The part that hates Danny for getting himself blown up and who embarrassed a beautiful girl in front of thousands because of petty jealousy.

I turn it up instead. My hands steer the powerful mower up, down, and across in tight rows through the rippling green grass. I don't have to think about it. They know what to do. Muscle memory. As soon as I could reach the pedals, I've been mowing. My shoulders ease, and I swipe at the sweat beading at my hairline. I readjust my ball cap, letting the breeze cool my damp scalp for a second before replacing it once more.

Down back and up again. Repeat.

The lyrics start to penetrate my thoughts, and I let them. In the back of my mind, I recall numerous conversations I had with my granddad and brother over the years. Even Fitz, though he's not the most openly devout person. I've fought long and hard to not need anything or anyone in my life. Life is loss. Love is loss. You can't tell me any different. Eat, drink, and be merry until you die from it all. What's the point of living if you aren't enjoying every moment to the fullest?

But am I enjoying it? Never mind to the fullest, just flat-out enjoying my life? Am I ever drunk enough to forget my demons? The pills, those fucking pills. Was I enjoying life on the pills? What about when I'm onstage? Does performing give me the thrill it used to?

I think long and hard. Fans screaming, girls hanging on my every word, my bank account swelling unreasonably for a not-quite-nineteen-year-old. Maybe if I sang my own songs . . . but the look of pure derision on Lora's face in my memories chases that thought away.

Not even then, really. Because what is it all for? *Who* is it for?

I don't know if I'm ready to change. I know Fitz thought I was playing when I said I wanted help with my drinking. But I wasn't. Not really. I don't know where to go from here, and honestly, it's all sort of embarrassing. Why is it the majority of the world's population can get their shit together and I can't?

Or maybe they can't. Maybe they're all pretending. But I know that's not 100 percent true. Annie has it together. Sure, she's damaged from her parents' deaths, but more than that, she's whole. Dented but filled. Bruised but carrying on.

I'm not carrying on. I'm treading water but slowly sinking. My breaths fast and furious, panicked and straining against the swelling waves.

I finish my rounds and end up at the border of the property, marked by a small fishing pond. There's a rickety dock covered in moss from disuse. A row of weeping willows shades the eastern rim. I turn off the mower and, leaving the iPod behind, hop down to the freshly mowed ground. I make my way to the water's edge and sit, unlacing my heavy leather boots. Then I strip off my shorts, specked in grass clippings. Next, I tug my shirt over my head, removing my cap with it.

Without overthinking it, I step into the water. The mud squishes under my toes, filling the spaces under and around my arches. I continue to my knees and waist. The water is warm but cooler than the hot sun, so I still feel goose bumps lift over my exposed skin. The pond is murky but not turbid, and there's a bubbling water feature on one end of the reservoir to keep the water fresh.

I inhale several long breaths, moving my arms back and forth, allowing the surface to ripple around and over me. I take another step, this one bringing me to my neck. There's a flutter of movement near my knee, curious fish darting around me.

I'm overwhelmed. Loss of family, loss of direction, the look on Annie's face when I betrayed her. It's as though I've forgotten who I'm supposed to be. What I *want* to be.

Do I even want to be Clay Coolidge anymore?

I know, in my gut, I don't. The truth threatens to drag me under. I don't want to be Clay Coolidge. I don't even want to be Jefferson Coolidge. As far as I can tell, he's barely a step above. Nothing about who I've been interests me. I've completely lost my way. I've become expendable. Worthless.

I imagine thousands of tiny tethers latched to my skin, tugging and weighing me down. Individually, they are nearly harmless, but as one, they pull me under.

I let go. I allow them to sink me. The water rushes over my head, and I close my eyes against the light filtering above me. Coolness washes over my skin, releasing the tethers. I stop struggling, and my face lifts, breaking the surface. I spread my arms wide and release my limbs. Invisible hands seem to support me on the top of the water. I open my eyes to a brilliant existence. Rich colors, musical sounds, sweet-smelling breezes wafting, caressing my skin.

An unfamiliar smile breaks across my face. Stretching the muscles in my cheeks and exposing my teeth. A laugh erupts from deep inside of me, and all at once, I can't stop. I have to stand up, tears streaming as I lose control in the wonder of it all.

I'm not Clay striving to be Jefferson anymore.

I'm someone new.

25

Clay

I fly home the next morning, early, before the sun is even up. I leave a note on the dining room table thanking Annie's grandparents for their hospitality and letting the rest of Willows and Fitz know I'll catch up with them at the next stop.

My lonely inheritance is calling me home. Time to face the music. Literally.

Sobriety takes some getting used to. It's not so much that my body needs the liquor as the rest of me does. The world is too sharp without the booze buffer. The airport is noisy and bright. The plane is cold. Indiana is terrifying, and I'm not ready for it.

It takes me another hour before I'm pulling down my dirt drive, and I curse as I see Fitz's truck out front in my spot.

Son of a bitch, the man has fucking unicorn magic or something.

I slam the door, pulling my duffel out the back of the rental car, and approach my front porch just as the man of the hour swings open my screen door to allow me in.

"Thanks for letting me in my own house, man," I mumble.

"Annie found me a flight with no layovers."

I drop my bag on the ground. The air smells like alcohol, and I grimace.

"It's all gone."

My shoulders slump in relief. "The ones in the barn?"

"Got them."

"There was a stash in Danny's—"

"—old room behind the Nintendo. Duh. Who do you think put it there? Gone."

My vision goes blurry around the edges, and I feel like the last two years are rushing behind my eyes. I have to swallow multiple times before I can choke out, "Thank you."

Fitz scratches the back of his neck. "I wasn't sure you wouldn't come home and throat-punch me."

I shake my head. "No. I planned to dump it all, but I wasn't sure I'd be able to once I got here."

"Same. After the pills, though . . ." He grimaces. "I wasn't gonna fail you again."

"*You* fail *me*? What are you talking about?"

Disbelief paints his face. "Clay. You can't be serious. You could have died."

"I didn't, and even if I did, that's not your fault. I'm the fuckup."

Fitz shakes his head, and I raise a hand to stop him as something hits home.

"Wait a minute. This isn't another one of your 'Danny' things, is it? He didn't leave you to take care of me. I'm an adult."

"No, that's not . . . well, yeah, of course that's always a part of it. But not the way you think. Danny didn't leave me in charge of you or anything, but Christ, Clay. You're all I have left. We're family. I care, you asshole. When you were laid out on the floor, blitzed out of your brain and bleeding . . ." He trails off, swallowing hard. My feet are frozen, stuck to the ground, my blood pounding painfully in my veins. Will I ever stop hurting the people I care about?

"I was ready to force you into rehab before Annie basically took charge of the situation and told me we were all going to her farm. Even then, I made some calls just in case. If you were coming back here to drink yourself into oblivion, I have an appointment at a place tomorrow morning."

He sinks into a kitchen chair with a weary creak. "I thought if I could keep an eye on you, it would be fine. I could keep you out of trouble. Lots of kids drink. Fuck, Danny and I drank like fish. We slept around. We got into all sorts of trouble whenever he was on leave. But then, we looked out for each other. I figured I could do the same with you and you'd grow out of it.

"But you don't drink to have a good time or scare away your nerves. You drink so you don't have to face things. That ain't right. You stuff that shit down until one day you'll explode. You taking those pills? That was serious. I know that's not the first time you've been given pills. The label hands that shit out like candy. But I was always there. You always told me about them. I mean, the first few times you handed them off to me to get rid of."

I open my mouth, but Fitz waves me off. "No. No explaining that away. One day you'll get it. You'll see it from our perspectives. Jesus H., Clay. You didn't see Annie's face when she first saw you."

"I didn't mean to scare—"

Fitz lets out a humorless chuckle. "Oh, she wasn't scared. I was scared. Kacey was scared. Jason wasn't, but that's . . ." He shrugs. "No. Annie was resigned. Cool. Calm. Ready. Because this wasn't her first time. She's been down this road before. *She* comforted *me,* dude. Told me you hadn't hit rock bottom yet."

My insides burn and sink at the same time. I think of the pictures at Annie's house of her parents. I've blown it.

"I'm done, though. That was rock bottom for me."

Fitz raises a brow. "Done with what? Drinking? The girls? And by girls, I mean Lora. What?"

"All of it," I say. "Drinking, girls, music, touring. I have to go back to square one. I can't keep going like this. I'm sorry for what that means for you."

"You think I care about any of that?"

I shrug. "It's your livelihood."

"Fuck my career. It's your life."

His words ring out in the silence of the kitchen. The clock ticks on the mantel in the dining room.

"Clay, what part of 'you're all I have left' did you miss? Family over fame, man."

I nod. "Family over fame," I repeat in a choked voice. After a beat, I say, "I'll finish the tour, though."

"And then what?" Fitz isn't challenging, just curious.

"Then . . ." My gaze skims around the dusty house, as though I'm looking for clues. "Then, I don't know. Maybe I'll take some classes or find a job."

"You're going to give up music?"

Even considering it hurts, and I rub at my chest. "I'm not sure. Maybe I need to go back to square one on that, too."

Fitz nods approvingly. "I'm hungry. Want some pizza?"

"Sure. But let's go out. It smells like a liquor store in here."

He grins and slaps my back as he stands. "But you're paying, brother. I'm about to be unemployed."

The next morning, Fitz and I go visit Lindy. It's my idea that we don't call her ahead of time. We've only got two days before we're due back on tour, and I'm afraid if she turns me down, I'll let the opportunity go again.

She answers the door with wet hair and a harried smile that falls the instant she sees me. "I wasn't expecting you—Clay! Is everything okay?"

"Everything's fine, Lindy." Fitz leans in to plant a kiss on her cheek just as Layla peeks from around her legs.

"More than fine," I add, feeling awkward. "I hope it's all right we came by."

Lindy's brows rise, but she stands back, allowing us into her small home. It's a tiny, gray ranch with two bedrooms and zero kitchen space. I've been here before but am suddenly taking it in as though I hadn't seen it. Her home is neat and clean but clearly worn. The walls are patched, and her kitchen floors slant toward one end. Her carpets are older and thin in spots from daily wear.

"I was about to head out back with my coffee. Care for some? Just brewed a fresh pot."

I nod, and Fitz helps himself, clearly familiar with the kitchen. He hands me a mug as Lindy slides open her back door and we all head out to her deck. The patio furniture is a heavy iron, sturdy, but with cracked paint. Lindy sits first, followed by Fitz. I stand, shifting my weight, and try to lean against the railing. It gives, and I straighten.

Here I am with more money than I know what to do with, and Lindy is raising my niece and I've left her to struggle on her own. Danny would wring my neck.

Fitz and Lindy are making small talk, but I'm distracted by Layla out in the yard. She's made her way over to a rickety swing set and a sandbox that's more mud than anything else.

Putting down my mug, untouched, I maneuver down the steps toward the girl.

She's talking to herself, piling up sand with a shovel. I grab another and squat down next to her.

"Can I play?" I ask.

She blinks, wide-eyed, looking so much like Danny, I can barely breathe. "Sure, Uncle Clay."

I swallow thickly, shaking off my grief, and dig in.

Layla and I play side by side for a long while. I really like the kid. She doesn't ask me lots of personal questions and doesn't look at me like I'm a ticking time bomb. She's a little bossy, but then so was Danny. There are worse things.

Lindy calls from the deck that it's time for lunch, and I startle, pulling my phone from my pocket. I've been in this sandbox for over an hour.

"Okay, Mama!" Layla shouts back in a high, sweet voice. I stand and brush off my hands before her little hand finds its way into mine.

"Mama cuts off my crust. She'll cut yours, too, if'n you want."

Fitz snickers, and I toss him a glare before looking down at the tiny girl still attached to my hand. "I actually really like the crust."

She freezes. "You do?"

I grin apologetically. "But your dad, he hated crust, too."

"He did?" She beams.

Lindy sniffs loudly, and I force myself to look at her finally. Her hazel eyes are watery and red-rimmed. She shakes her head. "It's nothing. I mean, it's everything, really. Thank you. I know this is hard for you, but she needs this." She gestures at our conjoined hands. "You're the closest thing she has to her daddy."

I swallow against the lump in my throat and clear it loudly. I look down at Layla. "Well, what a coincidence. You're the closest thing I have to my brother, Little Layla. Think we should stick together?"

We eat a lunch of PB and J with apple slices, and talk—while stilted at times—is more than it's ever been. I can see why my brother was attracted to this woman. She's strong-willed and pretty and protective as all get-out. They must have been great together. I wish I'd paid more attention, but I'd assumed I had all the time in the world.

"I was sort of hoping you'd bring that Annie Mathers back around with you. She's a delight," Lindy teases.

The image of sitting around this dilapidated patio with Annie by my side, visiting, is so appealing, my chest constricts.

"I don't think Annie will be coming back anytime soon," I say.

Lindy's expression is far too understanding, and I squirm.

"I know you and I aren't close, Clay, but I do know what it's like to love a Coolidge man, so I hope you'll hear me out."

Fitz settles back in his chair comfortably, crossing his boots. I clamp down on any words of argument, feeling my jaw clench. I don't want to hear the words *Annie* and *love* in the same sentence. I owe Lindy her say, though.

"You don't make it easy. You've been left a lot in your lives and prefer to do the leaving. Look at Danny." She waves a hand, taking a sip of her tea and swallowing before continuing. "Oh, I know he was military, so of course he had a noble reason to leave, and I don't mean to belittle his sacrifice. I'm proud as hell of him and will love him for it until the day I die. But he left. Always. If he'd lived, he'd still be leaving. I don't know the particulars of this visit, but I'll bet the roof over my head, you're leaving."

I don't disagree, and she continues.

"At some point, Clay, you're gonna have to be the one who stays put."

"My life's on the road," I say. I don't bother to tell her I'm thinking of quitting.

"You know that's not what I mean. Annie's been left behind, too. When you guys came to Taps, she defended you up and down. Convinced me maybe you weren't as selfish as you seemed. Said people grieve in different ways and you were grieving in yours. That girl spoke from the heart because she's been there."

"I'm not good enough for her," I say.

Lindy's lips spread into a blinding smile, and she taps the table with two fingers. "That's the best thing you could've said. Never forget it. If she chooses to love you anyway, don't you dare let her go."

26

Annie

sunday, august 18
chicago, illinois
wrigley field

A few weeks later, it's the last night of our summer tour, and I'm equal parts sad and relieved. I love to perform more than anything. I was meant for this. This summer has proved it to me. I love touring with Clay Coolidge. Jefferson and Fitz have become our family. Dysfunctional as we may well be.

More than that, even, I love to sing with Jefferson. Things are strained. His whatever-it-was with the pills scared the hell out of me. His visit at my grandparents intrigued me. His jump into the pond moved me.

But it's the end. Already the label is planning into the holidays, months in the distance. They are releasing our album in weeks. They've scheduled appearances on several late-night television shows and *Saturday Night Live* as the musical guest. I've even heard whispers about the Grand Ole Opry.

In all of this, I haven't heard a peep about Clay Coolidge.

The morning we arrived in Minneapolis, Trina intercepted Fitz at the door of our hotel. We left them in a hushed argument, but not before I heard her hiss something about Clay being MIA. Regardless, he showed up on time for sound check and looked bright and ready as ever. If anything, he seemed relaxed.

Which is good. Perfect, even. That's what the weeklong break was about.

Jason, Kacey, and I are slurping Thai noodles while sitting on tall black cases of stage equipment, watching Jefferson warm up. Fitz finally saunters over, and Kacey passes him her container.

He takes several distracted bites, watching his bandmate with an appraising eye.

"I think he's done," he says finally.

"Trina can't fire him," I say soothingly.

Fitz shakes his head. "No, she would never drop her cash cow. I mean, I think *he* is done."

"But he looks fine," says Kacey.

"He does. Better, actually, than I've seen him in a few years. Something's changed, though."

"Has he said anything to you about it?" I ask once I've found my voice. I can't say I'm surprised by this news, but it still pains me.

Fitz turns his penetrating gaze on me. "Music is in Clay's blood. Always has been, since he was a boy in his granddad's shop. He sent an email to all of us putting a stay on his contract negotiations. He was only given a one-album contract at signing, but we all thought they'd extend it in a heartbeat. He's supposed to meet with the label after Chicago, but he canceled the meeting. Said it was until further notice."

"Are you sure you're okay?" Kacey asks Fitz, rubbing his arm.

He blinks. "Definitely." And he sounds it. "Don't get me

wrong; I love my job, but I love Clay more. It's been like watching a car crash in slow motion this summer—maybe even this year. I have no doubt he's meant to sing, but I wonder if it all happened too soon. Too early for him? Too close to Danny's death? He never had a chance to deal, and the open road gives a guy way too much freedom at eighteen."

I swallow hard, and Fitz narrows his eyes at me. "I'm not talking about you, Annie. You're different. Even Clay has said so. You aren't sidetracked by your grief. You transform it into genius. Clay can do that, too, someday, maybe. But he needs to face it first. If that means taking time off . . ."

"But will the label wait?" Jason asks.

Fitz grimaces. "That's Trina's argument. She's not sure they will. All things considered this summer, it's a risk. By the time Clay decides he's ready, a new guy might've come along and stolen his spot. Fame is a fickle fucker."

"What do you mean by 'all things considered this summer'?"

Kacey and Fitz exchange a loaded look. Kacey lifts a shoulder, and Fitz turns to me. "I suppose it won't hurt, now that he's calling it. When I followed Clay back to Indy, I learned that before she left, Lora told him some rumors about you switching to Southern Belle. She seemed to think if you left, he'd be done."

"But that's ridiculous. This tour's been raking in money all summer long."

"That's not how they see it. They see it as *you've* raked in the money, and Clay's still a liability. If you left, he'd lose his contract."

"*What?*"

"Calm down, Annie. It doesn't matter. Like I said, Clay's done."

"But it does matter! I could've said something!"

"And that's exactly what he wouldn't want. Come on,

girl. Think about it. He doesn't want to be the weight on your line, dragging."

It hits me suddenly, how convoluted all of this has gotten: me thinking I can't love Clay without hurting him and him thinking he's not good enough for me.

We turn back to Clay as he holds a long, gravelly note that sends goose bumps up and down my arms. Fame might be fickle, but I don't agree with Trina. There's no one alive who could steal Clay's spot. If he took ten years off, even, it would only serve to deepen his lyrics and age his tenor. Jefferson will only improve with age.

Take your time, boy. Get your feet under you. I'll be right here.

"The label wants you to play 'You'd Be Mine' to close out the tour."

My eyes meet Trina's over Kacey's shoulders as she's smoothing out my curls. My tour stylist had to return to school, but it's fine. Kacey's been shaping my mop for years.

"Not happening," I say.

"It wasn't really a request," Connie says, backing up Trina from the doorway.

"Which label is asking?" I snip.

Connie rolls her eyes. "Don't get sassy. You know which label. After the way you shut it down with Southern Belle, I doubt any label will work with you again."

I sink back into my chair. "He shouldn't have brought up my daddy. Clearly, it would be a sore subject."

"He was offering you the moon."

We've been through this a dozen times, and anyway, Connie's just blowing smoke. I flat-out told her I wouldn't sit for the man trashing my dad, even if he was a selfish piece of work in his time. Only one person can talk shit about my parents and that's *me*.

"He could've offered me Mars and I still would've dumped his stupid mimosa down his overpriced shirt. What're you all sore about, anyway? SunCoast was more than happy to match his offer and then some."

"Speaking of," Trina butts in, preening in the mirror. "Tonight. 'You'd Be Mine.' It's happening."

"It's not ready for a live performance, and no one knows it. It'll kill the vibe we have going to introduce something unfamiliar so late in the game." I'm using every possible excuse in my arsenal. I could go all night.

Trina smooths her glossy lips with her fingertip in her reflection. "So replace 'Jolene.' You don't need to hide behind covers anymore, Annie."

"I'm bringing back the classics. It's an education."

This makes Trina pause in her grooming. She levels a look at me and then raises her heavily lined eyes up at Kacey. "As I said, it's not a request. Makes sure Jason knows." She walks out with a clatter of her heels, and Connie follows. So much for having my best interests. I slump.

"Well . . . shit."

Kacey presses her lips together around a mouthful of bobby pins, her fingers still gathered in my curls.

I shake my head, waving her off. "Don't look at me like that. It's fine. Who's to say he'll even hear it? Besides, for all anyone knows, I wrote that song long before this tour."

She fusses with the pins, placing them all carefully in silence. Then, "If he doesn't know, he's a fucking idiot."

This startles me so much, I giggle until I'm clutching my belly and laughing, tense tears pouring from my eyes and ruining my makeup. Kacey joins in. Jason knocks on the door while walking in, not bothering to wait for the invite.

"I just ran into Trina in the hall—"

"We know," Kacey sputters between giggles.

Jason rolls his eyes. "So . . . we're okay with this, then?"

I wipe at my cheeks, fanning my face. "It's an order from the top."

"But what about Clay?"

I sigh, finally composing myself. "It's the last show; maybe he'll miss it."

Jason taps out a rhythm on his thigh. I groan.

"Now what?"

"Yeah, so I was actually talking to Clay and Fitz when Trina told me. They heard you had a mystery song and were all over it. They wouldn't miss it."

"Of course not."

"They're huge fans," Kacey says apologetically.

"Maybe Jefferson won't read into it."

At this, Jason snorts. "Right. Because you never, *ever* base your songs on real life."

"Maybe he'll think it's about you."

"Maybe you're delusional."

I slam my hand down, and Kacey jumps. "Damn it, Jason! You're supposed to be supportive."

He raises a dark brow. "I don't know what you're talking about. This *is* me supporting you. I told you he doesn't deserve you. When he OD'd on pain pills and started rambling about being in love with you, I punched him in the mouth. What the fuck else do you want from me, Annie? I'm not your therapist."

Kacey winces at his slip, and my entire body flushes. "What did you say?" I ask slowly, each word being dragged from my lips.

"Okay, so I am your friend. I don't mean to be an asshole—"

I shake my head. "No, not that. I don't care about that. Did you just say he said he *loved* me?"

Jason's face pales. "I . . ."

"He said he loves me?"

"He was barely coherent, Annie. He's a mess."

"I know that," I snap. "Don't you think I know that? But he said he was falling in love with me and *no one told me*?"

Kacey releases a slow breath. Her tone is soothing, and I despise it. "No one wanted to get your hopes up. Fitz actually wanted to tell you. He has a thing about you two, but he's got blinders when it comes to Clay. He's his brother. He can't see how he could hurt someone like you."

"Someone like me? What does that mean?"

"Oh, don't get pissy with me, Annie May," Kacey says. "Yeah. Someone like you. Someone whose mom and dad are country music's biggest tragedy."

I close my mouth and slump back in my chair. I don't say anything else, just fix my makeup as Jason and Annie argue about something unimportant. Once I'm ready, I stand up, grabbing my guitar.

"We'll play it for the encore."

"But that's when—"

I silence them both with a raised chin. I'm not running from this. He'll hear it, and that's that. Either it's tonight at the show or its next month on the radio. I wrote it for him. I'd be a coward if I couldn't own up to that.

"Chicago, you've been the *best audience* a girl could ask for to end her summer! Whoever said Yanks couldn't party? Not me!" I wink and watch as the giant screens behind me amplify my movements all over the giant outdoor stadium. The crowd roars. "Who's ready for *Clay Coolidge*?" More roaring. I grin. "All right, all right, y'all. One more song from us and we'll get out of your way."

Booing. I smirk mischievously and wave my hand down, shrugging them off. "No hard feelings; those Coolidge band members have stolen our hearts for sure!"

I turn to face Kacey and Jason and release a calming

breath. They're waiting for my cue. I glance off to the wings, and there he is. Ball cap, jeans, gray V-neck. He gives me a happy grin.

Jefferson smile, I think automatically. But better, maybe. My heart flips in my chest. I turn to face the audience. Somehow, it's easier to reveal my gutted heart to thousands of people over just one.

"I hope y'all will hang with me here. Kacey, Jason, and I have had an amazing time on tour this summer. We want to keep it going and would honored if you all would come along with us. So we put together a little album that should be dropping in the next few weeks. This song is brand new. You're the first ears to hear it. It's called 'You'd Be Mine.'"

The crowd erupts in cheers, and it blows me away, still. Them cheering for me and a song they've never even heard. "It's a song about a boy," I say and start strumming. I swear you could hear a pin drop. The light of cell phones glitters back at me in an enormous waving sea of motion.

I shut my eyes and sing my heart. I can feel his eyes on me. His ears perked. His full attention laser-focused sends goose bumps over my skin as the lyrics unfold and stretch over the crowd. When I come to the last verses, I can barely choke them out over the emotion swelling, threatening to strangle the air from my lungs.

And, God, I hate myself for
Wishing
And lyin'
And thinking that maybe
You'd want to be mine

The damage is done. It's all been said. My heart's been torn open and revealed. Everything in me wants to glance back at the wings—to see for myself how he took my confession—but

I refuse. I can't. If there's even the tiniest chance in hell he didn't hear or didn't realize or . . . didn't feel the same . . .

I can't know it because then I can't unknow it.

I raise a hand, my guitar pick still gripped between my sweat-slick fingers, and beam at the crowd as though my heart weren't broken. They scream and stamp their feet, and it should be gratifying. It sort of is in a detached way, I suppose. "Thank y'all. You've been incredible. God bless and good night!"

The lights shut off, revealing only the dim glow of the backstage guides. I place my guitar back on its perch with more care than it requires and, in silence, turn at last to the wings.

Just in time to catch the stricken look on Jefferson's face as he strides away from me.

27

Annie

I'm back in my trailer when Trina comes knocking.

"You're up in ten," she says, letting the door flap shut again.

I rush to the door and swing it open. "Really?"

"Yes, really!" Trina yells over her shoulder.

"But I figured—"

Trina stalls midstride and whips to face me, her blond hair fanning out around her shoulders. "You figured wrong. Stop your pouting. You're a professional, Annie Mathers, so act like it. Get back out there."

I take the steps in one and jog to catch up to Trina's strides. She's muttering, "Goddamn teenagers. Making moon eyes at each other all summer just to go all *duh-rah-ma* on-stage before the whole world." She glances sideways at me. "Tell me, what did you hope to accomplish with that display tonight?"

"Me?" I sputter. "You're the one who said I had to sing it!"

"Obviously I hadn't realized who it was about, or I wouldn't have."

"I tried to tell you . . ."

Trina stops, placing her hand on my arm. "No, you didn't.

You gave every single excuse except the truth. I could have had him stay out of sight."

"Is it so bad he saw it? Maybe he couldn't tell," I offer, knowing it's bullshit.

Trina smiles humorlessly. "Oh, he knew. You're lucky this is the last stop for you two. Tomorrow the headlines will be fraught with speculation, and while you're riding high on your new album and your fame and Grammy nods or whatever, Clay's just given his notice."

"His what?"

"He's officially out. He's taking time off. Going back to Indy. Enrolling in college or some such nonsense."

"College?" I ask faintly.

Trina releases a giant sigh and squeezes my shoulder in an almost affectionate manner. "Look, I'm not really upset with you or even him. Despite what you all think, I care more about you kids than my bankroll. I've known Clay needed help, and I'm happy he's going to get it, and I knew when I heard your little low-budget clips on YouTube that you had your momma's blinding star power. So do me a favor. Just once, tonight, this last show, let him see the real Annie onstage. He's already decided to leave, and that's fine, but more than anything, the kid's been longing for something real. He's got the chops. Give him one last taste of what country music is really about." Her shoulders slither down, and she lowers her voice. "And if you do that, then maybe, just maybe, he'll find his way back to us one day."

I think back to the afternoon in June when I'd overhead Jefferson playing in his trailer. I nod. "I can do that."

We're at the back stairs now that lead to the stage. Trina releases my arm, and I shuffle up the steps alone. Someone holds out my guitar for me, but I wave them off. I won't need it for this. I see Kacey and Jason in the wings and come up behind them. Fitz shimmies over to us.

"Ready?"

"Totally," I say. I see Jefferson circle back to take a swig from his water bottle. "But I have a request . . ."

Fitz meets Jefferson in the middle of the stage, passing on my idea. Jefferson's face brightens as his eyes find mine in the wings. He nods once, easily, and I release a slow breath. Good. This is good.

"Ladies and gentlemen," Jefferson begins. "As with most nights on our summer tour, I'm about to bring out some very special guests to share a song with us. They've been our opening band, our lovely eye candy, and by now our very close friends and family . . . Jason, Kacey, and Annie from Under the Willows!" Another roar of cheering rings out into the navy sky beyond the bright lights of Wrigley. Kacey and Jason run out first, and I follow a little slower, taking it all in. The lights, the sheer massive number of fans, the balmy late-summer air. The scent of spilled beer and fried food. Jefferson glances down at my bare feet and grins, passing me a mic. I shrug before leaning over, as I do, taking in every detail of him as well. This is probably the last time I will ever share the stage with this man.

I swallow thickly before saying, "Are you sure you're up for one more Johnny and June?"

He wraps a strong arm around me, squeezing my shoulders. "I'd be honored." He reaches behind himself to pick up an older-model guitar with a slightly unraveled embroidered strap and secures it over his shoulder. "I don't know if word of our Johnny-and-June duets have reached you all out here in Chi-town, but we thought it'd be an appropriate end to our partnership, so Miss Mathers suggested a little song called 'Long-Legged Guitar Pickin' Man.'"

The stadium erupts, and we share a laugh. Either kids

have been shoring up their Johnny Cash knowledge or our reputation has preceded us. Either way, this song is really more for Jefferson than them anyhow.

He starts to pick out the opening chords, and I pick up my heels and twist on bare toes, kicking out my feet and waving my hands around my hips in an old-fashioned twist. He takes a long look at me before stepping up to his mic and belting out the first lyrics in his gravelly tenor. I bite my lip. Lord, he's all charm.

I raise my own mic to respond in like, not stopping my dancing. Kacey and Fitz are plucking away on their fiddles, and Jason is back on the shaker, probably paying more attention to the ladies in the front row than his performance.

But for me, it's all about the clear-eyed, handsome man in front of me.

There's an interlude, and as he artfully plucks at his strings, I twirl and clap with the beat. His eyes are crinkled at the edges, and I can tell I've made the right choice with this song. It's like watching someone in the comfort of their own home. He's genuinely at ease here. This style suits him, and my only regret is that the song is so short. We battle good-naturedly for another refrain before the song wraps.

But before I can manage to step off the stage, Jefferson is transitioning into another familiar melody. Not a duet. Chills roll up and down my bare limbs as he positions himself in front of the mic again. The stadium is absent of sound as though everyone is holding their breath. He sings "The First Time Ever I Saw Your Face."

Hot tears spring to my eyes, blurring everything around the edges. I'm frozen in place. In the back of my mind, I'm thinking I should move to a mic. I should harmonize. I should sway. I should grab that stupid egg shaker from Jason, but I can't.

I can't move. I can't think straight. I can't look away from his beautiful face. He closes his eyes as though he can't stand to look at me, and the pain of it threatens to overwhelm me in front of all these people.

It was pretend. It was supposed to be this act professionals do for laughs. For profit. For whatever it was until it no longer was any of those things for the two people that mattered: me and him.

It became so much more, and yet it doesn't matter because he's going home and I'm going up the charts. There is no what-if in this scenario. A gorgeous public offering is all we have. I said my piece, and now he's said his. When the song closes, Jefferson drops to his knees in front of me and takes my hands, kissing them. Tears pour down my cheeks, and I know my makeup must be running like crazy on the big screens, but I don't care. I laugh through my tears and tug him up before wrapping my arms around his neck and kissing him on the mouth. Only once. Quick and soft and lonely.

The tour has come to an end.

28

Clay

six months later
indianapolis, indiana

It's a packed house again tonight. Third Thirsty Thursday in a row that I've managed to fill every seat, and Petey looks about ready to kiss my boots. I don't mention in another life I filled stadiums twenty times this size. He might start charging me for my root beers, then.

It's not Wrigley Field, under the lights in August, but I get to wear my ball cap, sleep in my own bed, and sing whatever the hell I feel like. Tonight, I feel like a little Garth Brooks. I also tossed in a few newly written originals in between and no one's booed me out, so that's a good sign. There have even been a few women at the bar giving me eyes. They're not my type, but I bet Jason'd make a killing.

I ignore the pang in my chest at the thought of my friends. I'm able to compartmentalize Before and Now pretty well, even when performing, but occasionally the memories worm their way in. Like that one time last week when someone shouted out a request for Cash.

I won't play Cash. Not without *her*.

A rush of fresh air wafts its way up to the small stage. I squint through the cheap, bright lights as a familiar form saunters up toward the stage and takes a seat at a table in the front, never mind that there's been a party there all night. I smile to myself as he makes himself at home. Fitz is back in town.

Good. It's been too quiet around here. Of course, that'll last a week or so and I'll be texting his girlfriend to come get him again.

I lead the bar in the chorus of "The Thunder Rolls." I've considered playing one of my own hits, for old times' sake, but I worry I'd be pushing it. I've changed my name, going by Jefferson Daniels now, but everyone has camera phones these days and I don't need Trina to find me. I realize I can't hold her off forever, but I can for a little longer at least. Singing music is different from, say, being in a movie or on a Netflix series. Off the main stage, few people recognize me as Clay. They might think we sound similar, but I basically look like every other nineteen-year-old guy on the planet.

"Y'all have been incredibly gracious this evening. I hope you'll oblige me a little more before I take a break." A couple of boos ring out, and I don't bother to hide my grin. "Easy, there. A man's got to eat. But before I do, this next one is brand new. Let me know what you think."

I close my eyes, strumming gently on my granddad's old guitar. The frayed strap is like an embrace.

Take me away to where the sawdust spirals
Where it smells like fresh-cut pine and white oak
And it sounds like a song from green wilds
And a time when you were alive

I've been all around this great land,
Over ancient mountains, blistered in the white sand

Seen everything there is to see and
Chasing a mirage I won't ever catch this side of heaven

You were a kid, time transformed a hero
Dust in the desert sun, there could be no equal

Falling on some hard-luck times
When I remember how you and I
Dreamed every day about when we'd find
Out if we'd become better men
I raise every last drop of this pint
In memory of all those times
When you and I still tried
To be better men

You took my words with you over there
In the early morning light
Told me you listened with your men
Made them think of home on those lonely nights

I'll never play those words again
No point if you're never gonna hear them
I play for everyone else in your stead
But not those words, not since you're dead

Now I visit you under a stone
In the dirt, you lie alone, and I've—

Fallen on some hard-luck times
When I remember how you and I
Dreamed every day about when we'd find
Out if we'd become better men
I raise every last drop of this pint
In memory of all those times

When you and I still tried
To be better men

I tilt back from the mic, strumming an interlude while picturing Danny in my mind. Tall and strong and alive. Serious, not laughing. Because he knows what's coming up isn't funny. Dying at nineteen with a baby on the way isn't funny. Leaving me behind isn't funny. I press forward again.

I'm fighting mad at you and your noble cause
And I'll never forgive you for leaving me behind
But when it comes down to it, we both know who you became
You self-sacrificing son of a bitch . . .
Were the better man

Falling on some hard-luck times
When I remember how you and I
Dreamed every day about when we'd find
Out if we'd become better men
I raise every last drop of this pint
In memory of all those times
When you and I still tried
To be better men

You were the better man
You were the best man

I still the strings and open my eyes slowly to dead silence. Then a chair scrapes along the plank floor, and Fitz surges to his feet. Beneath the brim of his cap, his eyes are wet. He starts clapping, and that seems to wake everyone else up from their trances. Soon chairs are scraping and phones are glowing and people are clapping and cheering, and damn if it's not better than any standing ovation I've ever had before this.

Because this was my song. My heartache for my brother.

I wrap for a short break. There's a jukebox in the back that starts to play some classics, and I step off the stage toward Fitz. A couple of the people at the table move to give us space, and Fitz passes me a beer. I wave him off, and he raises a brow.

"It's just easier if I don't have any at all. Once I start, it's a lot harder to stop," I say.

He pulls the bottle back and passes it to a random guy sitting next to him.

"Nice place you got here. Standing room only, not that I'm surprised."

I accept a root beer from one of the waitstaff with thanks and then request a second for Fitz. "Yeah, I like it. All the wings I can eat, and it pays for laundry."

Fitz raises one eyebrow. I take a swig of my drink. We both know I could pay for brand-new clothes every single day if I wanted. For everyone in this bar. For the rest of their lives.

"So listen, Trina—"

I hold up a hand. "How about 'Hey, man. Nice to see you. You look good. How's it been? I like your new song. Are you growing a beard?'"

Fitz picks at his label. "Hey, man, nice to see you. You look better. I've always been a fan of your work, and you made me cry like a baby." He raises a rusty eyebrow. "Would we call that a beard?"

I scratch my hand against my whiskers. "It's filling in."

"If that's what you have to tell yourself."

Fine, I'll play. "I told Trina no."

"I know you did. I'm here to ask why."

"I'm without a contract, Fitz."

He shrugs. "By your choice, and the CMAs don't care about contracts. They care about viewership and audience numbers, and the fact of the matter is your tour brought in some of the biggest numbers last summer."

"Because of Annie."

"Only partially. Give yourself some credit. Besides, its tradition for the previous year's winner to present the Best New Artist category. That's you," Fitz points out in a low voice.

I narrow my eyes. "Trina said something about performing, too."

Fitz shrugs. "Maybe just a little something. I'm sure they'll throw you in a montage. You know they always put the up-and-coming artists in the back."

"I'm not comfortable being Clay Coolidge anymore."

"So don't be." He holds up a cheap neon flyer advertising the bar's stage schedule. "Be Jefferson Daniels."

"They won't be interested in Jefferson Daniels. He doesn't bring in the crowds."

Fitz looks pointedly around the bar, folks still pouring in even though it's filled to the brim and my set is already half over.

I chuckle darkly. "This is nothing, and you know it."

Fitz shifts his eyes, picking at the label again. I glance at my watch. Four and a half minutes to go.

"There's a way they'd let you play as Jefferson Daniels. It'd be a boost to your career, even."

I choke on a swallow of root beer, fizzing painfully in my sinuses. "Don't even say it," I sputter between hacking.

"Why? It was her idea. She cares. Loves your new stuff. You know she's always been a fan of the classics."

"You showed her my new stuff? Come on, Fitz. That was for you to learn, not to share."

"And I learned it. I'm ready to go. She happened to come by once or twice while I was practicing."

For some reason, knowing she's heard my raw cuts makes me feel all exposed and vulnerable, and I don't like it. Clay Coolidge was a tested-out persona. I was confident in his appeal. I'm far more unsure of myself now. Especially opposite Annie.

"It feels a lot like taking advantage."

Fitz huffs and points to the stage behind us. "What you just played up there? 'Better Man,' was it? That was the best song I've ever heard. From anyone. Not just from Clay or Jefferson. *Anyone.*"

He glances down at his phone and smirks before turning it to me so I can read.

WHAT THE FUCK WAS THAT

Trina.

"What did you do?" I ask.

"Don't even act like you're mad. You know there were at least a dozen people live streaming that song tonight from the bar. I just happen to have a heavier social media following."

His phone dings again.

I'M CRYING. ANNIE IS CRYING. JASON JUST "WENT TO PISS" BUT WE ALL KNOW HE'S WEEPING IN THE BATHROOM. GIVE CLAY OUR LOVE.

Kacey. I sigh heavily.

His phone keeps dinging, and I raise my hand before he shows me more.

"Later. I have a set to finish."

"In two minutes," he says. "So, CMAs? Duet with Mathers? Because she's not going to leave me alone after this."

"Is this before or after I hand her the award for Best New Artist?" I ask snarkily, ignoring the rush in my veins at the mere idea of singing with her again. I don't care about the millions watching. I could sing in a gas station with her and my life would be made.

Fitz is unfazed. "Don't be ridiculous; I don't know the schedule. If they're smart, though, right before."

I groan. "Did you know this is literally the first week we haven't been in the tabloids?"

"No, but I find it very telling that *you* do."

I wave him off. "A duet would clinch the speculation forever."

"Would that be so terrible?"

I narrow my eyes. It might be, just not for me. I feel different. Whole. Alive and happy. Secure. It seems too much to hope I'm any better for her than I was this past summer, though. "You're only looking to perform stadiums with your girlfriend again."

He smirks. "I like hotel sex."

I wince at the gleam in his eyes. "I need to get back to my set."

"Does that mean you're in?"

"That means I have to work and I'll . . . think about it."

Fitz settles back in his seat, taking a long draw from his root beer, looking satisfied. He has every right to. It *has* to be me who gives her that award, and if that means I have to play every Clay Coolidge song to do it—

Well, I would.

Three days later, I wake to barking at my front door.

I straighten, placing my bare feet on the worn rag rug my grandma made decades ago, and throw a T-shirt over my bare chest.

"Hush up, Brinks," I mutter to the blue-gray pit bull yapping at the door. I slide the sheers aside and scowl before pulling my door wide. Grabbing ahold of Brinks's collar, I let Jason Diaz in.

"What in the hell are you doing here?"

"It's ten in the morning; why're you still sleeping?" he asks instead.

"First of all, who are you to judge? And second, I work late. Fell asleep watching TV."

Jason pushes past me, walking straight to the fridge and tugging it open with a clatter of condiments.

Ignoring his all-too-familiar lack of manners, I pull out my coffeepot and scoop in fresh grounds. "Want some?" I ask.

"Sure."

He moves to my cabinets, opening and shutting them in turn. I finish with the water and sit down at the table, scratching behind Brinks's ears before he flops on his side, exhausted from his early guard effort. He'll probably nap all day after that.

"If you're looking for booze, you won't find any. I gave up on the stuff."

"That's what Fitz said," he mutters, still searching. "But I don't believe it."

He finishes with the last cabinets, and I point him to the bedrooms. "Go ahead and look. Search the place up and down. If I wanted a drink, though, I work at a bar. You'll just have to believe me. You can ask Petey, but he wouldn't serve me if I asked. Not until I'm legal, anyway. Said it's not worth losing his liquor license."

"How old are you, really?" Jason asks.

"Nineteen last month."

He freezes in his search and turns to me slowly. "No shit?"

I stand up and pour myself a cup of coffee, black. I need caffeine for this. "No shit."

"When'd you get a dog?"

"September. Found him at a shelter, abandoned by his last owners. Figured he was alone and I was alone in this big old farmhouse. Plenty of acres for him to get into trouble. I couldn't say no."

Jason nods and accepts the cup from me. "What about Lora?"

I lean a hip against the counter. "What about her?"

"Are you still together?"

I put down my cup and cross my arms. "Not that we ever really were together, but no. I haven't seen her since she left me those pills and told me to get a life."

"I didn't know. Sorry."

I narrow my eyes. "What's this about exactly? Did you seriously drive all this way to vet me before the CMAs?"

Jason folds his giant gangly legs into a seat at my table, cradling the mug in his hands. "Something like that. Fitz said you were planning to present for BNA and was saying something to Annie about a duet."

I grimace. "I told him not to do that. I don't want to rain on her night." Just this weekend I watched her perform her latest single on *SNL* to thunderous applause. The clip had millions of views on YouTube by the next morning. She's doing just as incredible as we all knew she would. Better than. "I'm wary about playing Clay Coolidge music. That's none of her concern."

"Yeah. I'm picking up on that. Listen. You know I'm not Clay Coolidge's biggest fan, but I saw your performance at the bar, and it was like nothing I'd ever seen you do before. The fact of the matter is *he's* the famous one. You're gonna have to meet in the middle. Reconcile that shit, or whatever. Show the world that Clay grew up and found his roots. Reinvention ain't new. Annie's been doing it all year. At any rate"—he straightens—"she insists on it."

My gut drops. "She does?" Of course she does.

Jason shakes his head, grinning fondly. "You know Annie. Bleeding heart, at least when it comes to you. So yeah. You probably already have an email from her about song collaborations."

"So you came down here to make sure I wasn't going to mess her around?"

"More like I wanted to see how you were dealing."

I raise one brow over my cup.

He shrugs, sheepish. "I know. I barely believe it myself. But as your onetime partner in literal crime, I wanted to see for myself that you were good."

"I am. Better than good."

"But lonely?"

I grimace, uncomfortable.

"Dude. Annie's my best friend, so I can say this with complete certainty. She's a once-in-a-lifetime girl. I haven't forgotten your drug-induced confessions of love, so I know you agree with me."

I clear my throat, straightening. I hadn't remembered saying any of those things at the time, but Fitz set me straight months ago. Still, the reminder stings. Of the confession and the pills. "Yeah, well, I'm fine. We both know I wasn't right for Annie. Look at how she's done since I left. Up for two CMAs. Her album's gone gold. I would have been a stone around her neck."

Jason studies me, putting down his cup and scooting back his chair. "Maybe. Maybe not. You do seem to be doing better, though."

"I am. Picked up a couple of woodworking classes last semester at the local college. Playing my own music at Petey's bar every weekend. I'm sober. I've got Brinks to keep me company. It's not a lot, but it's been good for me to be out of the spotlight and figure some things out."

"Do you miss it?"

"Nashville?"

Jason nods.

"I miss the high of performing my songs to thousands, yeah. And I miss singing with Annie."

Jason moves to the door, shrugging a heavy Carhartt coat over his shoulders. "That's all I needed to know, then. We'll see you in Vegas?"

"Sounds like. Hey, you leaving town right away?"

Jason shakes his head. "I don't have to. We have a few days off."

"How would you like to slum it with me tonight? Play backup? I could use a drummer to change it up."

Jason flashes a white smile. "What time?"

"Be there at 8:30 to set up." I point to a pile of dirty dishes. "Looks like Fitz is still around, so I'll recruit him, too."

"I'll be there." He stops the door before it slams shut behind him and sticks his head back in. "I'm happy for you, Jefferson. I'm glad you're doing better."

The door closes, and I hear his tires roll down the gravel drive before I sink back against the counter. I stand there, staring an indeterminate amount of time before Brinks shakes me out of my stupor with his whining to be let out. I shoo him out the door before trudging up the stairs to get cleaned up. I've been wanting to play more originals at the bar—from both Clay and Jefferson.

I think today is a good day to start. I've been hiding long enough.

29

Annie

march 13
nashville, tennessee

"Hey, Cora." I release a long, slow breath, stuffing my hands deep in my coat pockets and staring up at the gray sky. It's noon on a Friday, and the cemetery my parents are buried in is blessedly deserted. I've been here for two hours, but it took ninety minutes to force myself out of the car, then another thirty to find the tacky monstrosity bearing their names.

"You look terrible," I joke, my heart squeezing. "I mean, probably."

A crow flaps off with a squawk, startling me and setting the branch it was perched on to trembling. I watch the bare limb until it stills and then glance back at the marble stone. I don't allow my eyes to stray toward the side where my dad's name is carved.

I don't have words for Robbie right now. She left me by accident; he did it on purpose.

That kind of thing requires another trip on another day.

"They're inducting you into the Country Music Hall of Fame," I say, an edge creeping in. "Want me to sing 'All the

Roses' in your memory." My features twist. "Had to change the key. Seems my range is a bit better than yours. Sorry," I lie softly.

I run my fingers through the hair whipping around my face and tuck it roughly beneath my scarf.

"I turned them down at first. I want you to know that." My throat is thick, and I can feel the blazing-hot tears swelling behind my lids. I swallow them back, blinking rapidly. "You don't get my tears," I whisper. "You didn't earn them." Anger sears through me, until louder, almost shouting, I cry out, "You don't *deserve* me!"

My fingers clench at my sides, and I want to scream. Or throw up. Or hit something.

"I hate you, you know that? I hate everything about you. I hate that you chose everything over me. Singing, Robbie, *Roy, even*. You never even looked for those boots for me, did you?" I growl, my face hot. It's a stupid thing to say, but it's what I have. It's what she left me.

Once the first tear slips through, the rest are a torrent. "Why even have me? If you didn't want me? If you didn't care?" I sink to my knees on the spiky ground and begin clawing at the dead grass, digging into the frozen ground as if I could reach her. Too soon my fingers grow numb, and I start pounding at the earth with my fists. "Cora's perfect. Cora's beautiful. Cora had vocals from heaven. Don't you miss Cora? Didn't you love Cora? Didn't she break your heart into pieces?" The words spit out from between my teeth like rapid-fire gunshots. "More like Cora's *weak* and *pathetic* and an *addict* and *self-absorbed* and *vain* and *dead*. She's *dead*!" I'm striking out at anything and everything. Suddenly my father's name catches my eye.

"Why are you even here?" I scream, and I make a fist to strike the marble when a hand shoots out, grabbing hold. I struggle against it, but the grip is iron. *"Let me go!"*

The grip swiftly changes, and suddenly I'm being lifted and pulled back against something solid, my flailing fists tucked gently against my sides. I'm sobbing so hard now that I can't breathe. Years of heartsickness erupts in my stomach, and I drop back to my knees, gagging and heaving onto the grass.

When my stomach is empty, I peel open my swollen eyes, surprised to find myself still in the middle of a cemetery. The sky is still gray. The air is still cold. I swipe roughly at my face, my wool jacket scratching at my hot sweat-and-tear-damp cheeks. I barely register the presence behind me before a familiar whiskey tenor says, "I used to throw empty beer bottles at my brother's stone."

A large hand drops in front of my face, and I take it, standing. I let go and brush my hands down my front nervously. Jefferson leans back on his heels, shoving his own hands into his pockets. He's wearing a charcoal-gray jacket over jeans—a far cry from summertime touring Clay Coolidge—and his face is worried.

I smile to assure him I haven't completely lost it, but it's a weak effort.

"So these are my parents," I rasp, jabbing a thumb over my shoulder. He frowns, and I realize moments ago he'd pulled me away from that stone, away from my parents, and I'd probably struck him. *Hard.* A lot of times.

My hands shake as they reach to cover my face, and I slide to the ground again, completely overwhelmed. Adrenaline is pouring out of me at an alarming rate, leaving me boneless and dried up in its wake. I lean against the headstone, greedily gulping in air as Jefferson drops next to me. I'm reminded of the anniversary of my parents' deaths when we sat like this, shoulder to shoulder, at the foot of his hotel room bed.

I let my head drop to his shoulder just as before. I can't

seem to stop myself from leaning on him. Even after all this time and distance. Maybe this is what I've been waiting for. For him to be sturdy enough to hold me up the moment it all came crashing down.

For right now.

"Fancy meeting you here," I say, question clear in my tone.

"I flew in this morning to meet with the label and called Fitz to hook up with you all, but he said you were here. Alone. And I . . ." He shrugs. "I thought maybe you didn't want to be alone but felt like you had to be. So I just . . . came."

"Just in time for the main event," I say wryly.

"You've seen me at my worst. I'd say I owe you one. More than."

I nod, imagining him laid out on the floor, passed out and bleeding. "They're inducting her into the hall of fame and want me to sing in her stead."

He whistles low. "Are you?"

"Yeah. I couldn't figure a way out of it that didn't make me out to be bitter and all emo. Thought I should probably come out here and test the waters before getting onstage in front of millions and singing her praises."

"And how'd that work out?"

I hold out a scraped-up, dirt-and-grass-stained hand featuring chipped fingernails and bruised knuckles. "Better than I'd thought, actually."

He chuckles low, and my head bounces. He takes my messed-up hand in between both of his and gently cradles it. I thought I was cried out. I was wrong.

He doesn't say anything, just lets me sniff in silence, my hand in his.

———

He follows me back to my new place and pulls into a spot next to mine. I walk ahead, leading him through the entrance and past a doorman to whom I give a small wave. We stand apart in the elevator, quiet but not uncomfortable. Someone gets on the floor below mine, and Jefferson tugs down the brim of his hat automatically. I reach for his hand and give a single squeeze. He releases his breath.

The bell dings for my floor, and I pull him to my front door before taking out my keys. "It's not as cozy as my gran's place," I start to explain. "I just moved in a few weeks ago and haven't bothered to decorate or anything."

"No judgment here, believe me. I'm still using my grandmother's dishes. Lindy and Layla are moving in next month when their lease is up, so my house is currently 1950s housewife meets the modern toddler." His eyes crinkle happily at the corners.

I push open the door and kick off my shoes before reluctantly releasing his hand to remove my coat, tossing it on the back of the stiff leather couch Connie ordered for me.

"I didn't know Lindy and Layla were moving in. That's amazing," I say. Everyone needs family to come home to. "How are they? Lindy texted me a few months back. We made a date for coffee when I make it back to Indiana."

Jefferson shrugs off his coat, and my eyes take in his broad shoulders and scruff. Mercy, he's good-looking. It seems I've lost my immunity all over again. I hadn't the wherewithal to notice while I was having my graveyard breakdown, but in the small space of my studio loft, it's hard *not* to notice. "Jesus, take the wheel," I mutter before clearing my throat.

Just be cool.

"Give me a sec," I say. I dip into my tiny bathroom to splash warm water on my face to rinse away my tears and makeup and swig some Listerine. Adding a touch of gloss to my lips before rushing back out. "Sorry. I could still taste the meltdown. You were saying?"

"Yeah, the house sits mostly empty except for me and my dog and Fitz whenever he isn't shacking up with Kacey. Plus, I've re-signed with SunCoast, so I'll be back on the road soon enough. It'll be good to have the house lived in and loved. Should have done it years ago, honestly."

My eyes dart to his. "Back up. You re-signed? Really?"

He scratches at his neck, his eyes twinkling. "Yeah, I really did. Apparently, *someone* slipped some exec a clip of my new songs, and they want me back. Wonder who might do something like that?"

I press my lips together, opening my eyes wide. When I think I can pull it off, I shrug. "Probably Trina."

"Trina's in Cancún with her fiancée, Melody. Has been for a month, making up for lost time."

"Oh . . . right." I drop the pretense. "Okay, it was me. Are you mad?"

"Nah. They're letting me start fresh. They like my new sound, and they sure as hell prefer me sober. I'm grateful. Truly."

My shoulders relax. "They aren't the only ones who love your new songs. I think I've played that clip of 'Better Man' a thousand times. It's a beautiful tribute." He nods once, shyly, and I can't help but tease. "Think you might want to head out on tour with me this summer? Opening, of course."

"Obviously," he quips, giving me a lopsided smile, and suddenly I can't look at anything but his mouth. "Can I get back to you? I'm . . . taking it a bit at a time. I'm not worried about backsliding, but I want to make sure the girls get settled in and—"

I cut him off with my lips. I've waited long enough. Honestly, I'm impressed I made it this long.

It takes him half a second before he responds in earnest, engulfing me with his arms and fisting at the shirt on my back. My fingers thread through the longish sandy waves at the nape of his neck and push off his baseball cap as my tongue dances past his lips. We kiss until we're both breathless, and then I lower onto my feet as his lips chase me down, pecking softly once, twice, three times, before his hands relax their grip and his arms drape in a comfortable hug. I tuck my head into the perfect pocket of his collarbone and inhale, filling my lungs with him.

"Thank you for today, Jefferson," I whisper. "You were right. I didn't think I wanted anyone, but I actually just needed *you*." He responds by tightening his hold for a minute and then releasing me again. I tug him over to my couch.

"Want tea? Water? Expired milk?"

"Sweet tea? Blech," he says, making a face.

"Perish the thought. Hot tea, chamomile. Very macho."

"Water's great, thanks."

I grab us a couple of bottled waters and sit next to him, bending one knee under me.

He cracks open the cap and takes a sip before clearing his throat. "You know, you were right, earlier. At the cemetery. They didn't deserve you."

I swallow wrong and feel my cheeks heat. "You heard that? What else did you hear?"

"Most of it, I expect. I was just going to give you space to do your thing, but when I heard the screaming, I panicked." I open my mouth, but he holds up a hand, shaking his head. "My point is, you were right. They weren't good parents, and they didn't deserve you, but they . . . *she* was an incredible artist. You can acknowledge that while still being angry.

"Like with Danny. I'm still mad as hell he left me, but I'm proud to be his little brother. He gave up his life for others. I can be angry and still admire and love the bastard."

I let his words settle over me, soaking into my brittle pieces and mending them just a little bit. "So you're saying be angry but still celebrate her career."

He smirks. "Or be angry and show the world how Cora's daughter is even better than she was."

I bite my lip, but I know my smile is flat-out moony. I fan my face. "Dang, boy, you're all charm."

He tilts his head to the side and sinks back into my couch. "Only for you."

That settles it. I can't let him walk away from me now. Or ever, probably. Everything about him and me and this moment and his lips and that smile and the way his words are like a balm to my soul—all of it—means I can't let him go. He's mine now. In a way, it feels like we've belonged to each other all along. Even back when he was just a voice over the loudspeakers at Young Stars, my heart knew it was done for. We just had to grow up some. Still do, I'm sure. Only now, I'm ready to grow alongside him if he'll let me. "Where are you staying? Do you have somewhere to be?"

He sits up, tugging his phone out of his pocket and tapping in his pass code. "Told Fitz I'd crash in his room tonight."

I slink forward, holding his gaze before reaching out at the last second and stealing his phone. He watches me, his expression curious but open. With three swipes, I've pulled up his texts. I type out a quick message and hit Send before I lose my nerve, and pass it back to him.

He reads it before his eyes jump to mine, shining.

"I just got you back," I explain shyly. "And we never got to just be us on tour. Spend the weekend with me? Please? We can order takeout and turn off our phones and play guitar and—"

"Make out on your couch?"

"I mean, I certainly wouldn't turn you down, if it's on the table."

His smile is blinding. "I don't have a change of clothes or anything. I left it all at the hotel."

"I don't know if you know this, but I'm actually sort of famous. I'll have some delivered."

He laughs, tugging me so I'm lying across him, and he tilts my chin down, his eyes caressing my lips before his mouth follows suit.

"I may never leave," he warns in between kisses.

"Fine by me."

30

Annie

april 12
las vegas, nevada
country music awards

I haven't seen Jefferson yet, and everyone is acting like that's perfectly normal.

Our flights didn't line up, so we never got to rehearse together. Like, that's insane, right? I always assumed major award shows were meticulous in their planning. It's a live show. Why wouldn't they insist on a dress rehearsal? Instead, Connie shrugs and says, "You're a professional performer, Annie. Why should this be any different from playing in front of thousands in a concert? Just as live."

Which is perfectly true. Minus the teeny-tiny, itsy-bitsy fact of me not seeing him in *weeks*. True, in comparison to never, that's barely a glitch, but it's like they've completely disregarded my need for regular exposure. FaceTime barely manages a dent in my anxiety.

Jesus H., I will die. That's it. I'll have a stroke right there onstage in front of millions of viewers.

Why is this not obvious to anyone else?

I've been the consummate professional all along. Willows is up for Best New Artist, which there's absolutely zero chance of us winning, but it's thrilling all the same. We're up against two country rock duos, a pop princess who's looking to cross genres, and a diva whose caravan parked over the top of my allotted bus space.

We relocated. It's cool. I get it. We're only nominated because of my mom. Legacy winners make for good press.

Of course, young traditionalists do occasionally win. Jefferson won last year against all odds.

I rip a spaghetti strap clear off the fabric tugging it over my shoulder, and let out a growl of frustration.

Kacey rushes in, horrified. "Annie, your gown! We leave in thirty!"

"Scissors, please," I mutter. She passes me shears, and I unzip my dress, making quick work of the other three fastenings holding the useless straps to my gown. I zip it back up and turn to face my cousin. "Can you tell?"

She motions for me to spin. "Actually, not at all. Will it fall?"

I hop up and down a few times. "I'm good."

"Where are your shoes?"

"I wasn't planning on bothering. You can't even see my feet."

Kacey looks scandalized and shrieks, "But they will on the red carpet! You can't not wear shoes, Annie. This is the freaking CMAs."

I pull out a pair of glittery, overpriced slippers. "Calm down. I'm not a barbarian."

"Our wardrobe changes are already at the auditorium," she says, fixing her hair in my mirror. "Jason's on his way over."

"Where's Fitz?" I ask idly.

She smirks at her reflection, proving my nonchalance wasn't nonchalant. "I imagine at the auditorium already. No wardrobe malfunctions there."

Jason comes in. "Car's downstairs. Ready for this?"

I release a slow breath. "Go ahead. I need a minute alone, okay?"

They nod, Kacey grabbing my clutch and phone and closing the door behind her. I sink onto the bed, careful to not wrinkle my slinky magenta gown. I wipe sweaty hands on the down comforter before clutching them together in my lap.

"Lord," I whisper. "I wish I didn't want this so much. Help me to not make a fool of myself when I lose. Please don't let me cry. Please don't let me forget the words to my songs. And . . . tell Cora and Robbie I said hi and make sure they watch."

I'm up for two awards tonight. Best New Artist, obviously, but also Country Single of the Year for writing "You'd Be Mine." No one's talking about that one. Don't want to jinx it, Kacey says.

But that's the one eating at me. I want it so badly I can taste it. I want to prove myself a songwriter. It's something neither of my parents ever accomplished. The nomination should be enough. The recognition in such a prestigious field at my age so early in my career. Yeah, I should be content with that. It feels, I don't know, bratty to want more than a nomination.

But I do. Holy hell, I do. All my life I've been in my parents' shadow. The daughter of legends. The product of a tragic upbringing. I need the validation I'm more than just that—that I belong in my own right. I inhale and exhale a few more times before getting to my feet and walking to the door.

I completely understand why Jefferson wants to leave

Clay behind tonight, to publicly cut ties with his old brand. After all, it isn't only about how you see yourself. It's about how the world sees how you see yourself that matters.

I'm taken aback at how many reporters snag us on the carpet. I expected to walk past without notice, except for maybe CMT. Not only do E! and TMZ stop us, but the networks do as well. Kacey graciously answers all the fashion questions and fields comments on her fitness regime and how she came to have such killer arms. Jason oozes charisma, playing the part of the bad-boy drummer with aplomb. I fare well enough, for lucky happenstance has the pop diva crashing my TMZ interview to say she's played my single on loop and was a huge fan of my mom. My summer "romance" with Clay only came up once, right at the end with CMT. I laugh them off and give them my signature wink. We're being ushered inside, but not before I hear the reporter comment they would all be looking forward to the Clay and Annie reunion this evening live onstage.

"Is that what they're calling it?" I whisper to Kacey, feeling frantic. "The Clay and Annie reunion?"

Kacey grips my hand and squeezes tight as we walk into the decked-out auditorium. It's gleaming and golden and well-lit with glittering chandeliers strung high on arched ceilings. The royal-blue carpet is plush under my slippers, and I try not to think of all the famous people who've tread these very aisles before I have, including my own parents decades before. If I actually take the time to look around at everyone here, all the famous, ridiculous, and legendary musicians in this one giant room, I could easily pass out. I can't take it all in. My brain can't compute. It's too much.

Instead, I focus on the buttoned-up usher in front of me.

I focus on the feel of Kacey's hand in mine. Just like when we were kids on my gran's farm. My eyes trace the broad shoulders of my best friend in his tux. When the hell did Jason grow up?

I press my lips together to keep from crying, but this time, it's happy tears. We did this. Together. Forget my parents; three kids from a farm town did this. We traipse across the middle aisle and then down a long slope toward the stage. We keep inching closer, and I'm shocked when the usher stops three rows from the front. He gestures to three seats right on the end. I stare at Kacey, wide-eyed, and she giggles. "Holy shit, Mathers, we're in the hot-girl seats!"

I laugh, pulling her with me and sitting in the middle. I have this insane image of the three of us in a movie theater for the Saturday-afternoon matinees in junior high. Except my gown costs more than a car, and *oh my god, Dolly Parton is sitting across the aisle.* I wave at her weakly and sink back into my seat with a shaky breath. Man, am I glad I didn't plan to sing "Jolene" tonight.

Within minutes, the show gets under way. Kacey keeps turning around in her seat and fidgeting, and when I follow her line of sight, I realize with a start Jefferson and Fitz are sitting a few rows behind us. I drink up the image of him, at ease in his fitted suit coat and jeans. His face is smooth, but his hair is still the longer style he's been sporting since his "retirement," curling slightly over his ears. My fingers stretch of their own volition as if to reach for the wavy strands.

He winks at me, and I turn back around in my seat, feeling caught.

Kacey squeezes my hand again, and I remember to laugh along with the opening monologue just as a giant camera slides in front of my face, catching my reaction.

Whoa, is this stressful. Focus, Annie. It's only a wink. Basically, an overexaggerated eye twitch. My lady parts disagree, however.

Another usher comes to my seat during a commercial break. "Time to head backstage for your performance, Willows." I hop up, Jason and Kacey following behind. Dolly mouths, "Good luck, sweet girl," and I swoon.

"Dolly Parton just wished me luck," I say under my breath.

"I think Dolly Parton just pinched my butt," Jason whispers back.

I snort. "You win."

We're behind the wings when I finally see him. I don't think about my cousin or Jason or any of the stagehands or backstage reporters. All I see is him. I walk right up and wrap my arms around his neck, pulling him tight and inhaling deeply, taking in his Jefferson smell. He holds me in return, not releasing me a full minute.

"I've missed your face," I say simply.

He grins warmly. "Likewise, Mathers. You ready for this?"

"Born ready," I say. My nerves are gone. Jefferson is magic.

"Good. I have to get out there, but I'll see you soon." He starts to go but then rushes back. "No matter what this says," he says, waving the Best New Artist card, addressing all of us at once, "you were my favorite new artists, hands down."

He spins on his heel, gliding effortlessly onto the enormous stage from the wings. I creep closer to watch. He reads off the teleprompter, something anecdotal about winning last year and how much his life has changed, and then it's time for him to announce the nominees. They play a tiny clip of all our biggest hits this year, and hearing them all together, I honestly feel like any of us could win. We're so different.

But in the end, it's not just anyone.

"And the winner for Best New Artist is not only Country Music's favorite trio, but mine as well . . . *Under the Willows*!"

For a half second, I'm frozen in place, disbelief grounding my slippers to the floor, but then Kacey's bouncing and
Jason's dragging me forward. Jefferson looks directly at me,
and it's like magic all over again, and my feet move and I'm
drawn toward him and his stupid-happy grin. He pulls me
into a hug, swinging me around once before releasing me
and letting me have the mic.

"Whew," I say, fanning my face. "Holy hell—oh! Sorry,
Gram!—I just didn't think we would win!"

"*I did!*" Jason shouts from behind me to laughter. Kacey's
got tears streaming. Useless girl. I squeeze her hand.

"I guess I'm talking, and I don't have a speech prepared
because I'm not very good at planning, and I really didn't
think we'd win, so I'll just wing it real quick. Thank you to
my bandmates and best friends, Kacey Rosewood and Jason
Diaz, who are standing beside me. Always. I wouldn't be
here without them. Thank you to Clay Coolidge for letting
us tag along on your tour and to all the fans that came out
this summer to cheer us on. We fell in love with you all, and
you've changed our lives. Oh! Thank you to our families
back in Michigan, especially Gram and Pops for letting a
bunch of kids out in the world to make a ruckus! Thank you,
Jesus, for this gift. We promise we won't take it for granted."

We're ushered offstage as the orchestra plays us out, and
we're rushed behind a screen to do a wardrobe change during the commercial break. It takes all of thirty seconds and
more hands than I could possibly recognize to transform me
into something totally different before I'm shoved back onstage to a little *x* marking my spot in the middle. I don't see
Jefferson, but I don't have time to panic. I practiced my half
of the mash-up, so I should trust he did his. We'll follow the
cues, and it will be fine. I release a cleansing breath.

The host introduces us, including the fact that—squee!—
we've just won the New Artist of the Year and Clay and

Willows toured together this summer. "The country got a glimpse of real sorcery this summer when these two young people toured the nation, charming the pants off country music fans, and tonight they've reunited to give the rest of the world a glimpse of their legendary chemistry. Welcome to the stage, Annie Mathers and Jefferson Clay Coolidge!"

Soft white lights glitter on every surface, and I stand in the middle, in a gauzy white, floor-length gown. Kacey opens with a sweetly mournful melody on the strings, and I whisper my heart into the mic, singing "You'd Be Mine." Jason does a little march on the drums, and I wonder where Jefferson is. If he's watching me. If he's standing behind me. I'm afraid to look, so I close my eyes as I launch into the chorus, but I can hear them. The audience is singing along—some of the most famous vocalists in the world—and it's so powerful.

And then the song slows, Jason's percussion stutters to a pause, and Kacey's fiddle quiets, and I raise my mic to pick up the last, tragic verse, but before I can, Jefferson sings it instead, his sweet tenor striking a fissure into my heart as he does.

And, God, I hate myself for
Wishing
And lyin'
And thinking that maybe
You'd want to be mine

By the time he finishes the verse, he's in front of me, and the crowd is cheering his arrival. My eyes blur, but no tears fall. Instead, I smile, grabbing for his hand as we sing the last chorus together.

My glittering dawn
My twilight con

My overflowing cup
Of whiskey and wrong

My sweet release
My most, my least
My aching everything
My forbidden retreat

But if I close my eyes
And wish it all away
Pretend I'm someone else,
Pretend I'm here to stay
Gave us half a chance,
Let my stupid heart decide
There's no doubt in my mind,
You'd be mine

Before we can catch our breaths, we're moving forward into his hit single "Some Guys Do," and I'm relieved to lighten the atmosphere. This is what the crowd wants. Not moony eyes and declarations of longing. They want the sass we're known for, and we give it to them. He struts, and I swoon. I shake out of my floor-length gown to reveal a white pair of high-waisted shorts and a crop top, which he appreciatively flaunts by spinning me around the stage to grand applause.

We close with a duet, at the request of the CMAs. This year, they are honoring decades of music icons, and they asked if we could do our sort-of-famous rendition of "It Ain't Me, Babe."

"I want everyone on their feet for this one tonight. This little number's been on loan to us, and while we couldn't possibly top the original, I like to think there's a little of Johnny and June in all of us. Let's give them our best effort, y'all!"

Jefferson grabs a guitar from a stagehand, and I lead the auditorium in a clap to feed the beat. I've kicked off my shoes and twist on my toes as Jefferson hunches over the mic and laughs at my dancing as if it's the best thing he's ever seen.

And I realize right then and there that I never want to be looked at as anything less for the rest of my life.

I don't have time to say anything to Jefferson. I'm behind the wardrobe screen, getting back into my original gown before I can spare him a glance. They're announcing Country Song of the Year soon, and I must be in my seat before that blasted camera whirls in my direction. Funny, I remember watching awards shows as a kid and thinking they were so tediously long when I was waiting for my parents to be on-screen.

Ten minutes later, I'm back in my spot between Kacey and Jason. I sneak a peek behind me but don't see Jefferson and vow to try to find him after. Kacey and Fitz probably have plans. I'll just follow them.

Focus, Annie.

I'm able to (mostly) attend to the following awards. I even hop up on my feet with Kacey to dance to a country/hip-hop mash-up. I try to be as natural as possible and forget my uncoordinated square dance moves are being broadcast around the globe, live, and simply have a good time.

Before long, the final awards are being announced, starting with Country Song of the Year. This time, there's no hiding in the wings when they announce my name and play the sound bite of "You'd Be Mine." The crowd claps and cheers and I bite my lip, squeezing the life out of Kacey's and Jason's hands, all pretense at being cool gone out the window.

When they call my name, I promptly burst into tears.

Just make it up the steps, Annie. Eff it all. I didn't plan a speech for this one either. Did I already thank everyone?

I get up to the mic and swipe at my tears. "Y'all, my face is melting off," I say, and everyone laughs.

I inhale through my nose, trying to quickly regain my composure. "My parents never won this award. Maybe they didn't write enough, or maybe they just didn't live long enough, I don't know. But to me, this is an incredible feeling because this," I say, holding up the statue, "feels a lot like survival."

I release my breath and look out in the audience, catching Jefferson's eyes, shining with pride.

"I wrote this song for a boy. A boy I fell in love with against impossible odds. So this award is for you, Jefferson. If I had to choose my favorite, you'd be mine."

epilogue

It's hard to believe it's only been a year since Jefferson showed up on my front porch, hungover and put out that he'd been dragged to rural Michigan on a fool's errand from the label.

It feels like a lifetime ago. As if we've lived a lifetime in those months of push and pull and heartache and discovery. I expect if you'd tallied up our experiences in those months, they'd rival any college student's freshman year and then some. Maybe one day I'll know for sure, but for now, I'm head over heels for this life I've chosen, regardless of the fame merry-go-round.

Of course, that's easy to say right now. We leave on tour in a week, but for the moment, sitting under the willows, with Jefferson's head cradled in my lap and the laughter of our friends and family in muffled echoes around us, it feels like we can do anything. Even survive another summer on the road.

My fingers smooth over and over in the sandy hair falling across his forehead, and my bones seem to sink into the cool, dry grass beneath us. I think if we stayed here, I'd melt into the earth, I'm so content. Everything outside of this moment feels a million years away.

"Trina says I have to get a haircut," he mumbles softly, his eyes closed. He reminds me of a cat like this—his long limbs stretched, his tone barely above a happy purr. "Says I look like a surfer bum."

"I like your hair long," I reply, equally soft.

"Then you must like surfers."

"I don't know about that," I say. "Although there was this one guy my sophomore year who was on the swim team. Does that count?"

"You're ridiculous," he grumbles.

"He wore a Speedo," I continue. "It was very distracting."

"Poor, innocent fifteen-year-old you."

"Well, I wasn't so innocent after that."

"Wait. Didn't you date Jason your sophomore year?"

I pause my fingers. "Maybe."

"Diaz was a swimmer?"

"Not a real great one."

"You've seen him in a Speedo?"

I grimace at the memory. "I was a dutiful girlfriend and best friend, which requires some sacrifices, so yes."

"But you said it was distracting. Like, distracting how?"

"Why? Are you jealous?"

"I'm not sure yet. Answer the question." But he's smiling as he reaches blindly for my hand and gestures for me to keep up with my ministrations. I continue pulling my fingers through his hair, my eyes searching out where I know Jason is sitting at the picnic table with Fitz and Kacey and my aunt Carla. I force myself to think back to those days. The kid used to make jokes about swimming the breast stroke at least ten times a day back then. I wrinkle my nose. Lord, he was annoying.

"Definitely distracting in the way that it felt like I was seeing my brother's junk. It wasn't pleasant. No reason to be jealous." I know, objectively, that Jason's filled out and is a good catch for someone, but I can't ever unsee the Speedo days. I change the subject. "Kacey thinks he's got some secret love affair he's keeping from us, but I'm not so sure he's emotionally capable of that."

"Diaz?" Jefferson seems thoughtful. "I think you sell him short. He's got some depth to him. Not to mention, he's always glued to his phone. He's either got a Candy Crush obsession or a girl on the line."

I consider that. He does stare at his phone an awful lot. And he rarely dates. Not that this life is super conducive to dating, but . . . "Huh. Maybe you're right."

"Usually am. So speaking of secret love affairs, have you noticed anything different about the fiddling fiddlers?"

"Hardly a secret. If you mean have I noticed that they seem very domestic these days, then yes. He practically lives in her loft." Kacey and Fitz have graduated from hotel boinking to loft boinking. Which is perfectly okay by me. Last month, I needed to borrow Kacey's leather jacket and walked in on them in a very compromising position. Jason's Speedo days had nothing on Fitz in a cowboy hat and a smile. Jefferson, of course, thought it was hilarious. "She invited me to go to IKEA with them last weekend. Said they were picking out throw pillows or bath mats or something?"

"Thank God," Jefferson groans. "I told him if he bought one more stupid decorative pillow for my couch, I would make him eat it. I don't need that shit."

I twirl a strand and tug it gently. "Clearly. Who needs pillows when you have me?"

"Exactly. Nothing like it."

I bend over and give him a quick peck on the lips. "That was very cute."

"That's me," he says, flashing a charming grin. "Cute."

"It's cuter if you don't acknowledge it," I whisper.

"Noted."

"So you think he's getting ready to propose?" I say, getting back to our friends.

He shrugs against my thighs. "I don't know. He hasn't said it, but I wouldn't be surprised."

"But they're still so young!"

"When you know, you know."

"Do you really believe that?"

He opens his eyes. "Yeah. I do."

A thrill runs through me, even though I know we're not technically talking about us. It's just that something in his eyes feels like forever. Not like I'm in a hurry for forever, and neither is he. I'm still unpacking all my baggage from my parents, and he's still unpacking, period. But if I really gave over to the idea, I could see it. Him and me making a real go of it.

Him and me changing the trajectory of our lives.

"Me, too," I say simply, grinning. I cradle his head between both of my hands and run my fingers through his hair. He lets out a low moan, and for a second, I'm distracted by the sound. Just as I'm leaning forward to place a lingering kiss on his upturned lips, Jason comes barreling over.

"Dinner's ready," he says, his smirk telling me he's reading my thoughts. "If you can tear yourselves away for a hot minute and join us. You do realize you're in full view of God and your grandparents over here, right?"

"Easy, Diaz, it was just a kiss," Jefferson says, sitting up and reaching for his Cubs hat, replacing it over his mussed hair.

"That's not what Annie's face was saying."

Jefferson's eyes dart to mine. "Really?" He looks far too pleased with himself.

I roll mine, lightly. "Get over yourself, rock star."

Jason holds a hand out, offering to help Jefferson up. I watch them for a moment, feeling a rush of happiness at the sight of their bickering. Jefferson's heckling my best friend over the Speedo thing, and Jason's slugging him harder than necessary in the arm.

I haven't forgotten when Jason for real punched Jefferson, and I haven't forgotten when Jefferson deserved it. But I figure that's what makes us a family. Going through all the garbage and coming out the other end, still caring about each other.

The other day, someone from *People*'s country music issue came out to interview us. They wanted the scoop on our two bands. We answered questions about the tour from last summer, Jefferson's battles with drinking and grief, me living in the shadows of Cora and Robbie . . . our on-and-off-and-*on*-again love . . .

And when you lay it all out there like that, it seems unbelievable. Truly. The stuff of a country song, even.

But I don't know. Isn't life in general pretty unbelievable? In my mind, if it's not, you're doing it wrong.

"You coming?" Jefferson's a few yards ahead of me, waiting. I take in the sight of him: strong, standing tall, comfortable in his own skin. His face is shadowed under the brim of his cap, but I can still see his white teeth flashing in an easy, loping smile. He looks younger than when we first met. Less world-weary and angry. It shows in his music, too. He's going to blow them all away this summer.

If they thought bad boy Clay Coolidge was sexy, just wait until they feast their eyes on brilliant and glowing Jefferson. I'm gonna need to tattoo my name on his forehead to fend them off.

He raises his hand, holding it out to me. I reach for it, closing the distance between us and wrapping my arms around his neck, leaning back to see him more clearly.

"They can see us," he reminds me.

"Who cares?"

"Well," he teases. "Pops might. I don't think I could stand another night of old war stories from 'Nam."

"Could be worse. He hasn't taken to cleaning his hunting rifles in front of you like he used to with Robbie."

Jefferson shudders.

"For Pete's sake, Coolidge, your brother was a Marine."

"Yeah, but I'm a singer."

I press my lips together, and his eyes follow the movement, causing my stomach to do a little flip. A year later and it still flips every single time. I hope that never goes away. "You're so much more than a singer, Jefferson."

His lips quirk. "As long as I'm yours, I don't care what I am."

"Dang, boy. Where'd you get your lines?"

"My girlfriend's a songwriter. She's taught me a few things."

I press closer to him so that our lips are millimeters apart. "Maybe it's time you teach me a few things."

He groans, taking my lips against his. When we pull apart, he shakes his head. "You are evil, and your grandpa is gonna murder me in my sleep."

"You still love me."

"Couldn't stop if I wanted to."

"I have an idea."

"I'm all ears."

"We should go on tour together."

"I thought we already were."

"Shh. I know that. But hear me out. Last time, it was sort of forced on us. Like fate was pulling the strings or whatever. That whole speeding-train, inevitable-conclusion, we're-probably-hurtling-toward-disaster-but-we're-masochists-for-fame kind of thing.

"So I'm asking you this time. Forget the contracts and haircuts and set lists. It's just me, Annie Mathers, asking you, Jefferson Coolidge, if you'd like to sing with me this summer?"

Jefferson takes a half step back, his expression solemn. He holds our hands loosely between us, his thumbs stroking the insides of my wrists. His eyes pierce me, and he smiles.

"There is nothing in the world I'd love more. I'm in, Mathers."

acknowledgments

I will be forever grateful to everyone who read Annie and Clay's story and thought it might look good on a shelf one day.

To my agent, Kate McKean, who has the unenviable task of helping me to "cultivate my chill" and who's had my back from the very first. Every author needs someone so outstanding in their corner.

To Alicia Clancy. When it mattered most, you were one of *You'd Be Mine*'s earliest cheerleaders. Thank you.

To my editor, Vicki Lame. I'm fortunate to have found someone who really gets the rich history of country music but can also objectively edit kissing. It's a rare and beautiful combo and you have it in spades, my friend.

To everyone at Wednesday Books who took this story (and me) on. You're doing a mighty work in the industry and I'm thrilled to be a part of it. Thank you.

To my good friend and critique partner, Karen McManus. You deserve every bit of the success, glitter, and pies that come your way. Thanks for believing in me, even when I wrote terrible science fiction.

To my crew of talented CPs: Dr. Jenny Howe, "Twinsie" Annette Christie, and Meredith Ireland. Your thoughtful feedback and advice keep me going and make me look better than I am. You are far more than CPs; you're dear friends who are stuck with me for life.

To my early readers: Samantha Eaton and Jenn Dugan. Sam, you are Annie and Clay's fairy godmother. I hope your mom reads this and doesn't mind the lack of horses too much. Jenn, this book is missing *Teen Wolf*, but we have a lifetime of books ahead of us to remedy that.

To Deb Jenkins and Cassie Vrtis. Mom, I learned how to be a strong and fearless woman at the knee of Mary Chapin Carpenter, Reba McEntire, Martina McBride, and YOU. Cassie, I said it at the beginning. We did it, Little Sister.

To my siblings: Kyle, Krish, James, and Bridget. I thought it might be fun to see your names in print somewhere outside medical journals and honor societies. Love you, Smarties!

To the Vrtis, Jenkins, Hahn, Stomp, and Dick families: everything I write is colored with words and experiences I've shared with you. Special shout-out to Katie Childers, who helped me get Annie out of Indy, and Kristine Deem for knowing the name of "that one song you all line danced to" when I was pulling out my hair drafting this book.

To Mike. You spent three hours yesterday calmly searching YouTube videos because I couldn't get my keyboard to function. As I tearfully hiccuped back to work, you underlined the words "I love you" in my notes. THAT'S why you inspire every love interest I write. You are my best friend and biggest fan and I love you infinity times three.

To Jones and Al. When I thought of quitting, I couldn't, because of you. You are my Reason.

Finally, I am constantly overwhelmed by the generous mercy of God in my life. He lifts me up when I'm determined to be down and listens to me even when I cuss. "It makes no sense, but this is grace."